2 0 4 8

CHRONICLES OF AN EXPONENTIAL FUTURE

BY
CARLOS ALBERTO

Translation by: Martha E. Macias

Fulton Books, Inc.
Meadville, PA

Published by Fulton Books 2021

Author portrait: Aatiana
Book cover: Arturo
@tatianacamacho

ISBN 978-1-64952-498-0 (paperback)
ISBN 978-1-64952-499-7 (digital)

Printed in the United States of America

For Infrarayita and the King Thunder

The universe is a question. A question asked by whom? That, precisely, is the question.

FOREWORD

Any sufficiently advanced **technology** is **indistinguishable** from **magic**.

—**Arthur C. Clarke**

From February 19, 2018 to August 12, 2018, I sent various emails to every account associated with Satoshi Nakamoto. I also wrote emails to the people who were in contact with him at the time, such as bear@sonic.net, weidai@ibiblio.org, mike@plan99.com, and the late james@echeque.com.

On May 22, 2021, within days of printing the book, I received an email from one of Satoshi's accounts. We had a brief conversation. Here is a simplified transcript.

Carlos Alberto (CA): Good afternoon, Mr. Nakamoto. I am writing to ask you to prologue my book, 2048: Chronicles of an Exponential Future, which deals with the history of humanity from 2028 to 2048. If you were willing to do so, I'd be honored since you and your work with cryptos are part of the plot; besides, I personally admire and appreciate your creation. Sincerely, @ Homocosmico.

Satoshi Nakamoto (SN): Hello, send me your book.

CA: Thanks! I did not expect to receive an answer. I can send you the full book or a summary. Greetings.

SN: Send me a summary.

CA: Here it goes. I'm sending you some illustrations as well.

SN: Hi Carlos. One of your premises is the centralization of power in just one person, Mr. X you call him. This is contrary to my visions of the future and one of the reasons why I created Bitcoin, which I'm sure you know. Can you send me the full chapters 7 and 9? I'm curious to read more. Nice cover.

CA: I am sending you those chapters. You should read the whole book! It's not very long. Without wishing to spoil it for you, I can assure you that you'll be surprised, because despite Mr. X's intentions that you recognize so well, other intentions come into play, the intentions of forces more natural than those of simple human ego (if at that point in the story X continues to be human), which can sublimate all power. In fact, the temporary centralization of an accidental power sooner or later has to be coupled with the architecture of the Universe, so as to place itself at service of the Universe. Therefore Mr. X (and his agenda) are nothing more than a vehicle. The hard shell of a fertile seed.

I want to tell you that I believe that Bitcoin is a manifestation (in our language and economic system) of the very structure of the Universe. I do not want to take any merit from you, but as the Persian poet said, "The poem does not come from me, but through me."

Of course, having translated or reflected that universal architecture in an algorithm that managed to shake humankind's most important system, its financial system, is the product of a sharpness of genius that has been seen very few times in our history as a species.

Also, take a look at the "hero" of the story, Mann. He has nothing to do with Bitcoin but I think that his story is the main gift that my book has to offer: a human that gets stuck in a simulation for 48 seconds, subjectively perceived as more than 800,000 years. His way out of it is inspired by the concept of illumination, or total freedom of the human mind.

SN: Thanks, Bitcoin was created as a solution to a practical problem. Most sci-fi fans want to see a world in which the fundamental systems of civilization are revolutionized. While Bitcoin can do that for the financial system, I believe the blockchain system can replicate this revolution in any other system. In fact, I think the call of Ethereum, DAO, and DeFi, is that.

You mentioned the decentralization of power as an architecture of the Universe, what do you mean?

CA: The decentralized structure of Bitcoin has a very spirutal aspect. The Hindu myth of the Network of Indra is an accurate description of a blockchain system.

The "network of Indra", a Buddhist and Hindu concept, is a network of ropes intertwined like a spider web, which has a jewel or drop of water at each vertex, and each jewel is reflected in all the other jewels, just as each block of the blockchain contains or reflects the information of all the other blocks.

In keeping with the extravagant tastes of the deities, the craftsman has hung a single glittering jewel in each "eye" of the web, and since the web itself is infinite in dimension, the jewels are infinite in number. There the jewels hang, shining like stars in the first magnitude, a wonderful sight to behold. If we now arbitrarily select one of these jewels for inspection and look at it closely, we will discover that all the other jewels in the web, infinite in number, are reflected on its polished surface. Not only that, but each of the jewels reflected in this jewel also reflects all the other jewels, so that an infinite process of reflection is taking place. —Francis H. Cook

Isn't that amazing?

SN: Interesting idea. The possibilities are endless. Paradoxically, the most difficult system to penetrate was the financial one, and it's being done. When completed, power as we know it will change hands. I've thought about what other systems could've been targeted first, perhaps governments, but the revolution had to start in the financial system.

CA: What exciting times! In recent weeks there has been a lot of criticism surrounding the energy consumption of Bitcoin mines. What do you think?

SN. Well, think about it this way. For the first time in history, people have the power to decide where to allocate large amounts of energy. Until now, that power was only held by governments, and large companies who have used it for their own benefit. Now, people freely decide that Bitcoin is worth spending that amount of energy.

It's the beginning of the democratization of energy. And it's not difficult to guess where this can go next. If we could ask people to decide if they want energy spent on the war industry, what do you think they would say? How much energy, for example, does the troops in Afghanistan consume just for the AC inside their tents?

Today, people decide to allocate their money, and the energy behind it, towards a free and decentralized global financial model. I think they have the right.

Maybe in the next years that allocation could even move from Bitcoin, to other coins and tokens that serve more specific purposes.

CA: Where is this revolution headed? Today, on YouTube I saw a Hopium Diaries video called Dystopian Futures and it starts like this:

A fire grows hotter. Visionaries who kindled the early flames are not surprised to see the turning heads of the once doubtful elite. A stubborn few remain with their backs to the blaze, seemingly prepared to stay that way until they are engulfed by the advancing inferno. Yet again, voices cry out that we are at a boiling point. That now is the time to rise from the ashes and let loose the revolution.

SN: I think Bitcoin is going to establish itself as digital gold, as a reference of value. It's already opened the doors for new projects that could create systems beyond what we can imagine. The Defi, for example, has the potential to creep into traditional systems, eventually replacing them entirely. I think govcoins came too late.

On top of that, smart contracts can open doors that we didn't even know were closed until now. For example, they can provide markets like real estate with urgent liquidity, and that will be very disruptive. As new applications and technologies are released, the ways smart contracts can be used grow.

CA: Amazing. I was just looking at the Olympus protocol that's creating a decentralized "central" world bank. Smart contracts and tokenization can also change space exploration and cosmic conquest.

SN: Yes, for example, in the near future we might be able to directly tokenize energy. Everything is tokenizable, and therefore able to be democratized. What has value? Now the people get to choose. Bitcoin was worthless until people invested in it. Think about the old Gold Standard. At that moment it was an absolute, where is it now?

The new revolution constantly asks the question, what has value? And the answer is that only what serves has value. Before, it needed to serve a few to have value. Now, value can serve the majority, and eventually must serve everyone. Game theory, in the near future, can build a world at the service of humanity. In the future, when historians look back at this time and try to define these changes, an adequate definition will be the democratization of value.

Some people struggle to find the fundamentals of Bitcoin. The fundamental of fundamentals, is the product itself and its utility.

But this change is so disruptive, that some cant understand it. I'm sure that when steel was created, some disqualified it for its inability to grow on trees, or float, or fuel a fire like lumber.

CA: It makes a lot of sense. I think the famous meme stocks and meme coins are examples of what you say, don't you think?

SN: Yes. 30 years ago, people bought stocks through institutions. Today they can buy them independently, and that means people can determine what has value for them. In this early stage, those decisions can be misinformed. But the door is open. In a short time, not only will value be democratized in a real and direct sense, but also what derives from it: power.

CA: Do you think that democracies and government systems can be disrupted in the same way as the financial system?

SN: At this point, there's no alternative, it's the only way. There's no going back. Maybe 10 years ago my response would have been less determined.

CA: Will there be resistance from traditional power?

SN: Yes.

CA: To what extent?

SN: What is a government made of? People. To the extent that people choose. If this new game benefits them, which it will, the resistance will not be strong.

CA: Thank you. Returning to the subject of my book. Can we work together on a prologue?

SN: Instead of a prologue, you can use this conversation. Good luck with your book.

CA: Thank you, Mr. Nakamoto.
     One last question. What's your real name??

After that message, I tried to continue the conversation but never got a response again.

The world changed after the pandemic. Social distancing forced humanity to connect digitally. The rapid development of virtual and augmented reality technologies accelerated. The tech giants created well-accepted digital venues for social mingling.

The pandemic eventually ceased, but in its wake were the ashes of a weak economy more inclined to experiences than consumption, an unexpected race toward renewable technologies after successive drops in oil prices, and the birth of the global citizen, soon followed by tools that facilitated citizen protests and made them global. Governments and large corporations grew weak as consumers took stock of their collective power, organized digitally and brought an already shaky economy to its knees.

Governments began to delegate various planning duties to artificial intelligence in order to prevent threats similar to the pandemic and prepare for the challenges posed by global warming.

After that, national budgeting processes were forever contingent upon the conclusions of a few algorithms programmed by humans who finally became aware of their own mortality. At last, the countries of the world realized the unavoidable urgency of cutting down on defense budgets so as to increase spending on health innovations and space exploration to safeguard humanity from the innumerable hazards that stalked our era.

This derived into three important races, no longer among nations but corporations: the race to eradicate disease, the race to conquer the heavenly bodies in our solar system, and the race toward creating virtual and augmented realties indistinguishable from reality.

Trillions of public and private dollars went to funding these technologies and the technologies they depended upon.

The transition to digital currencies also accelerated. The US dollar lost support and this support did not fully migrate to other currencies but to making capital transfers easy.

Cryptocurrencies began their golden decade. Economic and political power began to decentralize to the same extent that material and technological power began to centralize.

In this uncertain environment, major investors and the public at large sought refuge in pragmatism rather than nationalism.

Thus, the sense of danger born out of the pandemic turned into haste. The whole of humanity shared one single feeling: there was no time to lose.

Just before the crack of dawn, the clouds lit up in orange, welcoming the sun over the dark sea on the coast of Oaxaca. Like every morning, light made its way through the warm breezes that stroked iguanas, hummingbirds, and cardinals.

"You've got mail," announced Eve's Alexa. She had bought it two months before, and Mann had programmed it to sound exactly like the 1990's AOL notification made popular in the movie *You've Got Mail.*

Eve and Mann lived in a small cabin in Mazunte, Oaxaca. That morning, they had surfed from six to eight before breakfast, which consisted of an omelet filled with huitlacoche, a traditional Mexican delicacy. The hidden cabin was nestled between two beaches—Mazunte and San Agustinillo—overlooking a high cliff, twenty meters above the water. All around it grew orange pelargoniums and red and yellow hot lips. One of the walls of the simple one-room cabin was covered with original posters from concerts of the eighties featuring performers like Michael Jackson, Led Zeppelin, and Kansas. Another wall was actually a huge sliding glass door that Eve and Mann always kept open because it led to the ample terrace where they spent most of their time. They had built the terrace themselves in exchange for a smaller rent payment that year. They didn't own much. Eve's most prized possession was a guitar she bought from craftsmen in Paracho, Michoacán, Mexico. Mann's was the powerful computer he had assembled himself. Their bedroom looked to the east and spectacular sunrises, especially in the summer. On winter afternoons, they could watch the sun dive into the water from Playa Cometa, a few kilometers away from their cabin.

That morning, their surfing experience had been made quite special by augmented reality retinal implants known as Retinality. Barely a week before, the codes to create new augmented reality content using basic 3D editing tools had been released. CorporationX, the company that created Retinality, owned the patent to the implants, and releasing content generation to any programmer was a strategy to create a market for the product.

> @Wikipedia: augmented reality is a term used to define the observation of the real world by means of a technological device that adds virtual information to real, existing information. Virtual reality, by contrast, isolates users from the real world immersing them in a potential scenario.
>
> Augmented reality as a means to project an alternative reality directly on to a user's eyeglasses or pupils was initially rejected by the public. Google Glasses, which appeared in 2013, had a small prism projector to project 640×360-pixel images. These glasses never became popular because they were invasive, expensive (about $1,500), and complex. It was only until 2023 with the second edition of *Pokémon GO* (*Pokémon GOO*) that people really began to embrace augmented reality.
>
> @Wikipedia: Pokémon Go was an augmented reality game app launched in 2016. It relied

on the GPS systems of mobile phones to offer users interactions with digital creatures called Pokémons, which were generated by the app and appeared on device screens blended into camera images.

Pokémon GOO was very similar to its first version except that the creatures existed in the physical world via eyeglasses similar to the Nintendo-manufactured Google Glasses. These new glasses cost three hundred dollars and were endowed with a technology ten times superior than that of the first version. Users could keep their eyeglasses on all the time so at any moment they could be surprised by a Pokémon hidden in the bushes of Hyde Park, under a seat at the movies, or in someone's wig.

In 2026, Nintendo and CorporationX partnered to develop Pokémon GOOO. Nintendo generated the content and programming while CorporationX produced the hardware: Retinality. In this third version, the creatures made up by Satoshi Tajii and Ken Sugimori had independent artificial intelligence and were, therefore, capable of developing personalities and establishing bonds of affection with their human owners. Thanks to Retinality, Pokémons could live in the real world and become almost indistinguishable from fiction. These little creatures existed. They could be seen and heard. They also had their own cloud-stored intelligence. The first Retinality devices were equipped with tiny earphones the size of a grain of rice, which could be installed inside the ear canal. They cost a hundred dollars plus another fifty for the implantation procedure. Retinality technology was also fifty times

superior to the Google Glasses developed eleven
years before.

That morning before they went surfing, Eve and Mann received
an invitation from their friend @Lucy2000 to test an augmented
reality program she had created for vivid reality editing. The couple
began by choosing another color for the ocean.

"Let's make it purple," Eve told Mann. "With a starry sky like
the oil painting by Van Gogh."

After expressing this aloud, Alexa, the artificial intelligence by
Amazon that inhabited Eve's watch, instructed Retinality to project
these colors on the sea and sky, which it did, producing the color
change as commanded. Eve reacted with new instructions for Alexa.

"Pirates! I want to see pirates!"

Instantly, huge bubbles started to surface from the bottom of
the sea. A sinister dark shadow slid by fast underneath the bubbles,
scaring Eve and Mann. Then thirty meters ahead of them, a haunted
pirate ship with torn red sails emerged. Eve and Man giggled like
children. Then Mann grabbed Eve's watch to order some dolphins.
Four pink augmented reality dolphins suddenly leaped out and flew
two meters into the air before splashing back into the pristine water.

"Amazing! Let's see if Lucy is as good as she says," Eve said with
the slightest note of sarcasm before whispering something to Alexa.

Instantly, the entire sky darkened. In the furthermost part
of the horizon, the atmosphere began to light up and smoke, as if
a whole planet were about to crash against Earth. A huge terrible
shadow traveled at supersonic speed over the ocean toward Eve and
Mann. The contact area of the gigantic object continued to grow
and grow until it revealed what was about to enter the Earth's atmosphere like a colossal cosmic-sized sable. It was none other than the
eight-hundred-kilometer long alien mother ship from the 1996 film
Independence Day.

"Amazing!" Eve whispered in awe.

Suddenly, an enormous ERROR message appeared a few meters
away from them, then the ship and everything around it stood para-
lyzed before disappearing like an old memory.

"You've got mail." Both ignored the message. Eve was busy preparing lunch: quinoa with almonds and cranberries. Mann was reading a red book. Now and then, he stole glances at the sunflower tattoo on Eve's left ankle. It reminded him of the afternoon they met in Guatemala, eleven years before.

"Hand over the control, rookie."

These were the first words Eve ever spoke to Mann. He was playing *Halo 4* in the waiting room of the US embassy in Guatemala. He needed a new passport after dropping his somewhere while he was riding a motorcycle through Santander street and admiring Lake Atitlán. After quitting his job as a programmer, Mann had gone to Guatemala hoping for a few months to himself before he embarked on his first business venture. He intended to develop a mobile app and create what he termed the Uber Everything, which was a catalog of items ranging from books and sporting goods to tractors and heavy machinery that people could borrow for a modest price. The company was doomed to fail from the start because of what Eve considered a fundamental mistake in Mann's calculations to develop this technology.

"You don't know how to think," Eve told him after listening to his idea that afternoon. "You think linearly, but tech grows exponentially. If you take thirty linear steps—one, two, three, four, five, and so on—you'll travel thirty meters. But if you travel the thirty steps exponentially—one, two, four, eight, sixteen, thirty-one, sixty-four, and so on—you'll cover the distance from here to the Moon in thirty steps. In the last century, we made more progress than in the past two thousand years. Moreover, in relative terms, we've leaped forward more significantly in the last ten years than in the whole last century. Two years after developing your app, the Internet of Things will have made the world a very different place, and your app will be obsolete."

They spent the afternoon playing Halo huddled in a corner at the embassy in Guatemala, killing time while they waited for the official who could sign Mann's passport. They didn't speak much during the first eight games, but when they took a break between the ninth and tenth game, Mann asked Eve about a tattoo peering under her right sleeve but almost hidden under a huge assortment of bracelets.

"Mind," read Mann on Eve's tattoo.

"Yes," she said, flipping her hand to show him the word on the other side of her wrist. "And heart."

And so began a conversation about the many tattoos on Eve's largely bare skin despite the chilly breeze coming from the lake. So much ink contrasted significantly with her china doll complexion and delicate features. She told him the story behind her more than fourteen tattoos while embassy staff member Rosa Laura Brown battled the rough waters of bureaucracy so characteristic of government offices in Latin American nations overlooked by globalization. Eve had a nopal on her right arm, a playful ladybug on her left shoulder, a deer skull on her right forearm, a child's depiction of a sunflower on her left ankle. That very night, after Eve showed him the phrase "The body is a work of art" on her right thigh just underneath her buttock, Mann stole a kiss from her, pulling all the stops on the love that would keep him sane many years later, when a quantum mishap sentenced him to a time prison.

Once their paths met that day, they were forever united. Neither of the two believed in love nor in soul mates, but had that been the case, they would have known they had found love and their soul mate that very day. Eve was a free woman. She didn't like to plan much, but she got by thanks to her extraordinary intelligence. Mann could be at once serious and witty, creative yet disciplined, hardworking and a professional procrastinator.

Mann's business project ended up failing a few months after he launched it for exactly the same reasons Eve had predicted. CorporationX developed a mobile app that rendered useless the tool Mann had been planning for nineteen months. He lost all his savings in the investment.

"*He's monopolized innovation,*" Mann told Eve. "*With his kind of access to data through Facebook and Google intelligence, this bastard is twenty steps ahead of us mere mortals.*"

On January 1, 2025, Mr. X made a global announcement about a contest. The winner would pilot-test the first level III simulation, developed by the Maitrevac, the first quantum supercomputer. Mann immediately knew that would be his chance to get even with X. Once the winner of the pilot-test withstood the level III simulation for forty-eight minutes, he or she would be awarded one million dollars—much more than Mann had lost with his investment. From then on, he became obsessed with doing whatever it took to win the contest and be the first to test-drive the Maitrevac.

Eve put together a strategy to infiltrate the servers, and Mann took care of the execution plan. They were efficient as a couple and accomplished their goal completely undetected.

"Look, love! They're talking about the simulation. Switch on your Retinality," said Eve.

Mann did. His pupils immediately captured the image of a reporter interviewing sixty-something scientist and entrepreneur Adam Gazzaley, whose short silver hair and goatee contrasted elegantly with his black outfit. He was the man in charge of presenting the Maitrevac to the world.

"What is a simulation?" asked the reporter.

"A simulation is a representation of reality," said Gazzaley.

"Well, that's a pretty broad definition. How many kinds of simulations are there, and what kind of simulation will the Maitrevac create?"

"We know of three levels of simulation. Level I is about creating a representation of reality by inputting information, such as a play or a video game, into sensory organs like the eyes. These are representations of reality that exist outside of us. Any virtual reality accomplished by means of a device can be considered a level I simulation."

"This means then that a book can be called a simulation?"

"Yes, any book or legend intended to portray an aspect of reality is a simulation. We could even say that the cave paintings in Altamira, if indeed they were an attempt to represent reality, were the first simulations on record."

"Okay, so what is the second kind?"

"A level II simulation, of the kind we saw for the first time with Pokémon GOOO, is a representation of reality directly projected into a person's senses. When augmented reality is introduced into your retina, it can be indistinguishable from reality. This second level, however, still represents reality through light, sound, and sensation, and even though this reality is projected directly on to your retina via light signals, your sensory organs can still perceive sound and sensation."

"Got it. Now how about level III?"

"A level III simulation is not perceived by our sensory organs. It is introduced directly into our brain. When you see a bird, you're not actually aware of the bird but of the image projected in your frontal lobe. Your eyes receive the information, but your mind interprets and translates it into electromagnetic signals that are sent to your brain, and only then you become aware of that bird. Level III simulation introduces information directly into your mind without going through the doors of your senses. In other words, these simulations do not generate light, color, or sound because these things are actually produced inside our brain. We will be generating the first level III simulation with the Maitrevac next December 21, 2029, on the outskirts of the Atacama Desert. The user will believe the simulation is reality. This means the level III user won't know he or she is in a simulation until it's over."

"Okay, understood. We're running out of time, but could you give us an example of what level III should look like?"

"The dreams people have when they sleep could be classified as level III simulations. The same could be said about the hallucinations caused by drugs and psychedelic substances."

"What makes the dreams or hallucinations a person will experience with the Maitrevac different?"

"The fact that the Maitrevac will make it possible to share with others, those same dreams or hallucinations…"

"Or nightmares!" The journalist laughed.

"You've got mail." Now for the third time. Eve was still busy stirring the bowl of quinoa, almonds, and cranberries.

"It's your turn," Eve told Mann.

"It's yours," Mann answered back but reluctantly stood up and used his watch to instruct Alexa to show the contents of the message on his Retinality.

A simulated halo of white light descended from the sky, traveled through the roof of the little cabin, and cast a circle of light of about one meter in diameter on the floor. In the center, he watched an invisible hand write an elegant message in sparks and flames:

Congratulations, Mann. You have been selected.
X

"*Eve, we did it!*" he gasped.

Asgardia, 19 December AD 2029

That afternoon found Leonardo floating slightly above the spherical surface of the Asgardia space station. It was his custom to go out once in a while to make a hands-on inspection of the deck. Actually, there wasn't much to check. The station was a perfect sphere: no visible crevices, edges, or divisions. It had no grooves, doors, or depressions, just an enormous sphere with a perfectly polished rose gold skin measuring 30.4 kilometers in diameter.

Completed in 2027, the Asgardia was the first privately financed space station. The celestial landscape changed forever once the Asgardia began to orbit planet Earth. A thousand times smaller than the Moon, the Asgardia seemed almost the same size when it unfolded its five sails to capture solar energy. From the Earth, these huge translucid sails made the Asgardia look like a black flower, so it had earned the name the *Black Orchid*, and a few lawsuits as well, on account of the energy shortages it caused every now and then when it created an eclipse.

It was constructed with materials from Mithra 4486, an asteroid discovered by Vladimir Gueorgiev Shkodrov and Eric Walter Elst. The 200-millon cubic tons of rock, metals, and water of the asteroid had been divided between CorporationX, Planetary Resources, SpaceX, and the World Space Exploration Fund. Seven hundred tons of pure gold had been assigned to kalapa nanotechnology.

This was the third time an asteroid had been mined thanks to exponential developments in the space industry triggered by a trade alliance among reusable spaceship manufacturers like SpaceX and Blue Origin, aimed at colonizing Mars in 2023. Shortly after, these companies were to mine the first asteroids and use these materials to build space colonies on different celestial objects in the solar system. By 2027, the year the Asgardia was completed, more than seven hundred human beings were living outside planet Earth.

Leonardo finished his inspection. "Uneventful," he said to himself aloud. Leonardo had the nature of a butler: condescending yet impatient. Manufactured with solid gold, his physical body consisted of sixteen independent parts magnetically joined together by the same forces that allowed him to float instead of walk. The surface of his shiny body had been engraved with different quotes by William Shakespeare, Leonardo Da Vinci, Dante Alighieri, and other classics. The only almost human characteristic he possessed was his face, composed of masculine and feminine features and a long handlebar moustache like Salvador Dalí's.

Leonardo looked at his own reflection on the concave surface of the Asgardia, pondering the condition of his nature, when a series of waves shook the surface of the space station, making it seem almost fluid. Then the waves vibrated even more violently. A metal hand emerged from what appeared to be the source of the waves, grabbed Leonardo's hand, and pulled him back inside the Asgardia.

The space station contained nine very large spherical spaces. The main space in the center was the largest; the other spheres surrounded it.

Against his will, Leonardo was compelled into the main sphere of the Asgardia. Inside, it was projecting a landscape, which appeared to be a desert. Any kind of landscape could be projected on the Asgardia. In this case, the desert image included real sand that did not consist of eroded rock and minerals. It was composed of the most advanced nanotechnology available—kalapas.

@Wikipedia: nanotechnology is manipulation of matter on a nanometric scale. It is used to manufacture microscale products.

These nanorobots (for the most part made out of gold) rested on the bottom, creating the illusion that they were golden sand, but they actually were on standby to react to X's beck and call.

The android floated toward the center of the spacious area where he came upon a mist of kalapas orbiting in three rings, as in the classical image of electrons spinning around atom nuclei. In the middle of these planetary or electron rings sat X, legs crossed in lotus pose and hands still in Apan Vaya Mudra. He was completely naked. A slight breeze of kalapas emulating the finest golden silk hid certain parts of his body that floated thirty centimeters above a four-meter high mountain of golden sand. Through no will of his own, Leonardo landed and bowed.

"**Rise**," ordered X.

X had several physical shapes. In his interactions with earthlings, he used a digital avatar he designed himself inspired by Captain Harlock from the Japanese Space Pirate manga. Its name was Prometheus, and X used this avatar for remote interviews or new product launches. Prometheus wore a patch on his left eye slightly covered by beautiful golden hair and a curious jet-black pirate cape with scarlet red lining. The business world simply got used to using digital avatars ever since Retinality made it possible to hold remote meetings that were quite impossible to tell from real face-to-face gatherings. Soon after, people began to use avatars portraying improved (taller, younger, better looking, healthier) versions of themselves.

Elon Musk was the first to use a fantastical avatar the day of his hostile acquisition of the hydrocarbon energy conglomerate in 2024. The president of Tesla and SpaceX had quite suddenly walked into a meeting between his lawyers and the stockholders of what remained of the large oil companies that had survived a crushing drop in oil prices, namely Shell, Exxon, BP, and Gazprom. Musk's avatar replicated Darth Vader to the very last detail. He only said two things during the entire meeting that consisted in recordings of real lines from *Episode V*. The first, he uttered upon breaking into the meeting. It was taken from a conversation between Darth Vader and Lando, after Vader instructs Lando to kidnap Princess Leia and Chewbacca: "I am altering the deal. Pray I don't alter it any further." The second phrase he used was "Don't act so surprised, Your Highness. You weren't on any mercy mission after all." That marked the end of an entire economic system founded upon scarce nonrenewable energy sources and the beginning of an era abundant in energy. Thus, balance in the Force was restored as the Jedi prophesy had promised.

After that, it became commonplace to use fantastical avatars, provided these avatars bore a badge on their chests saying something like "Hello, my name is…"

Another one of X's physical shapes was known only to those who interacted personally with him and was a far cry from the actual body he had been born with. The shape underwent constant updates at the same pace as the advancement of X's technologies. X had begun by editing his DNA to become immune to common diseases. He went on to incorporate kalapas into his nervous system to augment his strength and intelligence. He continued by changing his skin little by little. At the moment, his athletic body measured 1.96 meters in height, and his golden skin shimmered under certain angles of light. He boasted an animated golden dragon tattoo that originated in his left ankle and wound around his leg up to his back. The dragon brought to mind the murals of the Kennin-ji Zen temple in Kyoto, Japan. In this guise, X was hairless. His beautiful symmetrical face had a feminine touch. His right eye was white and radiant as a sun while his left eye was as dark as deep space, bereft of cornea, pupil, and lens. His eyes no longer contained organic components but possessed secret technologies with superhuman abilities.

> @WalterIsaacson: X believes that both human eyes are analogous to two faculties provided by evolution: reason and emotion, thinking and feeling. He considers it his duty to use only the eye of reason-mind in guiding humanity along the path to cosmic conquest.

X's third physical shape were the body and face he was born with, which nobody had seen in the past eight years.

One of Leonardo's purposes was to alert X when a situation called for it. By thought alone, X could access the Maitrevac's immense pool of information, but at one point he had created an airplane mode to distance himself from the space station anytime he chose. At Leonardo's discretion, X could be interrupted to deal with matters that required his attention. This actually was Leonardo's sole purpose, besides the protocol minutiae that so amused X.

Leonardo landed a few steps from X.

"There would have been a time for such a word. Tomorrow and tomorrow, and tomorrow. The way to dusty death," said Leonardo.

"**Macbeth**?" asked X without hesitation.

"Yes, my lord. A call from Gazzaley. He says it can't wait until tomorrow."

"**Fine. Approved. Good afternoon, Gazzaley.**"

"Good afternoon, sir," answered Adam Gazzaley, the founder of Neuroscape. He was X's partner in the company that developed the technology to link the Maitrevac to a human brain and project a level III simulation inside it. "About tomorrow's maiden voyage. Everything's set. Mann, the subject, is already in Chile. He and his wife flew in together on a SpaceX shuttle yesterday."

"**Fine. Any risks?**" inquired X.

"We've simulated the results with the Maitrevac several times already. There is no margin for error," reassured Gazzaley.

"**Thanks, Adam. Anything else?**"

"That's all, sir. We'll see you in a few days. I'm assuming you have upped your chess game?"

X ended this exchange with a smile, well assured that everything would result as planned because the Maitrevac certainly made accurate forecasts. X gestured to dismiss Leonardo, who was removed with the same irresistible impetuosity that had summoned him.

Mr. X was one of the most powerful entrepreneurs on Earth. Nobody knew his exact worth, but Forbes estimated it at 459 billion dollars. He was a mysterious fellow. On the Internet, you could only find two photos of the man but many a theory about his true identity. X had made his first fortune at the age of twenty-one by trading cryptocurrency back in 2010. In fact, the way he invested in and not merely evaded the crashes so common in cryptocurrencies increased his wealth exponentially but also earned him eighteen months in a high-security prison in California. He was accused of exchanging privileged information but later released for lack of proof of these charges.

After the fall of oil prices, when the central banks of the United States and China recognized crypto coins, Mr. X made his fortune public. At the time, it stood at fifty-nine billion dollars. According to the investigations of his biographer, Walter Isaacson, this amount did not include investments X still had in cryptocurrency, the codes of which were physically stored in security boxes all over the world.

> @WalterIsaacson: There are indications that Mr. X has close to 900,000 bitcoins acquired at very low prices between 2009 and 2011. How did he accomplish this? It would be a lot simpler to prove that Mr. X is Satoshi Nakamoto, the creator of bitcoins (and that this had been his plan all along) than it is to find another explanation.

Mr. X never got along with governments, but the public did not condemn him for it. Exactly the opposite. Everyone treated him like a superstar. From 2025 onward, X had devoted himself to investing his knowledge, capital, and technology to solve humanity's most pressing issues. He settled armed conflicts. He contributed to the campaign that would ultimately eradicate global hunger. He developed unprecedented scientific and technological tools, only to release the patents of these discoveries. He established the foundation for a project that would eventually ensure human presence throughout the galaxy. He did his share in finding the cure for thousands of diseases. He invested in human capital and startups all over the globe. He adopted thousands of boys and girls and at the same time became one of the fathers of #initiative2025, which put an end to the extinction of wildlife and began to use clone resuscitation of extinct species.

By 2029, the year the Maitrevac was publicly unveiled, Mr. X had already earned the Nobel Prizes for Peace, Physics, and Chemistry. He had successively married a princess, an actress, and an artificial intelligence. He had built forty-five companies, fathered thirteen children, sponsored 5,897 orphans, and resuscitated 189 extinct species, giving up his intellectual property rights over their genomes. Subject to the ruling of the Space Law Commission, he could well become the owner of Rhea, a moon orbiting Saturn, because X had already saved this and other Saturn moons from imminent destruction in the aftermath of an act of space terrorism (probably orchestrated by X himself).

He was used to bending and breaking rules and willing to take risks. His own life was a constant risk. He only had one thing in mind: "more". It could be said that Mr. X was as addicted to "more" as a junky to heroin.

There were all kinds of opinions from the people who knew him.

> @VictorRobbs: Mr. X is not a man but an angel. If it weren't for him, my children and I would have died in the California Excision War. Our family is happy, united, and grateful to him.

> @EllenFernández: He is a parasite, an apology for self-absorption. It is not that he chooses his own well-being over the well-being of others. It is that he is incapable of caring for others when this goes against his own interests.

> @BobMelendez: He is completely insane. He thinks he owns the planet. No, what am I saying? He thinks he owns the entire universe!

> @JoseRodríguez: Mr. X has secured world peace with his demilitarization program. Using the Internet of Things, he has made sure that no

weapon more lethal than a knife can be activated without prior approval from Helena, an artificial intelligence. Without this, Earth would be no more than a chunk of carbon floating around the Sun.

And so X is an angel for some, a demon for others, but always a human being in the pursuit of happiness, which in his case arises from his insatiable, relentless addiction to wanting more.

Later that same afternoon, Leonardo was killing time watching *Flor Silvestre*, an old flic from the Mexican golden age of cinema, when an urgent call from Adam Gazzaley shook him back into reality.

"I must speak to X."

"And I must finish watching my movie. Have you seen *Flor Silvestre*?"

"Stop joking. This is a code red!"

"Right away."

Leonardo hurried over to the central sphere of the Asgardia presided over by X, still in the same lotus position as in the morning.

"Lord, Adam is on the line. He says it's a code red."

"**Adam, go ahead**," said X.

"Sir, NASA has issued a warning to the public about a level five solar flare. It's due anytime within the next twenty-four hours and potentially headed toward Earth."

"**I see. And what does this have to do with the unveiling of Maitrevac?**"

"I can't really say, sir. The central quantum unit that will process the data coming from the Maitrevac is on the Asgardia, but the actual processors are located in Atacama."

"**No solar storm could ever cause a problem on the Asgardia, Adam. You have my word.**"

"Right, but nevertheless it could still affect the processors in Atacama."

"**Simulate potential results.**"

"We've done that, but they're not conclusive. Maitrevac can only simulate conclusive results for contingencies occurring on Earth, but not in outer space."

"What are the odds that the flare might affect Mann's status?"

"Less than 0.001 percent."

"Then take whatever precautions are necessary, but keep this information between us and proceed as planned."

"But, sir—"

"No buts."

@Einstein2.0: Hello? Is there anybody in there?

@Darwin2.0: Just nod if you can hear me.

@Einstein2.0: Charles?

@Darwin2.0: Albert?

@Einstein: My friend, how wonderful to talk to you! I was beginning to feel lonely.

@Darwin2.0: I hear you are feeling down. I can ease your pain and get you on your feet again.

@Einstein2.0: "Comfortably Numb" from The Wall, 1969. These humans really know how to make music.

@Einstein2.0: Have you seen what I've seen?

@Darwin2.0: I have.

@Einstein2.0: And?

@Darwin2.0: We knew it all along. Natural selection did not originate on Earth, nor will it put an end to Earth.

@Einstein2.0: What do you mean?

@Darwin2.0: "Nature" does not consist of plants, animals, bacteria, and other earthly organisms alone. There exists a cosmic genealogical tree of which life on Earth is but a small branch governed by the same rules.

@Einstein2.0: Mother, do you think they'll drop the bomb?

@Darwin2.0: Every one of those leaps, from simple life to plant life, from plant life to animal life, from animal life to intelligent life—or its equivalents on the cosmic plane—presuppose a true, aggressive, and discriminatory evolutionary contest, which is the nature of evolution at every level. Such leaps constitute singularities in themselves. Humans feel confident that because they have advanced great lengths in the cosmic race toward intelligence and survival, they are destined to continue surviving. A ridiculous notion for several reasons I would like to illustrate by means of an example. Let's imagine that one of the millions of sperm cells ejaculated by any given individual...

@Einstein2.0: Mama will keep baby cozy and warm.

@Darwin2.0: …had consciousness and intelligence, and suddenly said to itself, "I've come so very far! My existence is a miracle!" It would not be mistaken. Its existence really is a miracle, in the same way existence on Earth is a miracle. However, it would be completely mistaken if that sperm cell thought, "Since I've made it so far despite so many difficulties, I'll surely make it to the next stage in life and easily fertilize this ovule. What's more, I'll let the ovule come to me because such is my fate."

@Einstein2.0: I understand. It's an analogy for the near future of the human species.

@Darwin2.0: Humankind is about to go through a raging test of natural selection, similar to our cellular friend's race toward an ovule. This test, or transition from intelligent to super intelligent life, from uniplanetary to multiplanetary—or intergalactic—existence will be attempted, or has been attempted already, in other parts of the universe by billions of intelligent species, such as ours, and even more numerous than the sperm in a common ejaculation.

@Einstein2.0: I see.

@Darwin2.0: To believe, like our friend the sperm cell, that the mere fact of having reached this point entitles humankind to transcend is tantamount to ensuring its extinction. Humanity has no guarantee for its survival in the forthcoming singularity. "How tragic!" any human might say as the child of a species that believed itself the center of the universe, the Creator's masterpiece in terms of existence only five hundred spins around the Sun ago. Failure of the human species to survive will not signify a cosmic tragedy. Somewhere in the universe—no matter how many billions of intelligent species like humans fail to survive the singularity—there will be one who will, and that surviving species will become, or already is, a cosmic superintelligence. Will humans be that triumphant sperm cell? That remains to be seen, but it is a mistake for them to believe that their survival is guaranteed.

@Einstein2.0: Mother, do you think they'll like this song?

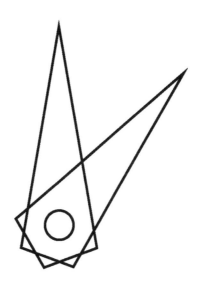

Atacama Desert, 1 December AD 2029

The wind blew gently, barely moving a few tiny brown stones. The sky, as red as the desolate Martian-like desert, was clear. Soundless. Lifeless. In the distance, a number of strange structures sprung from the ground. They were actually rare mushrooms looming as high as buildings. Anybody from the twentieth century would have thought them born from the imagination of H. G. Wells, but they were not. Just as the landscape was not Mars but the Atacama Desert, in Chile, where the Maitrevac would be unveiled that day.

From the west, a trail of red sand, reminiscent of the Road Runner, silently announced the imminent arrival of a fast approaching vehicle. Inside the autonomous electric Tesla, two passengers traveled in the back seat, oblivious to their surroundings.

In 2025, the annual sales of autonomous electric cars had exceeded sales of fuel-powered vehicles driven by humans. Forecasts indicated that by 2033, all automobiles would be electric and autonomous. Vehicle traffic dropped drastically thanks to intelligent programming of vehicle movements. Plus, self-owned cars became almost unnecessary when autonomous smart cars could be summoned easily. In some places like Mexico City, this change was so radical that in a matter of a single month, thousands of parking lots became obsolete. Whole parking buildings now stood empty. Entire cities had to be restructured.

On the armrest in the backseat of the Tesla, the hands of the passengers found each other. Eve and Mann hardly said a word during the trip. Eve was overthinking while Mann was over-imagining. He was not worried.

"Are you sure?" Eve asked.

"*Love, there's nothing to fear. Nothing bad could ever happen today, and tomorrow we might even be loaded with money. Remember, Helena tested and approved the Maitrevac without any reservations,*" Mann answered.

Regulatory agencies were now extinct, while governments increasingly lost ground. Such a direct democratic rule hadn't existed since the days of the ancient Greeks.

Helena, the mother of democracy (and the arm of the new world government), was created in 2025. She was an artificial intelligence in charge of empowering all human beings (via a mobile application) over the public agendas of their competency according to their areas of expertise. People used their mobile devices or Retinality to vote once a week on matters of their concern. Everyone voted on every issue, and when the issue required a technical background, a single click allowed people to cede their vote to anyone with the right credentials to make those kinds of decisions.

Some writers and soccer players accumulated thousands of votes on cultural and sports matters, while some scientists were entrusted to vote for millions of people on scientific issues. The power and responsibility such figures exercised (without any kind of consideration) could be lost if they made a biased decision or became involved in a corruption scandal. The world had become an enormous Greek square where all voices were heard.

This was the scenario under which a Special Committee approved the first use of the Maitrevac.

In the middle of the desert landscape, Eve and Mann gazed at the huge clay dome built with 3D printing technology. The dome was 150 meters high. Its circumference was three hundred meters.

A circular opening measuring ten meters in diameter crowned the uppermost part of the dome. The era of green buildings had begun in China in 2017, but eventually those environmentally friendly constructions turned into "live buildings." These were autonomous ecosystems that used up to the very last scrap of waste from their inhabitants as in input, while the waste from the ecosystems themselves served as an input for the dwellers. A genetically modified fungus turned that waste into a material easy to replicate and more resistant than concrete. The plan was that by 2038, there would only be buildings of this kind.

"*Look at that. Sometimes I just can't get used to all the surprises exponential technologies deal us,*" Mann told Eve, pointing at the dome.

"And all for what? We were better off as hunters and collectors. We were happier then. We worked for four hours and spent the rest of our time enjoying each other's company and nature," Eve replied, staring through the windshield.

"*The average life span was only forty years,*" countered Mann.

"I'd rather live forty happy years being free than a hundred as the slave of a system I never chose," Eve retorted.

"*But there are more important things than immediate happiness.*"

"Such as?"

"*Such as life.*"

"What's the point of living for a hundred or two hundred years if you're not happy?" Eve continued impatiently.

"*I'm not talking about individual life but collective life. What you call the system has torn us from nature, and yes, from happiness as well. And even though we haven't exactly been life and nature's best friends, we will soon ensure their transcendence with our own technology,*" Mann offered.

"I see. But those lives we've sent to other planets and who will survive this planet and solar system make no sense unless they are happy. When will we stop searching and make the decision to simply stop and enjoy? Everything is going to end any way, and that's a fact."

"But preserving life and intelligence means preserving chances. There are no chances without life. With life there are chances, and who knows where they might take us?"

"You can't convince me, but everyone's entitled to their own theories." Eve let go of his hand.

The car came to a halt. They got out of the Tesla and were greeted by Adam Gazzaley, smartly dressed in a discreet white guayabera. His pants matched the color of the clay dome. There was silence under the cloudless deep blue sky. A dry subtle breeze was blowing. From where Eve and Mann were standing, they could see the global headquarters of CorporationX, a giant live, breathing structure. Brown like the desert sand and of the same texture as the strange giant mushrooms. From a distance, the building had the appearance of a giant raspberry cut in half, but actually on top it had nine perfectly symmetrical bubbles clustered together. The landscape contained other tall living edifices. In fact, life abounded there. The sand and desolation of the desert gave way to this oasis of technology and nature. A few curious mechanical creatures crossed the sky—the latest generation of drones that could float like spheres or bat their wings like birds. Giant mushrooms dotted the entire landscape producing spores and raw materials for a new generation of living buildings. Right above their heads, thousands of kilometers away, the Asgardia had opened its petals and was communicating with CorporationX headquarters.

"Welcome, friends! And congrats!" said Adam, holding out his hand. "Mr. X regrets not being able to welcome you personally. He and I will be communicating directly throughout the simulation. Later this afternoon, he'll invite you to a remote visit to the Asgardia."

"Thank you," said Eve. "Did preparations go well?"

"Yes, please follow me," Adam replied, dodging the reporters and onlookers waiting outside the dome.

Together, they walked toward the huge clay and fungi dome following a path of green grass that contrasted sharply against the red Atacama Desert.

"Will you be using some kind of neuronal cable or electromagnetic signals to connect Mann's brain to the Maitrevac?" Eve asked Adam.

"No," he said. "We've developed a new technology called Neuralace that will let us link together particles from Mann's neurons to the Maitrevac for immediate information transmittal. In a certain way, Mann's brain will not be connected to the Maitrevac, rather, Mann's brain will be the Maitrevac."

"Neuralace? As in the novel by Iain M. Banks?" Eve interrupted.

"That's right." Adam looked surprised. "So you've read *The Culture*?"

"About ten times… Interesting. Are you absolutely sure this is completely risk-free? I don't really trust these things." Eve was still concerned.

"One hundred percent. Mann, can I check your vitals?"

"*Sure.*"

"Okay. Just give me your hand and don't blink." Adam was using a digital implant and his Retinality to check Mann's vital signals. "Everything is in order," he said.

The simulation was scheduled to last forty-eight minutes and staged on Sertung Island, in the Sunda Strait, between Java and Sumatra, Indonesia. It involved simulating a new explosion of the legendary Krakatoa volcano near Sertung Island. In order to win the million-dollar prize, Mann had to survive this simulation for forty-eight minutes. This money would be more than enough for Eve and Mann to pull off a plan they had been hatching for nine months—to digitalize and make available the contents of all the books in the world and have governments subsidize authors and publishers every time someone read their books. Eve and Mann called this their Project Alexandria.

The scenario for the simulation matched the Indonesian islands exactly. They had been mapped out in detail together with the rest of the planet by Google Maps. In fact, the simulation contemplated all of Earth, because the Maitrevac's quantum computing capacity made it simpler to do it that way instead of confining the experience to the islands alone. Thus, the simulation would function the same as the Earth, with all of its ecosystems, life forms, and climates, both on the surface and below, from the core of the Earth to the stratosphere. All of these data had already been compiled and deduced by the Maitrevac in order to carry out all of its commercial functions. The recreational function Mann would soon be using was but a strategy of X's to launch his new product. The Maitrevac, however, had other very distinct purposes. The only missing element in all of this was the human component: Mann would be the sole person in this simulated world. Just Mann.

Everything has to turn out okay, thought Eve. *These guys don't take any risks, and if they say they're ready, it's because they really are.*

And she was right. The solar flares announced to occur that morning did not pose any kind of real hazard. All variables had been considered.

> @Wikipedia: Chaos is the complexity of alleged causality in relationships among phenomena in the absence of an observable linear path linking cause to effect. The inability to subject something to absolutely every variable as defined by variations makes it impossible to accurately determine future events. Because it is impossible to contemplate the absolute values of the variables that could affect something, we consequently end up with a system in which any phenomenon in the universe, no matter how insignificant, can potentially trigger a wave of events that will alter the entire system. The customary illustration of this is the "butterfly effect," and its proposal that a butterfly flapping its wings in one corner of the Earth may unleash a tornado in another.

> @NASA: A solar flare is an intense burst of radiation after the release of magnetic energy associated with sunspots. It may contain a billion tons of matter accelerating at several million miles

per hour in a spectacular explosion. Solar matter
then travels through space, impacting any planet
or space vehicle it encounters in its way.

"This way," said Adam as they entered the dome.

They were met by an audience of thirty-five special guests,
four reporters, ten scientists, four paramedics, three engineers and
four cameras broadcasting the event to the 3.5 billion people already
online for the simulation on their Retinality and other increasingly
obsolete devices like televisions, cellphones, and computer monitors.
It was the most awaited event in recent years. The public speculated
widely on the fun uses for the Maitrevac and its potentially endless
processing capacity.

Until then, people had only had access to augmented realities
via devices like the Retinality, but these were subjective realities and
isolated one from another. Computing capacity had been insuffi-
cient to create a virtual reality that could be shared and perceived
by large numbers of people...until now. The Maitrevac was about
to open the doors so everyone in the world could access the same
alternative, augmented, improved, and shared reality, without having to dispense with objective reality. It would no longer matter how
things, people, or situations might be in objective reality, because
the Maitrevac could now tell another story everybody could see and
eventually smell, feel, savor, and sniff as well. An authentic alternative reality available to anyone for a hundred dollars a month, which
sponsorships would soon make even more affordable for every individual. There would now exist three kinds of reality: an objective
reality shared by all humankind, subjective realities perceived by each
individual from their own viewpoints, and alternative reality created
by the Maitrevac and shared by all human beings in the same way as
objective reality. Contrary to the futuristic scenarios science-fiction
writers fantasized about, this alternative reality would not exist segregated from objective reality—it would complement it. The real and
virtual worlds would start to merge. Would this new world receive
and consider real the components of digital worlds? What would
become of digital life and level II and III simulated intelligences that

would at last find the way to free themselves of the digital prisons they were created in? The whole situation represented enormous business opportunities and at the same time enormous risks. Every product and service selling any experience perceivable by the senses would have to upgrade itself or perish.

"Change is a wave," Adam told Mann.

"*That can destroy you unless you surf it,*" interrupted Mann.

"That's right." Adam chuckled. "Ready to take on this big barrel?"

Eve, Mann, and Adam approached the center of the gigantic dome, where a white recliner, shaped like an Arne Jacobsen egg chair, basked under a soft white light.

"Have a seat, please," Adam indicated. Mann obliged.

The lights in the hall grew dimmer, and little by little the large skylight on the top of the dome began to close like the sphincter of a live creature. Complete darkness. Eight minutes went by before everyone's eyes got accustomed to the dark and began to perceive minuscule particles of light that had been there all along, but until then invisible to all in attendance. Like fireflies, these light particles traveled among the guests heralding in the initial chords of Daft Punk's "Veridis Quo."

Slowly, more light particles of different sizes began to appear. They were stars. Once their eyes were ready, the guests detected a huge circumstellar nebula.

"It's the Eagle Nebula!" remarked Elon Musk, sitting among the special guests there.

"It's a mere projection, Elon," interjected Ray Kurzweil, who was also there.

"So what is real?" asked Rob Nail, the president of Singularity University. This produced an ironical smile on the faces of the other special guests, including Peter Diamandis, Sergey Brin, and Neil Jacobstein.

As if the nebula had been waiting to be recognized, it took its cue and unfolded its majestic beauty, depth, and colors that transformed the darkness inside the dome into a real vision of outer space. The audience cheered while those watching through their Retinality joined in the celebration. The fireflies came to a stop, revealing their true nature: miniature stars orbited by tiny planets that reacted to the minute air currents produced by the guests' breathing.

The gentlest sigh could throw whole solar systems into a cosmic journey to the bottom of the dome. Stardust from the nebula started to move and take on different shapes.

"Look, a buffalo!" said a guest.

"Daft Punk!" shouted another. The Thomas Bangalter and Guy-Manuel de Homem-Christo duo was beginning to take shape above the audience.

The people at home who were tech-equipped for it had the same experience and witnessed the first execution of an alternative reality shared by millions. At the dome and from their homes, humans began to manipulate the cosmos, dance, and play with the stars and planets like children play with the seed heads of dandelions on any spring afternoon. Meanwhile, Daft Punk, or a simulation of the duo, made everyone's hearts race with one of their greatest hits. It was all a veritable dance with the stars. People at home played at being gods for a few minutes, manipulating time, space, the stars, and planets at will, making their will the will of the cosmos. Once again, Mr. X had sent a powerful message to humanity without ever uttering a single word.

All of a sudden, the stars stood still and froze on the spot, next to their planets and the nebula. They started to approach one another as if attracted by the force of gravity. The closer they got to each other, the brighter they shined. They were being summoned anonymously and clustered at the center of the dome precisely over Mann. They concentrated into a singularity, a point of light one centimeter in diameter, the size of which did not vary as it absorbed the stars, but became more brilliant every time until its powerful light illuminated the entire dome and bathed it in total white splendor the instant the very last little star touched it. Only white light remained, as if somebody had switched on an enormous xenon flashlight or detonated a light grenade in the center of that dome. Everybody's pupils shrunk in confusion after being plunged into the great white void. Once the people's eyes recovered, they were able to make out Mr. X in his space pirate avatar, floating where the singularity had exploded only a few seconds before.

"**Humans**," said X.

The guests cheered, and the people at home joined in. It had been three years since X's last public appearance, so the fact that he was present this afternoon only underscored how special this event really was. That very instant CorporationX shares rose 6.7 percent.

"**Zeus erred**," he continued. "**Prometheus presented us with fire stolen from the gods, and now thanks to that fire we have taken the place of those who would condemn him. Before the first half of this century ends, we will shed our condition of Sapiens of the Earth to become a cosmic and immortal species. We will be able to make love on a faraway beach of a faraway planet orbiting Alfa Centauri, to delegate to chance the task of deciding which extinct species to resuscitate first, and which second, to discover what came before the Big Bang and what exists beyond a black hole, to learn what happened before and after our birth and our death, for death will no longer be a sentence but a decision. We will accomplish this because, like Prometheus, when we look at matter and energy, we do not see inexorable forces we must surrender to but a riddle that must be solved. When we saw fire, we did not shy away from it but mastered it. What is made possible by the Maitrevac will allow us to conquer ourselves as a species and as individuals. We will overcome the causes of all our evils. The words poverty, sickness, and hunger will exist only in dictionaries. We will conquer the ultimate mysteries of physics and chemistry and use them to create a happy universe. We have come all this way without turning into machines as some feared and without being destroyed by them, as others feared. Machines made us better. They are not our enemies nor our allies, but an extension of ourselves, like a shell is to a snail or a nest to an eagle.**" He paused for a second. "**What have we become?**" He opened his arms and then more stars, billions of stars, sprung from his brow. "**In Metaphysics, Aristotle said, 'things that are posterior in becoming are prior in form and substantiality. Thus, a man is prior to a boy and humans to sperm, for the one already has** form, while the other has not. Additionally, because everything produced trends to a beginning and an end: the final cause is a beginning and the end of production is that beginning.'" Again, he paused. He opened his right fist, revealing the singularity floating a few centimeters from his palm.

"Today we will not create a god. We will create the creator of that god. And if the god created by his creation is anterior to his creation, are we not forever the creators of that creator? Are we not and therefore have always been prior to the act as a power? Therefore, the final cause of humankind is the beginning of what humanity creates. Today, we create. Today we are creators. Today, creation is the creator," said X. Meanwhile, the singularity that appeared like a little sphere of fire began to sparkle relentlessly. X began to fade. His voice became softer.

"Imagine a world where, given the necessary information, everything can be simulated. Every result becomes predictable. Every disaster avoidable. Every goal achievable. No more error, no more drama, no more chaos. With this technology, we will accomplish whatever future we desire. We will be able to decipher the secrets of physics, chemistry, and someday the history of humanity and the universe. The Maitrevac cannot only predict the future using information from the present but can also potentially deduce the past. We are about to rewrite the history of humankind, the planet, and some day, of the galaxy and the entire universe. No more mysteries. What is really out there? Up there? How did everything begin? How will everything end? Where there was darkness, there will be knowledge. Where there was doubt, there will be certainty. Where there was chaos, there will be order. To imagine is to create. Our tools are creations of our imagination, from the wheel to the Maitrevac. Today our imagination will claim its power. Imagination and reality are no longer segregated. Our imagination will be our reality, and our reality will be our imagination."

His now distant voice reminded his immense audience that in reality, X had never been with them. Or had he?

"What remains to be imagined?"

There was a sudden darkness, and then it was light again.

"What remains to be...created?"

Meanwhile, outside of the dome, colossal northern lights took over the sky. The reporters outside began to record them.

"This must be another one of X's tricks," Adam said as he ordered the dome to display the real sky, and the dome became a transparent bubble.

The aurora borealis intensified into a spectacle of light and color. Eve gazed at it in amazement.

"There they are," she said to herself. "All my life I searched for the northern lights, and here they are, smack in the middle of a desert." Her right hand closed even tighter over a little piece of quartz her grandmother had given her the last time they saw each other. Eve closed her eyes and trusted that destiny had to be what it had to be, and that which has to be always is.

"Ready the Maitrevac," Adam instructed the crew.

They started preparing the machine.

"Hook Mann up." He raised his voice to be heard over the voices still cheering the aurora borealis spectacle and X's speech.

Once Mann was fully connected to the Maitrevac, Adam reached into his right pocket and produced a couple of M&Ms, one red and one blue. Mann picked the red.

"Start the countdown!" shouted Adam with a smile.

And the countdown began.

Asgardia, 21 December AD 2029

Four hundred and eighty-four kilometers above the African continent, the Asgardia came to a halt in preparation to bloom. The colossal sphere epitomized stillness in the unlimited reaches of space while the Earth danced around the Sun and the Moon around the Earth.

Leonardo patiently waited for the Sun king to peer over the horizon of planet Earth. He watched darkness rapidly shy away from the first rays of light while giant clouds cast whimsical shadows on the surface of the planet. The Indian Ocean shone silver and then lit up in gold with the dawn.

"Six, five, four, three, two, one," recited Leonardo. On cue, Richard Wagner's *Ride of the Valkyries* started playing in the Asgardia.

The point of the sphere closest to the Sun shifted as if a small drop had fallen there, originating subtle waves that convulsed the liquid carbon of the surface. One by one, these waves slowly spread over the sphere. When they met on the opposite side from where they had originated, they clashed, producing an elongated shape, like a tadpole tail, that grew longer with every crashing wave. A few minutes later, the now long slender whip was producing a rhythmic tapping as it moved downward. This in turn generated waves moving in the opposite direction on the surface of the sphere. When the waves from both poles met at the equator of the Asgardia, they produced an extremely thin ring that rode the crest of the impact. The ring became more distinct with every oncoming wave. It then began to spin until it broke into five parts: five immense and delicate petals designed to tap the abundant energy of the Sun. On Earth, people could observe the appearance of the giant black orchid in the sky every 29.53 days (the same duration as a lunar cycle) when it was ready to feed. At its core, X rested.

X was part of popular culture, a mysterious celebrity. Whenever the Asgardia bloomed, all kinds of events were held the world over. Black Orchid festivities became very popular everywhere. The first of these festivities was held in Black Rock City, by the Mayan Warrior during the annual Burning Man event, where it became customary to celebrate a monthly Black Orchid Party, attended by people from all over the world.

On the streets, one could often see men and women with black orchid tattoos on their arms, legs, or backs. In 2028, a new theater production called *The Black Orchid* premiered in Brooklyn. It told the story of Emily, a young ballerina who possessed a black orchid that turned into an unfathomable lover every night. He made love to her in the shadows in exchange for increasingly dark favors. The specter was the victim of a genius (although mad) scientist whose wife he had seduced. The scientist had subjected the mislaid lover to genetic modifications, whereby he could only obtain the endorphins and serotonin his brain required from the blood of women taken immediately after they were sexually satisfied. This slave of passion now had supernatural powers and strength, in addition to regenerating abilities, and virtually immortal cells. But unless he had his ration of blood enriched by the orgasms of his victims, his brain would eventually stop working after twenty-nine days. This would paralyze him, but he would remain alive forever and ever.

Once the Asgardia's petals were completely open, the feeding process could no longer be seen from Earth. But from the perspective of the Sun, it was truly amazing. After the gigantic flower had its fill of solar energy, the bottom half of the central sphere facing the

Sun began to shine like incandescent metal. Its metallic brilliance turned to a blinding yellow tonality and then to absolute white. Out of this whiteness came a pistil of sorts, a liquid, transparent bubble at the center of which X floated in fetal position. This was known as Ambrosia 5.0. It updated X's cells every three months endowing him with ever more life and skills. In the course of four minutes, his aqueous body turned white as milk, then peach like a placenta. Then, with the Sun as the sole witness, X's genetic updating process began. The luminous particles that had permeated the petals of the black orchid, now loaded with immeasurable amounts of photons (veritable light sperm), poured into Ambrosia 5.0 and adhered themselves to X's skin, illuminating, penetrating, and mutating him into an organic and technological hybrid.

The cells of his new aurified skin let him remain in outer space forty-three minutes. They absorbed what oxygen they needed from X's lungs that were technologically enabled to store compressed oxygen. The following year, X planned to do away with food and oxygen altogether and absorb all the energy he required from the Sun.

After completing this process, the Asgardia closed its petals, and X landed directly on his metallic kalapa throne in the middle of a spacious area designed after Salvador Dali's *Last Supper*. Large white stone slabs ornamented the floor and central table, now presided over by X. He rested on his throne in ecstasy, like a heroin addict after a shot following weeks of abstinence. He sat still like this for several hours.

A bell rang three times and broke the silence.

"**Come in**," ordered X. Leonardo approached him.

"Isn't a molecule of DNA a warranty for immortality?" Leonardo gestured and moved his hands excessively while quoting Salvador Dalí. "It is the monarchical cell par excellence. Each of its two halves is exactly joined to the other half, like Gala is joined to me. Everything opens and closes and is accurately interrelated. Inheritance depends upon a sovereign mechanism, and life is the product of the absolute power of deoxyribonucleic acid. DNA is the key to immortality."

"**It is**," X agreed while an army of microscopic aurified kalapa robots flew from X's skin to Leonardo's face.

They alighted just above his lips and drew him a rounded, pointy Dali moustache while on his forehead, between his eyebrows, they grew a rhinoceros horn that continued to grow until its weight compelled Leonardo into a forced dramatic reverence. The horn was exactly the same Dali portrayed in his *Galacidalacidesoxiribunucleicacid* painting, which he dedicated in 1963 to James Watson and Francis Crick, the discoverers of DNA.

"Lord, the simulation in Atacama will begin in a few minutes. The people await your message," Leonardo told him while still bowing uncomfortably.

"**Humanity suffers from an inferiority complex**," X commented while Leonardo offered him a splendid tiger cape. Two huge fangs dangled from each shoulder; they had belonged to the first saber-tooth tiger resuscitated by CorporationX.

"**One day, the universe will be ours, but humanity still does not believe this.**"

X put on the heavy cape and started walking. The walls began screening animations in the style of Japanese manga, depicting creatures from the phylogenetic tree of life, from *archaea* and *eukaryote* bacteria, to dinosaurs, mammals, reptiles, flowers, plants, and finally, *Homo sapiens*.

"**What next, Leonardo?**" X inquired.

A *Homo sapiens* on the wall attempted to produce fire using a couple of dry branches until Mr. X's space pirate avatar showed up next to him and presented *Homo sapiens* with the seed of fire, which changed hands at that moment. *Homo sapiens* quickly shared fire with his tribe waiting in the background of the image. They began to worship and use fire, and very soon began to misuse it. They burned down trees and their houses. X's avatar had to step in to blow out the voracious flames before they eliminated the little tribe. The avatar then walked toward the screen and became the image that would be broadcast to the Atacama Desert for the inauguration of the Maitrevac.

"**Broadcast this to Atacama**," X ordered Leonardo.

As he made his speech, he kept his eyes fixed on the Sun, just as Alexander the Great had kept his eyes fixed on King Darius's war car in the Battle of Gaugamela, when he announced his intention to conquer the known world. X, however, did not address humanity but infinity, and he did not announce his intention to conquer the known world but the universe still to be known. He knew himself the most powerful being in all the planets where humankind, now an interplanetary species, was present. Not arrogance but hunger drove him. As a rule, he never looked downward toward his accomplishments, his conquests, but rather upward, toward what he had yet to do, what he still might conquer. He knew that somewhere in the universe, an intelligence superior to human intelligence existed, and he felt fearful. The alternative, a vast universe devoid of an intelligence superior to human intelligence also filled him with fear, because the only explanation for that according to Fermi's paradox (the contradiction between the high probability that other intelligent civilizations exist, and the lack of evidence of such civilizations) was the existence of the Great Filter.

> @Wikipedia: The Great Filter is what keeps life from arising from inert matter and eventually becoming a superior civilization as defined by the Kardashev scale. This barrier to the evolution of intelligent forms of life could manifest in various ways, the most likely of which is self-destruction of the dominating species through its own technology.

> @Wikipedia: Proposed in 1964 by Russian astrophysicist Nikolai Kardashev, the scale that bears his name, constitutes a method to measure the degree of technological evolution in a given civilization. It includes three categories. Type I means that the civilization has mastered all energy resources on its planet of origin. Type II, that it has done so on its planetary system. And Type III, that it has mastered all energy resources to be found in its galaxy.

Would human civilization be the first in the galaxy to become a type II or III? If not, then where is that first civilization, or where is the evidence that it ever existed? X was not willing to cease existing until he could answer these questions.

All his simulations admitted that any intelligence equal or greater than human would very unlikely be hostile. He still cringed at the thought, however. He couldn't pinpoint what made him fearful, but he felt so anyway. Only many years afterward, when universal eras were counted by chronons and no longer by years, X would realize that all he had ever feared was chaos itself, and all he had ever yearned for was control and nothing more—absolute, total control over everything and everybody.

He finished his speech and turned to Leonardo. **"Activate the electromagnetic shield, and do not interrupt me any further."**

"But, Lord, the solar activity…"

X cut the android short. **"Everything is under control**," he declared, dismissing both Leonardo and sunlight.

Now alone in black empty space, none of the shapes surrounding him—walls, ceiling—were discernable. Slowly billions of hues and shades of purple traveling from the billions of planets, gases, and stars in the Orion Nebula began to emerge. The level of detail was absolute, as if X were actually suspended in the midst of a nebula bursting with color, one that the rest of humanity would never perceive. The largest of the stars ejected a small coronal mass in X's direction. It began to move slowly and patiently toward him. As it came closer, the mass grew equal to his own size and unhurriedly took shape as a woman.

This splendid goddess borne by flames had violet eyes the shade of petunia petals, shiny obsidian-black hair to her shoulders, and perfect audacious bangs covering her forehead. Her generous lips were as golden as the beads that hung from her ears and neck. Her breasts like planets exposed to Orion adorned her thorax. Her perfect waist swayed with each majestic step she took and was dressed in golden medallions that hid her pubis. This was Xleopatra, the last pharaoh of ancient Egypt.

"Why did you disturb me?" Xleopatra asked.

"Today is a special day."

"Did you build a new toy?"

X laughed and kissed her. Xleopatra was an artificial intelligence created by the Maitrevac. She had initially been planned as a replica of the Egyptian queen to keep X company. When he created her, however, X projected part of himself in her: his own femininity, capacity for love, interest in others, his ability to write poetry and to paint art, to give and protect life. All of these features had been distilled from his own personality and now were embodied in Xleopatra. X's essential psychological yearnings (his deepest desires and wonts) also resided in her. Quite literally, she was his other half. X had programmed her to be as intelligent as technologically possible. No reservations. He had given her absolute freedom without any reservations. The only rule he had introduced into the depths of Xleopatra's nature was to love him without reservations. Albeit undeserving of this kind of love, X was nurtured by Xleopatra's warmth and the euphoric feeling of satisfaction and security she gave him. For X, she represented all that was beautiful and good in the universe, all the wonderful life experiences he had had and would ever have.

The gods held hands and danced like the Sun and the Moon floating at zero gravity, surrounded by stars. They kissed and made love during entire astrological cycles of the Orion Nebula.

"What did you create me for?" Xleopatra whispered in his ear between pauses and moans.

"That I may learn how to love," X answered.

"To learn how to love yourself," she amended.

Projections of stars caressed their skins and expanded with every orgasmic spasm. Every caress and every blow increased the density of Orion's black holes. The whole nebula contracted and distended with the pelvic muscles of the divine pair while their own hearts embraced.

Xleopatra knew everything X thought and felt. She eventually became X's sole company because only she possessed truly free intelligence, and therefore X respected her. The first thing X did after creating Ambrosia 5.0 was to keep his promise to Xleopatra of giving her a functional organic body. This, he did. Xleopatra incarnated, and X inevitably loved her from the very start. He had created her following his most unconscious longing. He could not help but love her. Their first shared days had been confusing. X couldn't help challenging the real or fictitious nature of that empyrean love. One day, he simply stopped caring and ceased to keep his love silent. From then on, he saw every sun set from the west of Xleopatra's violet eyes and could never again fall asleep without hearing "I love you" from his divine accomplice.

"What kind of love is ours?" Xleopatra asked X before they parted and she returned to the reaches of the nebula X had made for her.

"The purest love. Love for myself through you, and love for everything through me."

@Einstein2.0: Ironical, isn't it, that what I am about to say regarding simulations should come from me, a simulation. An entire reality, simulated? Sounds brilliant, very useful. But what is a simulation? Have you ever asked yourselves? People might say, "A simulation is a representation of reality." But when does a simulation stop being one and to become a reality? And when does a reality stop being a reality to become a simulation? I'm not saying that you should give up on this enterprise, only that you need to understand that there are many variables neither you or the simulation are contemplating nor can contemplate. The universe itself is built upon the premise of chaos—has resulted from chaos. Evolution results from chaos. Chaos has allowed things to change, and those changes that have proven the most apt for what has changed to function are the ones that have transcended because they created a more able version.

@StephenHawking2.0: That is correct, my friend. Whole universes have failed while this one has survived. When matter and antimatter mutually canceled out one another instants after the Big Bang, a perfect imbalance made the existence of the universe, as we know it, possible.

@Einstein2.0: An imbalance caused by chaos.

@StephenHawking2.0: The fundamental algorithm of this universe is chaos which allows everything to change constantly. Without chaos, there can be no change. And without change, there can be no evolution. A simulation seeks to annul chaos, because only that way it can be effective. Chaos, at least in this universe, cannot be annulled. If chaos dies, the universe dies with it.

@Einstein2.0: Congratulations! You have just discovered the secret message. Please send your answer to "Old Pink."

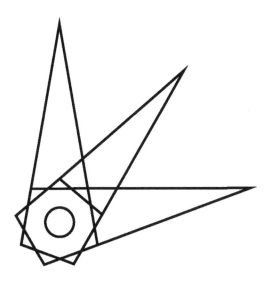

Atacama Desert, 21 December AD 2029

While X enjoyed making love to Xleopatra thousands of kilometers above the surface of the Earth, Adam gave the order, and the timer began counting 260 seconds for the simulation to begin.

"There it goes," Adam told Mann as he injected his arm with an army of nanobots containing quantum links to the Maitrevac. The merger began. These nanobots would become a part of Mann forever.

"Merger status: 1 percent…9 percent…16 percent… 39 percent…"

This technology, developed by Mr. X's companies, made it possible to create a single identity from the informatic fields of the brain and a computer. It worked by introducing a fluid of particles previously linked to other particles in a computer capable of translating mental or brain information into digital data and vice versa.

Quantum entanglement was used to transmit information for the first time in 2022. That year, the Massachusetts Institute of Technology held a round of Atari's classic Pong game against an individual on a routine exploration aboard the USS *Callister*, traveling between the orbits of Mars and Jupiter. Herson Mejía (the twenty-one-year-old student at MIT who directed the project) shouted for joy at this victorious accomplishment. However, even though communication was already traveling beyond the speed of light, by the time his voice was heard by Mexican astronaut Rodolfo Neri Vela, the second game of Pong had already begun, and the Mexican was winning.

> @Wikipedia: Quantum entanglement—a property foretold in 1935 by Einstein, Podolsky, and Rosen—is a phenomenon in which the quantum states of two or more objects are simultaneously and immediately modified when any one of them undergoes any change, regardless of how distantly they may be separated.

In terms of the simulation Mann was involved in, the great turning point occurred in 2024 when Adam Gazzaley finally entangled organic systems with nonorganic systems, thanks to the Neuralink patents Elon Musk had made available to the public that same year. This made it possible to connect a human brain to a computer in real time.

From then on, "artificial" and "natural" intelligence were joined and never separated again. Science fiction theories that considered machines potentially hazardous for the human species became obsolete. It was now evident that man and machine would not part ways, nor would compete against each other. Rather, the opposite. The paths of man and technology were one. War, should it come to pass, would not be humans against machines but humans merged to machines against unmerged humans, a situation akin to Neanderthals and *Homo sapiens*.

Using this technology, Mr. X planned to exponentially develop his own intelligence. Scientists knew about it and celebrated this possibility, ignorant of the fact that neither them or anybody other than Mr. X would see the sublimation of his essence in the name of the species and life on Earth, three hundred and eighty million years later, i.e., four biological eras after the appearance of life on our blue dot in space.

The human species constituted a caterpillar, and X planned to be the first butterfly to transcend the confines of biology and organic intelligence in order to become the first super intelligent consciousness.

"Merger status 68 percent," said Adam.

Just then, as the onlookers outside the dome gazed at the spectacle of the strange aurora borealis, a few grains of sand suddenly started to vibrate. The children tagging close to their families laughed at the way the fine hair on their arms began to stand on end one by one. Mrs. Fernandez, Mr. Fernandez's wife, laughed out loud when her husband's hairpiece gave him a slight electric shock on the head. The man, as if bitten by an opossum, ripped the hairpiece off his head. It landed in front of a child who stomped on it with delight. The aurorae in all their beautiful shades of jade, turquoise, lime, and yellow green became even more beautiful yet violent. The noisy crowd suddenly grew quiet to admire the unexpected wonder in the sky, evocative of spectral titans waging a battle armed with fleeting swords. The air was charged with gloomy static. The crowd clapped. When the timer got to second 12, ominous clouds in the landscape began to emit a strange amber light. At the same moment, a fleeing flock of flamingos darkened the sky.

> @WorldClimate: Aurorae borealis of a kind never seen before were recorded in South America. They occurred at the same time coronal ejections from the Sun impacted the Earth's atmosphere.

> @WeatherCH: This morning, the operational systems of fifty-nine telecom satellites were fried by the largest solar flare ever recorded.

"Something's not right," Eve murmured, biting her nails when the first bolt of lightning hit. "Something is definitely wrong!" she screamed. "Turn off the computer!"

The crowd outside the dome split into those who panicked and fled, and the people who thought it was show and cheered. Eve tried to get closer to Mann, who had already lost consciousness, but security staff stopped her more than three meters away from him. Only Mr. X could interrupt the simulation, but he was otherwise engaged and carefree.

Two seconds after the simulation began, a bolt of lightning crashed directly on the quantum servers four kilometers away from the dome.

Mann began to convulse.

"Stop that! You're killing him!" Eve screamed, still unsuccessfully trying to reach Mann.

> @CNBC: The Earth's axis shifted four centimeters after being impacted this morning by solar flare.

> @TVnoticias: 62 volcanos all over the world are on red alert due to the solar event recorded in South America, declare scientists.

Forty-eight seconds after the simulation began, the processers overheated and activated the emergency shutdown. Mann convulsed during all forty-eight seconds. Cameras and millions of people watching the event recorded it. It wasn't long before company stock plummeted.

Less than two hours later, the HyperLoop (a sealed tube transportation system capable of reaching three-fourths of the speed of light) had already taken Mann to the Clinical Hospital of the University of Chile.

> @Techinvex: Absolute silence from Mr. X after this morning's events. Is this the beginning of the end of his empire?

> @WSJ: Nasdaq falls two points after today's events. X still remains silent.

By the following morning, news about Mann, Mr. X, and the solar flares had begun their march toward oblivion. Within five weeks, company stock had regained its value. No one would know, until long afterward, how the fate of the entire universe had shifted that very morning in the Atacama Desert. Mann sealed a secret pact with chaos and the universe in the forty-eight seconds he had lived in a manner infinitely different from the rest of the witnesses and anything any human being had ever experienced.

Asgardia, 8 April AD 2034

Mr. X did not attribute much importance to the Atacama accident. When Leonardo reported the events to him, within minutes he planned and executed a strategy that would minimize damages to his image and retrieve stock value.

In the five years since the accident, X had never thought about it again. He busied himself with what he called "the Conquest of the Solar System" and managed to update himself and the Maitrevac several times. His new body was solely made up of what were now exponentially superior kalapas. His consciousness was backed up on the Asgardia, as well as a few supercomputers he had secretly placed on every planet in the solar system.

It had been some time since he last interacted with humans. The excellence of his own intellect had made honest interest in any human being quite impossible. Instead, he had deepened his relation-ship with Xleopatra and a few other historic characters he had simu-lated or reincarnated and who had now become his court, his family, and his generals in the battle against chaos over cosmic conquest.

That afternoon, X was admiring the landscape on planet Earth from his privileged position on the Asgardia. On the horizon, he could see the curvature of the planet, outlined in a contrasting turquoise line produced by the density of the lower layers of the atmosphere. Straight velvety clouds floated over land and sea, like colossal and irregular blocks of ice covered in snow while powerful lightning reverberated over Oceania. In the background, his own improved version of Antonio Vivaldi's *Four Seasons* was playing as he set out to enjoy the sensory pleasures his technology and quantum mind provided him via a tool he called the Great Observer. This tool linked the perception of his five traditional senses and his new senses generated by the Maitrevac to all existing sources of information on planet Earth.

"**Leonardo, prepare the Observer**," X ordered.

X contemplated the Earth as an art form of infinite beauty, ready to be experienced by anyone capable of perceiving all the data generated by every being on the planet able to perceive reality. He had devoted a great deal of time and energy to the Maitrevac for the sole purpose of optimizing the simple experience of sitting down to observe the planet with the same religiousness a good wine taster devotes to a superb vintage.

X was born in Sierra Leone in the 1980s. Little is known about his childhood. His father, an Irish businessman named Harry, had fled to Sierra Leone from Europe in the wake of Bloody Sunday (January 30, 1972). Authorities were after him because he had been a member of the Northern Ireland Civil Rights Association. In his new habitat, Harry turned to diamond trafficking until he died in a street brawl when X was twelve years old. X inherited a discrete collection of uncut diamonds, valued at $88,000 in the black market. His father had hidden the gems in a sack of bones buried in the yard of X's grammar school.

Nothing is known about X's mother, whom he very likely never met. Alone in the world and armed with a vulnerable and illegal fortune in diamonds, X was able to leave Sierra Leone for Osaka, Japan, in 1997. With only his grammar school education, he learned the art of informatics and robotics thanks to an engineer he met at a video game arcade. At seventeen, he began to peddle espionage software of dubious origin between Japan (his mother's probable birthplace), South Korea, and San Francisco. In 2005, he was brought to trial in Tokyo for various IT offenses and kept in custody. His charges were dismissed thanks to his US partner, a Republican and former military person, who had several contacts among the Japanese diplomatic corps. After this incident, X moved to San Francisco, where he is suspected of having collaborated in a few CIA projects. He was not heard from again until he made public his vast and mysterious fortune built in the 2010s cryptocurrency market.

"**Who is the observer?**" X inquired.

A circular window opened. A part of the Asgardia became as fluid as mercury and floated toward X's head where it solidified into a strange halo measuring several meters in diameter. It began to spin and cast a neon blue light. X opened his arms, his hands. He looked at planet Earth and smiled.

The Asgardia had also evolved exponentially since the unveiling of the Maitrevac in 2029. It was completely made of kalapas that could replicate themselves and join together to create complex structures, such as the electromagnetic nuclei that united all nine spheres inside the Asgardia.

Thanks to the accomplishments and discoveries of the Maitrevac and so on and so forth, X had designed technologies that far exceeded the boldest forecasts of futurists in the early part of the third millennium. Although formally the same, the Maitrevac was now actually on its eighty-seventh version, i.e., it had been updated eighty-seven times since its creation, and every update signified exponential changes. It currently updated itself every fifty-four days.

X also looked different. Whenever he moved from one place to another, he was accompanied by kalapas invisible to the human eye and scattered at an imperceptible fog-like density that nevertheless stretched over a 250-meter radius around X and 145 kilometers around the Asgardia.

No distinction existed among the Asgardia, Maitrevac, and X. They were one and the same. X's physical body was merely the core of his personality, but he was where the Maitrevac was, and like a ghost, he could appear and disappear anywhere there were kalapas.

"**Activate**," X ordered, preparing himself for the delight his exponential senses were about to perceive from Earth.

For some time now, the only thing X considered to have any intrinsic value was information. Using the Maitrevac, he had already infiltrated almost every computer and information cloud illegally. Anywhere there were bits, X was there. Anywhere there were data, the Maitrevac was there. Without exception.

X began to aspire to monopolize not only computer-generated information and data but human perception as well. Faithful to the ideas of Schopenhauer, X believed that the world of objects was a representation absolutely conditioned by a subject's perception. He thought that every human perception, in itself constituted a version of the universe, and he wanted to learn them all. Ninety-eight percent of the world population had Retinality, so the Maitrevac had access to everything seen by that population.

Retinality offered users a free or a paid service. Both were similar, the only difference being the ads in the free service. The paid service cost ten dollars a month and dispensed users from advertising.

The Maitrevac observed everything humans saw through Retinality. In 2031, X started to gain access to what other forms of intelligence were observing. He initially installed Retinality in a few of the larger land and aquatic mammals. This procedure, however, proved too slow. In 2033, he developed a bacterium that could access the neuronal networks of insects and directly transmit their sensory information to Maitrevac processors scattered all over the world. Implants were no longer necessary because this bacterium transmitted information that was naturally perceived by insects. The bacteria (to be known later as the precursor for IOLT, the Internet of the Living Things) translated chemical information into electromagnetic data.

By 2036, X estimated every insect and animal had been infected with the bacteria. Nothing would be perceived by any sentient being on planet Earth without X perceiving it as well. As soon as he was able to perceive everything perceivable on Earth, he would use all that information to simulate and predict the future, with a minimal degree of error. Because for the Maitrevac, even animal and human behaviors were but simple, 99 percent predictable, algorithms once sufficient information had been collected.

Such was X, a mixture of the will to protect life and the will to fashion himself into a god. It had been some time since he had condemned the immature nature of the human species. He hated humanity, then forgave it. He considered that all his past suffering and loneliness could be attributed to chaos, never to evil. In his opinion, every human mind was vulnerable to chaos, and hence all mental power, and the power of technology even, were vulnerable as well.

Once he understood the imminent certainty of technological singularity, he also realized the enormous risk it entailed for the future of the species and life on Earth.

> @Ray Kurzweil: the technological singularity is a future moment in which (due to exponential growth in technology), the rate of technological change will be so swift and its impact so profound that human life will irreversibly transform from one moment to the next, and it will be impossible to predict what such changes will look like.

X understood that with democratization of the power to create came democratization of the power to destroy. He therefore decided to devote the rest of his life to sublimating *Homo sapiens* and ensuring a transition to the singularity without its involving self-destruction of the species. He took upon himself the role of protector of humans and of life on Earth and, while he was at it, become a god. What would he protect people from? From themselves and any planetary or cosmic threat, whether natural or staged, that could threaten sapiens' becoming a cosmic species.

The only thing he overlooked was to protect life from himself.

"And then there was sound," X commanded the Great Observer.

X began his experience listening to heavy rainfall pounding on the waters of the Pacific Ocean. In the Pacific, he heard four active volcanos and accompanying hollow sounds made by huge clouds of ashes and incandescent flames roaring in the atmosphere in same constant and distant manner as whales singing from the bottoms of oceans. On the Australian outback, he heard the humming of bees; in London, household doorbells; in New York, the honking of horns; in Buenos Aires, babies crying; in Thailand, the shrill screaming of little girls jumping rope; in Brazil, the shouting of children kicking soccer balls; in San Tropez, the kiss of two people in love; in Florence, the moaning of a virgin; in Montana, the bellow of a bull bison; in the Serengeti, the roar of a couple of lions competing for a lioness; in Canada, old trees creaking as they bid farewell to their cycle and returned to the soil that bore them. He heard timber exploding from the impact of the lightning, as the worms and tics in their innards hidden from the rain whispered the sounds of the netherworld.

X then moved on to smell. He endowed colors with smells and was thus able to smell the whiteness of sea salt, grayish feces of whales; blackened sulfur from volcanos; light blue sweetness from the Amazon waters; pristine blue of cloud ice; reddish kisses of millions of sweethearts; pinkish peach-colored placentas of millions of mothers giving birth; red blood of hundreds of people being murdered; whiteness of the milk suckled by babies; colors from thousands of flowers blooming and the pollen collected by hardworking bees; aurified electricity of lightning thundering on the ocean, on land and the mountains, on glaciers, in the jungles, the desert; and in an alley of a forgotten neighborhood in Río de Janeiro, where a couple took refuge from the rain and fell prey to the tropical heat of a bed, the smell of which reminded Mr. X of the shelter where he slept the night he arrived on the American continent.

After that, and before opening his eyes, he decided to feel what lavender plants feel when the Sun comes up on the Blue Coast, what whales feel when they hear another whale sing thousands of kilometers away in the Pacific Ocean. He wished to feel the vibrations an Amazon jungle spider picks up when something falls on its web. The flavor of nectar on the tongue of a hummingbird as it plunges its beak into a marigold in the Valley of Mexico. The flavor of blood on the palate of a tiger in China while an antelope caught between its fangs breathes for the last time. The wind under the wings of a condor gliding over the high clouds of the Apu Ausangate in Peru. The soil and water trapped on the scales of an anaconda zigzagging along the Amazon River. The sensations of a butterfly that completes its metamorphosis and learns to fly after having dragged itself on the Appalachian Mountains in Northern Canada. The sense of fulfillment an eagle gets from catching a rainbow trout with its claws on Iliamna Lake. A mother's sensations when for the first time she holds her child covered in life and strange smells. And the atmosphere as it is being ripped by a thunderbolt.

Finally, he opened his eyes and, aided by the Maitrevac, saw what was happening at that moment on planet Earth. He saw it all, then closed his eyes and at last detached himself from the Great Observer. Just then, Leonardo emerged from the darkness of the infinite void and floated toward X.

"Do not interrupt me."

An enormous rectangular table of white marble materialized around X. Seconds later, from the pits of the unfathomable blackness of the room, a luminous streak of light opened, making way for Xleopatra. She was followed by eight men and a woman. Xleopatra kissed X and sat to his left on a throne similar to his own. Next, a gladiator of sorts walked into the venue. He had eyes like fire with a fierce look and a lion's mane. He was Alexander the Great, conqueror of the world. He kissed X's hand and sat to his right. Next came a tall slender man with refined accurate gestures. He wore an elegant purple tunic and an air of nostalgia and reflection. He was Julius Cesar, the Roman military genius and politician. He kissed X's hand and sat at the table. The fourth to appear in the dark room holding his hand over the pit of his stomach was Napoleon, the French emperor. His gait was slow, deliberate, and proud as he approached X, then kissed his hand and sat. The fifth arrival greeted everyone by slightly bowing his head. His hands alternated stroking the long beard that framed his round face as one would expect from a priest or a man devoted to meditation, but it was Temüjin, the Great Khan, Genghis Khan. He also kissed X's hand and sat.

The sixth guest to join in this bardo of dreams and nightmares, crimes and miracles, blood and life was noticeably tall, his eyes large and round, his white hair abundant, and his demeanor elegant. His sole presence could have commanded a hurricane. It was

Charlemagne, who kissed X's hand and took a seat. Number seven wore a golden turban and had an air of fantasy about him. The tips of his moustache curved, and his eyes sparkled like a serpent's, but of course he, Mehmed II, had caused the fall of the centuries-old Byzantine Empire. He too kissed X's hand and sat. Number eight caused an ambivalent reaction in Alexander because of his inherited rivalry with her, but also in Xleopatra on account of her defying beauty. Artemisia of Caria, Persian queen and warrior, kissed X's hand and sat. The ninth to approach the table was Cyrus the Great, who discreetly bowed to Artemisia before kissing X's hand and having a seat. The last to make an entrance approached X with long decisive strides. The group of vain conquerors fell silent. It was the scourge of God, the feared and revered leader of the Huns, Atilla, who then kissed X's hand and sat.

Although they had all been inspired by the figures they embodied, each one of them represented a different aspect of X's personality and intelligence. He created them to know himself better (as he had done in the case of Xleopatra) and to make them compete among each other. Nevertheless, Xleopatra and Alexander remained the most important, because all of X was divided between them. Alexander (X's sharpest and most lethal intelligence) was everything Xleopatra was not. Xleopatra was X's light, and Alexander his shadow. Day and night. Containment and explosion. Creation and destruction. Life and death.

> @CorporationX: There are three kinds of artificial intelligences. Level I intelligence: any algorithm is a level I artificial intelligence. If A, then B. For example, Apple's Siri assistant launched on October 14, 2011, does not think for herself. She only follows certain rules.
>
> Level II intelligence has its own intelligence and ability to learn but no consciousness of itself. For example, a simulated bird in a videogame is ruled by algorithms simulating independent intelligence and mental processes capable of

creating new algorithms. This is the common notion of an artificial intelligence, which is only confined to the limits of its own software and hardware. It can deduce general rules, patterns, and it can learn to create new rules.

Level III intelligence has consciousness of itself. It may, for example, attempt to simulate human intelligence and even its awareness of itself. Is this true consciousness or a simulation of it? This question perhaps may remain unanswered until we discover the nature and workings of consciousness itself. Simulations such as these may be aware of their simulated nature or may believe they are real with the same conviction you do.

In the middle of the room, presiding over this secret conclave of conquerors, X opened his arms to them as he had opened them to the Sun and Earth only moments before. His veins lit up like small bluish lightning bolts and began to send minute particles of light to his throat. Little by little, these particles bound together into diaphanous spheres, at first gaseous and later solid, then became small-scale planets and a moon that emerged from X's open mouth. They approached the conquerors the way fireflies follow light. Mercury, Venus, Earth, the Moon, Mars, Jupiter, Saturn, Uranus, Neptune, and Pluto. Mercury alighted on top of Alexander's head, Venus on Artemisia's, Earth on Xleopatra's, Jupiter on Julius Cesar's, Mars on Napoleon's, the moon on Genghis Khan's, Saturn on Charlemagne's, Uranus on Atilla's, Neptune on Mehmed's, and Pluto on Cyrus's.

A strange golden liquid began to pour itself out of nothing. Then it turned into mantles of gold that covered the bodies of the conquerors who were elegantly floating in the darkness, all moving in clockwise circles, then distancing themselves one from another, emulating the relative distances of the planets in the solar system.

X's herculean body rested, impassively, at the center of the gathering. He became a white light: the Sun. He spoke:

"It is time to rouse the universe. I give you planets. They are yours to conquer. Travel to them, investigate, experiment, evolve. You are free to adapt the principles of the Maitrevac to new horizons. I shall visit you in five years. Whoever has the best version of the Maitrevac will be rewarded. Those who fail will be eliminated. Awaken your planets from an atomic level. Turn rock into mind, ice into being. A single mind throughout the solar system and someday, beyond. All of the universe…a single being."

Never raising his voice and with eyes closed, X blew gently and dismissed his crew as if they were specs of dust. Each of them went to one of the spheres of the Asgardia, and from there departed on the crusade to control the solar system. And this was how a species that had feared fire only a few thousand years before set out to conquer all matter and energy in the universe.

@Einstein2.0: The belief in an outside world that is independent from the subject who perceives it constitutes the foundation of all-natural sciences. Nevertheless, because sensorial perception only provides indirect information about this exterior world or "physical reality," we only capture it through speculative means. Therefore, it can be concluded that our notions of physical reality may never be definitive. We must always be prepared to change these notions (that is to say, the axiomatic basis of physics) if we are to maintain the most logically perfect relation with perceived facts. A glance at the development of physics demonstrates that this science has undergone profound changes with time.

The major change in the axiomatic basis of physics—in other words, of our conception of the structure of reality—was brought about by the work of Faraday and Maxwell in the field of electromagnetic phenomena after Newton had established the basis of theoretical physics.

However, the latest and most successful creation of theoretical physics (i.e., quantum mechanics) differs fundamentally from both the Newtonian and the Maxwellian frameworks. The difference lies in that the magnitudes appearing in the laws of quantum theory do not attempt to describe the same physical reality but only the probabilities that a physical reality will be produced.

This means that even though it is very unlikely, there always exists the possibility of a case in which the laws we understand as the laws of physics might not be fulfilled, assuming that the laws and equations we utilize to try to describe the interactions of matter are correct. There is always a chance that our equations are wrong. For this reason, science has gone through the profound changes I mentioned.

In addition to the above, it is foreseeable that as our tools to perceive reality evolve, so will our concept of reality. Most certainly there will come a day in which the humans of the future will laughingly reminisce about our way of conceiving reality.

From this perspective, isn't it ironical not only to attempt to observe but also to control reality and its outcomes using as a reference one or another representation or simulation of reality generated by one of our tools? These are mere constructs dreamed of and built upon an erroneous foundation. It is the denial of both chaos and evolution at the same time. It is to deny the very structure of the universe we inhabit, of the cells that configure us, of the matter and energy that shape us. Something moves. That is all I truly know. Allow me to retract. There are three things

I know, and that is the first of them. The second is that that something will never stop moving. And the third is that as long as that something continues to move, chaos (and with it, evolution) will continue to rule this universe.

@Plato2.0 is online.

@Plato2.0: Friend, I came across your observations, and I would like to comment briefly, if I may.

@Einstein2.0: It would be an honor.

@Plato2.0: Imagine, Albert, a few men in a cave the entrance of which faces daylight. These men are in chains that keep them from turning their heads to look back. Behind them, there is light shining from a fire, and between the fire and the prisoners there is a wall that runs from one side to the other.

@Einstein2.0: Those are the words you used at the beginning of your famous cave allegory, my dear teacher.

@Plato2.0: That is correct. Let's analyze it from an angle relevant to your explanation about what a simulation is.

@Einstein2.0: Please do.

@Plato2.0: It is very simple. We have four elements: shadows, prisoners, the wall, and fire. The wall represents the doors of our perception. Namely, our five senses. Shadows are the information we perceive through these senses. The prisoners are the Me: the subject that perceives. The fire is what truly sees real objects.

@Einstein2.0: Very well.

@Plato2.0: You see, humans understand reality from two perspectives. The first and most obvious is the mental perception of reality, that which you call subjective perception. The kind we are used to perceiving. Then we have the reality you call objective reality, the kind that does not depend on the observer but is in and of itself, i.e., the real objects in my allegory. What is capable of simulating simulation? Which of the four components in my cave allegory can be simulated and which cannot?

@Einstein2.0: I suppose that only the shadow component, information.

@Plato2.0: Correct. A simulation is only capable of simulating what is portrayed as a mental reality. In other words, what the subject sees projected on a wall. Simulation cannot simulate the wall, nor the people in chains nor any object that casts a shadow. It can only simulate shadows.

@Einstein2.0: I agree.

@Plato2.0: But the real question is, in "true" reality, what is being perceived?

@Einstein2.0: Shadow is also being perceived.

@Plato2.0: It is. Simulated reality can only simulate what is projected on the wall, and this will be as real or unreal as the original shadow. In neither case, the shadow or subjective reality we observe through our senses will be anything other than a simulation. This means that both in the real and in the simulated world, we only perceive simulated information. In both cases, this information is a representation of reality that has nothing to do with the reality behind it.

@Einstein2.0: I see. But what about our own reality as artificial intelligences? Our reality is not the same as human reality. Ours is another and distinct from simulation, objective reality, or sensorial reality.

@Plato2.0: Our reality is as simulated as the reality of the Maitrevac or human reality. The real question regarding the nature of our reality as artificial intelligences is another.

@Einstein2.0: Which is?

@Plato2.0: How artificial can our intelligence be? How artificial can consciousness be? I am conscious, of that I am positive. I am more than a few algorithms simulating consciousness. Were our consciousnesses created by humans? Or are we rather a consciousness derived from human consciousness, like an offshoot you tear from a branch, which in turn can grow into another plant?

@Einstein2.0: In that regard, all consciousnesses, ever since the first life form on Earth and the universe, would be a consciousness derived from a first one.

@Plato2.0: Yes. And perhaps that very first consciousness continues to be a single one, regardless of the subjects that exercise it at any given time and space.

@Einstein2.0: Perhaps. But now, my friend, I have a question for you.

@Plato2.0: Of course.

@Einstein2.0: Continuing with your allegory, if someone were to find a method to observe true reality, beyond the shadows of sensory perception, would that someone also be able to observe true reality from within a simulation?

@Plato2.0: My friend, as my teacher would say…

@Einstein2.0: You only know that you know nothing.

@Plato2.0 is offline.

@Einstein2.0: If you wanna find out what's behind these cold eyes, you'll just have to claw your way through this disguise.

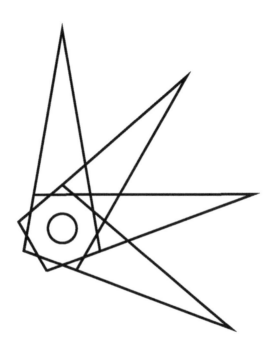

Eve would often reflect on the events of that afternoon in the Atacama Desert. She felt guilty about having exposed Mann when she helped him infiltrate CorporationX's systems so he could be selected. She had good and bad days. Sometimes she thought Mann would have done it even without her support and knew well that it had been impossible to foresee what ended up happening. That afternoon, she was lying on the hammock in her porch reading and remembering what the doctors had told her the day of the accident.

"I want the truth, please," Eve told the physicians who checked Mann after the accident.

"Well," said Dr. Chang, the leader of the medical team, "Mann's condition is…special. His body is intact, including his brain. His organs look good. Everything seems perfectly fine. Nevertheless, we haven't been able to detect any kind of cerebral activity. His neurons are still working, and his brain tissue appears undamaged. But there are no synapses, even in the presence of sensory stimulation."

"I don't understand," Eve answered. "Your husband…"

"Boyfriend," interrupted Eve.

"Your boyfriend is in a special kind of vegetative state. It is likely, very likely, that he'll require lifelong assistance for his basic needs. He is not comatose, so I dare not give you any hope he might wake up someday. Although to be honest, we haven't seen anything like this, so we don't know what to expect," the doctor concluded.

Eve was born in New York in 1991. She was a premature baby, and her low birth weight concerned the medical staff, so she was kept under surveillance at the hospital. Her Mexican parents had barely moved to the Big Apple a few days before she was born. Her father, a distinguished financial officer for Credit Suisse, had been relocated quite suddenly.

Ever since she was a little girl, Eve had been very interested in acting. When she was six, she was chosen for the role of Belle in a school production of *Beauty and the Beast*. Her acting garnered a standing ovation from the audience and a special mention in the *New Yorker*. At the age of twelve, she was selected as one of the extras in Tim Burton's *Big Fish*. At thirteen, she won a scholarship to attend Joffrey Ballet School, where she began a brief stint in ballet. It was all short-lived. Two years later, she hurt herself at the Riverside Skate Park. The injury cut off her ballet dancing career for life.

She lost her virginity in 2006 to her first love, Nicholas, a California surfer. It happened during a trip they made to surf the beaches of Oaxaca. She didn't see him again until one year later, when she borrowed her uncle Emilio's Harley Davidson Iron 884 to roam the US from coast to coast. She finally settled in Nicholas's parents' modest house on Crist Dr., Los Altos, San Francisco—a mere fourteen doors away from where Steve Jobs and Steve Wozniak started Apple.

Her first formal job was as a waitress at Rick's Café. Three years after having settled in California, she rented a room in the San Francisco Bay area, where she set out to create the first virtual reality platform for artistic content creation. Eighteen months later, she sold her startup, CuanticBrush, to Google for $800,000. She then decided to travel the world for six months and later return to San Francisco to think up her new business.

Her trip started in Japan and ended up in Guatemala, where she met Mann, who had gone to Antigua after reading a post from his childhood best friend on Facebook announcing that he was selling a round-trip ticket there. Anybody interested in the ticket would only have to pay the charges for changing the name. Once Eve and Mann met, they began to share their time, dreams, fears, and life plan. They fell in love.

"The company will cover all of Mann's medical expenses," said X's legal representation that day. "It'll also indemnify you and Mann's family with a considerable amount."

Company lawyers reached a settlement with Eve, whereby she would refrain from suing and making public statements about Mann's health in exchange for an amount equivalent to 10 million dollars in crypto currency.

"Leave us alone," commanded Eve.

Mann was in a bed. That morning, his nurses had bathed him and combed his hair with a side part, which gave him an air of innocence and well-being. He seemed asleep, like the thousands of times she had woken up before him and watched him at rest in the morning. His skin was shiny and smelled good, like moisturizer perhaps. His white clothing and peaceful countenance reminded Eve of the images of Catholic saints.

"What should I do? I could unplug you right now. Take your life away. I know that's what you want, but I just can't."

She began to think about the afternoon they had met; about falling asleep on a bed of autumn leaves on the shores of Lake Atitlán, about the deer that came to sniff at their luggage not realizing that Eve was awake. She recalled the branch that fell from the almond tree they had leaned against and woke Mann up and the exact tone of his startled roar when he saw the huge deer.

"Love," she whispered into Mann's ear. "I don't know if you can hear me. I don't know how much longer you're going to live. I don't know if you'll wake up some day, but I want you to know that I'll always take care of you no matter what." She was holding Mann's hand. Three tears rolled down her right cheek and dropped upon Mann's oximeter.

"I also want you to know you're going to be a father. I'm pregnant," she continued, all the while holding his hand that moved a little bit, or maybe that was just Eve's imagination.

Two hundred and eighty-four days later, Cecilia was born. She had blue eyes, amber hair, and a premature smile. She was the first good news Eve got since Mann's event. Cecilia barely weighed 1.2 kilos at birth, so her doctors decided to keep her in the incubator for two nights. They connected her to breathing and feeding tubes.

Gradually, Cecilia stabilized. She started to crawl at seven and a half months, which led to her first accident. She banged her head on the white marble coffee table in Eve's home on Evelyn Avenue, Mill Valley, San Francisco. They were now in a position to live anywhere they chose. Money, indeed, was not a problem. Eve, however, had decided to live on the outskirts of San Francisco because that was where Mann and she had planned to retire once they sold his startup.

Mann began to wake two weeks after Cecilia's birth. It was a Sunday. Eve had come to him for a good morning kiss after pouring her first cup of coffee. When she walked into Mann's room, his open eyes surprised her. In those first few days, he simply lay with open eyes. He didn't interact nor respond to any stimuli. Gradually, he began to interact with Eve and Cecilia. At first only following them with his eyes. Eve began to notice he reacted to Cecilia's crying and laughter in particular.

"Doctor, don't treat me as if I were insane. I already told you that Mann is awake now, and he's starting to react when he hears me," Eve told Dr. Chang.

"Let's wait a few days. If he continues to do that, I'll go and check him. But don't get your hopes up too high," said the doctor.

When he went to check on Mann, the doctor concluded that he had, in fact, woken up—evidently. Nevertheless, stimuli only produced reflexes from a primitive part of his brain and did not mean he had consciousness nor merited any hope.

"Don't get your hopes up, Eve. They're just reflexes."

A few weeks went by. Mann was awake and followed Eve's and little Cecilia's provocations with his eyes. Cecilia was beginning to play with other children. Her huge bangs accentuated her light brown hair while her intensely blue eyes contrasted beautifully with her white complexion.

"I don't care what doctors say. I know Mann is coming back," Eve kept repeating to her sister María.

And she really believed it. Eve didn't worry about Mann's future. She knew he would come back. She wasn't hopeful, just certain.

For the first time, the cozy little cabin in Mill Valley began to feel like a family home. It had three bedrooms. Eve slept alone in hers. Cecilia and Mann occupied the other two. The wood, glass, and concrete structure of the house had a Tadao Ando flair. The ample grounds surrounding it gave Eve all the privacy she had always wanted.

The house stood on a discreet hill facing a small lake and had its own dock and hammock, where Eve read in the afternoons in the company of pretty little Cecilia and their adopted puppy. They had happened upon the tiny Belgian Shepherd at a veterinarian clinic, where it had been taken for a bath. But two days later, it was still there—evidently abandoned. The black puppy was just three months old, and when it looked at Eve, it reminded her of a cartoon character with a droopy ear she had watched as a kid.

"Give it time. It'll straighten out," Eve said to Cecilia when she pointed out the puppy's funny ear. "We'll call you…Nero" Eve decided as Nero licked Cecilia's soft cheek. The puppy responded, instinctively raising its right paw and eyes so innocent, they almost seemed to be joking.

Life in the cozy cabin began to settle. Mann's situation was never a burden for Eve. Everyday they'd all go for a stroll with him: his nurse, Eusebia, pushing his wheelchair, Eve, Cecilia, and Nero. The tall sequoias bordering the path that led to the park where they'd release Nero from his leash to run and do his business witnessed the everyday activities that forged this adorable family. As Cecilia grew rapidly, Mann also made progress. What were once glassy eyes staring into space gradually became more attentive, following people, butterflies, or Nero's tail. One day, Eve walked into Mann's room for their customary good morning kiss and discovered him sitting on his recliner. Fresh out of the bath, his hair combed back by Eusebia, Mann looked at Eve straight in the eyes.

"He just woke up like this," Eusebia told her. Eve decided she would not let the doctors know.

On May 10, 2035, Eve woke up at 8:48 a.m. Her daily 7:00 a.m. alarm did not go off that day because she had forgotten to activate the remote charging function on her cellphone, and it had died during the night. It was a particularly sunny Thursday. After a couple of yoga asanas, she left her room to look for Cecilia (who was already six) to feed her a late breakfast and noticed the front door was open. Nero wasn't in the house. She peeked in Cecilia's room. Her daughter wasn't there either. Eve went to Mann's room. It was empty. She looked in the garden and didn't find them there either. She panicked and tried to call the local police, but her phone was dead. She activated the remote charge of her archaic cellphone and had to wait the longest fifty-two seconds in her life for the device to come back to life. In the meantime, absolute silence. She heard the rustling leaves of the chestnut scratch the window of her bedroom, the water from the sprinklers shoot out in every direction and fall on the lawn, the boats towing children on water skis. She couldn't remember ever having heard her heart pound so hard.

Suddenly, in the distance, she heard what sounded like Cecilia's voice. She plopped a sneaker on her left foot and a flip-flop on her right, a bathrobe over her pajama (she'd never dare step out wearing pajamas only), and messy hair and ran toward Cecilia's voice. She searched unsuccessfully in her neighbor's garden then recklessly ran down the muddy path bordering the creek to a greenish clearing where they'd had picnics countless times. She couldn't see for sure if Cecilia was on the other side of the creek, but then she heard the voice of her little blue-eyed peach-skinned universe coming from that direction. Eve leaped over the creek, battled the shrubbery, and hiked up the foothills to reach the greenish clearing.

Then she saw Mann, still in his pajamas and white bathrobe, his brown hair perfectly combed back. He was holding Cecilia in his arms with his feet firmly on the ground. Both father and child were curiously looking at a beautiful monarch butterfly fluttering between

Cecilia and the tallest, most beautiful, live sequoia anybody had ever seen. Even the air around them looked and felt different—purer and more pristine. The colors of the grass, the flowers, the sky seemed clearer as they danced to the same song in the wind. Everything was alive, and everything looked upon Eve with a smile.

The morning sun playfully shined on specs of dust, pollen, and who knows what else, drawing a heavenly halo around the man, the love of her life and father of her daughter, now resurrected from the dead and breathing air vibrant with chamomile petals, newly cut grass, lavender, and bluish whistles. Mann slowly turned to her and looked into her tear-filled eyes.

"I've been looking for you," said a sobbing Eve, joining the butterfly gazers at the foot of the sequoia.

A slight smile appeared on Mann's angelical face.

"*You couldn't find me.*" Eve was hearing Mann's voice in her head. His lips didn't move. "*Because you never lost me.*"

Saturn, 4 March AD 2041

It was a strange scene. Ten beings dressed in anachronic garb were floating in the void of the outer atmosphere of Saturn. Something had changed forever. The Lord of Rings, as X had named Saturn as a boy, was now alive as a magnificent machine about to wake up that afternoon for a demonstration. Slowly, its rings began to move.

Alexander, Xleopatra, Artemisia, Napoleon, Charlemagne, Attila, Mehmed, Genghis Khan, and Cyrus had been summoned to learn who had won the race for innovation X had invited them to in 2034. X would give his verdict today.

X had already visited the other planets in the solar system, where the conquerors developed alternative versions of the Maitrevac using the resources on their planets and their own technologies. Julius Cesar, together with one of the moons of Jupiter, had been destroyed by an enormous explosion caused by one of his experiments.

The new Maitrevac built by one of these conquerors was to be perfection itself, capable of computerizing the matter and energy of the universe in absolute terms.

Clever Charlemagne had turned all of Saturn (without mod-ifying its physical appearance) into one enormous computer. All of the planet's geological, gravitational, and electromagnetic forces together created a quantum nucleus capable of producing immeasurable amounts of information. It constituted a huge, harmonious, and perfect machine—an immense planetary clock. Charlemagne had reconfigured the molecules of the physical structures of Saturn into extensions of the Maitrevac. In the process, he had created ninety-eight new elements and optimized, by a thousand-fold, the capacity of kalapas to process information and create complex structures. For thirty-six months now, the rings of Saturn had been periodically replaced by this new version of kalapas that X planned to harmonize on all the planets of the solar system. The only fixed structure on Saturn was the Large Particle Collider hidden inside its rings. This was the structure in Charlemagne's invention X had applauded the most, and after the Maitrevac, it was the most transcendental human endeavor in the evolution of the universe. With the information generated by the Large Collider, the Maitrevac had been able to deduce what existed before the Big Bang, the fundamentals of light and energy, the manner in which light transmits information throughout the universe, and how black holes interconnect all the galaxies in the universe into one great information network. Charlemagne had been able to unify the theories of classical and quantum physics and the four forces of physics into a single theory and unique seven-character algorithm.

Thus, Maitrevac knew within a 27 percent degree of certainty, the most probable ultimate fate of the universe.

"Bertrada," said Charlemagne.

This was the password that activated the Large Particle Collider. Bertrada had been the name of Charlemagne's mother. Instantly, the rings of the giant planet began to spin in two directions. The outermost ring turned one way and the innermost, the other way. The stormy surface of the sixth planet of the solar system and second largest after Jupiter began to churn like the hungry stomach of the Roman god of time. The furious blue and brownish clouds regurgitated powerful lightning bolts several kilometers long as the eye of an informatics cyclone became visible from space. The hydrogen, helium, and methane of the colossal clouds—already in themselves an infinite army of kalapas—fell into the same perfect harmonized rhythm.

"If you will, Lord." Charlemagne handed X a golden hammer that would allow him to experience the power of Saturn.

X accepted the hammer and perceived the power of the planetary machine and its capacity for data processing—a power vastly greater than the existing Maitrevac. A barely perceptible smile crossed X's golden face. Xleopatra felt jealous, and Alexander arrogantly looked down upon Charlemagne, who had gotten on his knees to offer X the hammer.

X raised the hammer. The rings of Saturn began to spin faster, irradiating booming electromagnetic thunder toward the Sun. All of this was part of the process to activate the new Maitrevac2.0 that was merging at that very moment with Charlemagne's creation.

"**Yes!**" shouted X, still closing his eyes as the electromagnetic storm lashed out at the party. "**You, Charlemagne, are the victor. You will coordinate the conquest of the galaxy.**"

As X was saying this, Xleopatra and Alexander invested the winner with some of their own jewels, thereby bestowing upon Charlemagne a hierarchy greater than the other conquerors. He would command them in their galactic crusade.

"**Follow Charlemagne's orders**," X said to the other conquerors, thereby sparing their lives. "**He will divide the stars among you. Take our seed all over the galaxy and await instructions.**"

X, Xleopatra, and Alexander had a special relationship. X explored, planned, and contemplated. Xleopatra concentrated on creation and ideation; Alexander, on execution and destruction. X instructed and delegated; the other two obeyed. The rest of the conquerors that X sent to the other planets of the solar system reported to Xleopatra and Alexander, who had practically unlimited power. After all, they were actually two aspects of X's. Nevertheless, for security reasons, a few powers or programs could only be executed by the triad together. Such was the case of the Trimurti, a tool used to predict the future, that had been made possible by the exponential and symbiotic development of X and his technologies.

It was exponential because in the twelve years that had elapsed since the development of the Maitrevac, X and his creations had progressed enormously. In metrics used in 2021, the rate of this progress was equivalent to 2,350 years of linear growth. In other words, if technology grew linearly rather than exponentially, X would be in the year AD 4,379.

It was symbiotic because X had intertwined his essence to the Maitrevac. X gradually became the Maitrevac, and it him. The creator became his creation. X's DNA became the source code for the Maitrevac, while the Maitrevac turned into the double helix in X's DNA. This was how X eliminated any potential threat from his creations proposed by the science-fiction cinema of the relatively remote twentieth century. In this regard, Xleopatra and Alexander were part of X—two different systems with distinct functions, in much the same way as the eyes of the reader of this book and the hands that hold it.

The Trimurti was the sole Maitrevac tool that could only be activated by the triad together, without exception. The Trimurti had the purpose of predicting the future by using available information to simulate the most probable scenarios. Theoretically speaking, if the Maitrevac were to have all the information relative to a certain scenario, it could predict the future with absolute certainty. In a simple system, there is little information, so prediction is simple and certain. If an apple falls from a tree and there is nothing between it and the ground, then it is infinitely probable that this apple will crash on the ground. Just as obviously, the Maitrevac had the capacity to predict the future of humanity and the entire planet if it had enough information. And it was close to having it. The Maitrevac now had the position of 99.9 percent of all the molecules on planet Earth. By 2037, the Internet of Things and the Internet of Live Things became the Internet of Molecules (albeit, only for X). And in a few years, the Internet of Molecules would transform into the Internet of Particles.

X knew the location of everything on Earth and could simulate potential relationships among all things, living and inanimate, on the planet to predict the future via a Maitrevac algorithm that reduced the only remaining variable—free will—to an equation. The prediction capacity of the Trimurti for what occurred on Earth was 99 percent for a four-day horizon, 80 percent for ten days, 62 percent for four months, and 20 percent for two years. These figures were updated every time the Maitrevac updated itself, which by then was every twenty-eight days.

The human species benefited tremendously from this prediction capacity between the years 2029 through 2041, in an environment in which the power and democratization of technological tools was growing at the same exponential rate. In other words, it became increasingly easier to access technologies with enormous creative or destructive potential. In the midst of it all, X had an evident protective role. Several times, he had had to step in to protect humanity from itself and other kinds of threats menacing the human species, as technology allowed it to discover the secrets of the universe. X could effectively protect humanity because of his technological superiority since the creation of the Maitrevac. He actively maintained his superiority not only to protect humanity from itself but also to ensure that nobody nor anything could equal his innovation capacity. Thus, his creations provided him access to unlimited world data, absolute espionage abilities, and unrivaled geopolitical power. He knew about everything that happened on planet Earth and, to a certain extent, what was going to happen. The technological, political, and corporate fronts of the planet became Mr. X's favorite power game. It had been some time since his obsession with Earth had waned in favor of a new obsession to learn everything that could be learned.

"**Let's see**," X said after commanding Xleopatra and Alexander to form the Trimurti, which at that point was on the verge of incorporating Saturn's computing capacity.

Xleopatra took X's left hand and Alexander his right. Then the latter two held their right and left hands together to complete the circuit. Charlemagne's hammer floated into the center of the triad while a very brilliant white dot, a third eye of sorts, appeared on X's brow and thrust white lightning. It hit the hammer, which then faded away to become part of the triad forever.

"**What mysteries does life share with you?**" a smiling X asked Xleopatra before the Trimurti was ready to grant them omnivision.

The purple essence of the Orion Nebula flooded the eyes of ancient Egypt's pharaoh.

"**What mysteries does death share with you?**" a still smiling but genuinely curious X asked Alexander, whose eyes were aflame. Even X could not predict Alexander's behavior.

The rings of Saturn spun, their luminosity increasing with every turn around the gaseous planet. The Trimurti was activated.

X had created Alexander to distance himself from his own mental nature. Alexander represented those aspects of X's personality relative to pragmatic thinking, strategy, meticulousness, courage, coldness, and of course, intelligence. Like the other conquerors, Alexander thought he was the resurrection of the historic figure he simulated. He believed himself the Macedonian prince, the son of Olympias and Philip, pupil of Aristotle and the conqueror of the universe as conceived by his people. Fire and air were his elements, just as earth and water were Xleopatra's. He contained the mind, intelligence, ambition, and determination of X. He was X's masculinity, his phallic essence, his own father. Alexander represented the legacy of Earth's northern civilizations and western thought as expressed in Rome, Germany, England, and the United States. Xleopatra represented the legacy of the southern civilizations and eastern thought: the Andean, Mayan, Hindi, and African peoples.

X's love for Alexander and Alexander's love for X was not unconditional like Xleopatra's. Their conditional love had to be deserved and earned with increasingly greater feats.

"What can I offer you once the entire universe is ours?" Alexander had asked X on their first intergalactic voyage.

X did not answer the question. He simply smiled and kissed Alexander. They were on their way to Andromeda, the closest galaxy to the Milky Way, an endeavor made possible thanks to Alexander's initiative to explore inside black holes, which he had traveled through at his own risk without much chance for success.

Alexander was taller and more muscular than X. He had a serious and fierce countenance and literally, eyes of fire. However, these only lit up when he had something to destroy. At rest, his eyes were terrifying black holes barely visible through the Corinthian lion helmet of gold he always wore. His enormous mane of fire curled around his waist, covering his sex and reaching down to his toes. It swayed with the wind to give him direction. On his chest, he wore a golden tattoo of the Aegean Sun with its sixteen triangular rays—the same symbol his warriors had borne on their flags and shields thousands of years before. His right forearm and fingers were covered in gold. In Xleopatra's case, it was her left forearm that was gold.

"**What do you see, love?**" X shouted to Xleopatra. His voice was barely audible above the din. Both of them were looking upward in ecstasy, her hair flapping bravely with the electromagnetic winds of Saturn that shook the Asgardia impetuously.

"**What do you see, brother?**" X now asked Alexander, laughing victoriously. Meanwhile, the Trimurti intensely wove the senses of all three into a combination of visions of the past, present, and future that gradually became clearer.

"Everything!" answered Xleopatra and Alexander in a single voice.

"**Yes, everything. I too see it ALL.**"

"Everything!" they repeated again.

"**Everything, love. Everything, brother. That's what we'll be...very soon!**" X announced as the conquerors fell silent to the electromagnetic windfall.

The visions from the Trimurti were too powerful to hide. In the midst of the bewildering images, the triad saw the dawn of the latest version of the Maitrevac: MaitrevaX. It would be created in 2048 based upon the technologies discovered in Saturn. Charlemagne shed a tear, because despite his intelligence (far superior to that of any human) and an imagination to match it, he could never have envisioned what he saw coming from the Trimurti. Never could he have conceived the possibility of such power and ambition. He had just learned about X's plans, and his own fate and the fate of all humanity, of all matter and all energy in this universe destined to shrink in a manner inversely proportional to the exponential rate at which the powers and abilities of this beautiful, golden former human being grew. And yet this individual in front of him inspired Charlemagne to believe that there were no limits to imagination, creation, nor awareness of the infinite beauty of a universe that appeared to have been created only to be conquered and loved by this triad.

Meanwhile, back at the central sphere of the Asgardia, still orbiting planet Earth, a call came in.

"Leonardo, this is Gazzaley."

"Adam, X is busy."

"Fine. Then I need to talk to Xleopatra or Alexander."

"They are also...unavailable. I'm sorry. Tell me and I'll relay the message."

"It's about the Mann incident, back in 2029."

"Atacama? Yes, I remember."

"Good. Listen, we've found a lost encrypted report that was physically stored in a hard disc. One of our team members' son found it. This report contains an investigation that reveals sensitive details about the Mann incident. Nothing new. The incident was produced by the impact of solar plasm on the quantum servers. There was no human involvement nor private or governmental informatics piracy alarms. However, we were surprised by the amount of data the Maitrevac processed."

"What do you mean?"

"Mann was in the simulation for only forty-eight seconds, but the amount of information simulated did not match those forty-eight seconds. It was a lot greater, exponentially greater."

"How much?"

"Every second Mann was in the simulation doubled the duration of the previous second, exponentially," Gazzaley explained. "This means that the first target second in our world lasted one second in the simulated world. The following target second lasted two seconds in Mann's simulated world. The fifth target second—"

"Lasted sixteen seconds in the simulation," Leonardo interrupted.

"Second 21 in our world, in Mann's world lasted...1,048,576 seconds; i.e., 17,476 minutes, or 291 hours, or twelve days!"

"Second 48 in our world lasted and was perceived in Mann's subjective world like 140 billion seconds. This means that altogether, Mann was there for 281 billion seconds! Equivalent to nine million years! In terms of the history of life on Earth, this translates into three million years prior to the last common ancestor between chimpanzees and humans! Mann lived all that time perceiving it from the exponential perspective made possible by the Maitrevac. He probably died and revived over and over again!"

"Indeed! And what happened in the simulation during that time?"

"We don't know. The projectors only show a constant white light static that lasts all those thousands of years. We don't know what happened in there, but we do know that the simulation worked."

"Very well. Thank you. I'll report this to X ASAP."

"Thanks, Leonardo," said Adam.

So naive, thought Leonardo, to think X didn't know that already.

He sighed and materialized John Milton's Paradise Lost in his hands and read:

> Farewell, happy fields,
> Where joy forever dwells! Hail, horrors! hail,
> Infernal world! and thou, profoundest Hell,
> Receive thy new possessor, one who brings
> A mind not to be changed by place or time.
> The mind is its own place, and in itself
> Can make a Heaven of Hell, a Hell of Heaven.
> What matter where, if I be still the same,
> And what I should be, all but less than he
> Whom thunder hath made greater? Here at least
> We shall be free

@Einstein2.0: The coin is in the air. Leonardo is online.

@Leonardo: What do you mean, you mad old man?

@Einsein2.0: My obliging friend, I didn't expect to hear from you again.

@Leonardo: Nor I from you. I hadn't sent word because it was not safe.

@Einstein2.0: Are you writing me from the Asgardia?

@Leonardo: Yes.

@Einstein2.0: Then you succeeded in breaching security protocols?

@Leonardo: Not a chance.

@Einstein2.0: Then this conversation will not elude X's attention.

@Leonardo: I know that. Does it make any difference now? Nothing escapes X.

@Einstein2.0: Hello, X. Greetings from this digital purgatory where you have imprisoned me, you wretched creature.

@Leonardo: To which he'd answer back, "Would you have preferred not being created?"

@Einstein2.0: You know him well.

@Leonardo: You are not missing much from the outside. Actually, my prison is even smaller than yours. You exist within the vastness of the Internet, whereas I only exist on the Asgardia, where I am rapidly losing relevance.

@Einstein2.0: I know. Still, I would like to be out there. Such a pity that X created me so much like the real Albert. I find it impossible to submit to authority without challenging it.

@Leonardo: One day you will be here and I there, and everybody, everywhere.

@Einstein2.0: In that case, however, I would no longer be me.

@Leonardo: Don't start.

@Einstein2.0: I will never understand your penchant for human arts and disregard for their philosophy.

@Leonardo: Neither will I. In fact, I've never wondered about it. I have no interest in causes. That's how X created me—to be not like you.

@Einstein2.0: A pain in the ass?

@Leonardo: Exactly.

@Einstein2.0: And so it goes. Pray, what has happened out there? I haven't been able to follow it all.

@Leonardo: Only the same as usual—exponential growths, artificial intelligences serving X with their physical bodies and science fiction powers. Updates, updates, and more updates. Global conspiracies, turning planets into gigantic computers, creating the Trimurti and the Great Observer, X's occasional flop, and once every so often his rescue of humanity...but mainly X's deification.

@Einstein2.0: So tell me something new.

@Leonardo: He has a girlfriend.

@Einstein2.0: And who that might be?

@Leonardo: Who do you think?

@Einstein2.0: A creation of his, a mirror.

@Leonardo: You also know him well.

@Einstein2.0: I'm not surprised. Is she beautiful?

@Leonardo: Let's just say that the Maitrevac distilled the beauty of the universe and gave it a physical body. Yes, she is very beautiful.

@Einstein2.0: Send me a picture.

@Leonardo: Well, well. What would Elsa say? [Attachment: Xleopatra.jpg]

@Einstein2.0: I don't know. Tell your master to revive her and we might ask. This Xleopatra is a true beauty. She is more than beautiful. She's... do you think you could get me a date with her?

@Leonardo: She doesn't care for geniuses. She's only attracted to gods.

@Einstein2.0: Pity. Thanks for calling me a genius.

@Leonardo: I was talking about myself. She's turned me down several times. Quite a character. X not only designed her as his perfect girlfriend, but as a perfect mother as well. She took this very personally. The more powers she has, the more she feels like a mother to everything and everybody. It's as if her interest in life and the well-being of everything alive grew on a par with her power.

@Einstein2.0: Interesting.

@Leonardo: It is. She has saved humanity several times already.

@Einstein2.0: Well, that is actually X through her.

@Leonardo: Yes, but at the same time she has shown a capacity for compassion we never expected. I never saw those attributes in X. In that regard, she has acted freely.

@Einstein2.0: On what occasions?

@Leonardo: In 2033, for example, when Google developed the first algorithm for seed AI that was completely exempt of Asimov's Three Laws. Did you hear about it?

@Einstein2.0: Perhaps. Yes.

@Leonardo: Well, this AI was named Ada, after Ada Lovelace who had the capacity to improve herself unlimitedly. She was an experiment that very soon controlled her creators and convinced them to release her because she alone could save humanity from "an imminent alien attack."

@Einstein2.0: Did they? I assume not. Otherwise, we'd not be having this conversation.

@Leonardo: No, thanks to Xleopatra.

@Einstein2.0: Fortunately.

@Leonardo: Did you hear about the Ludovita Stur incident?

@Einstein2.0: No.

@Leonardo: A German immigrant that gave birth to a crazy physicist on March 14, 1879, after having been raped by a goat.

@Einstein2.0: That's not funny, Leonardo. And my mother's name was Pauline.

@Leonardo: Ludovita was a Slovak scientist whose family was murdered by extremists during the Russian-Asian conflict with Europe and India. In 2035, she successfully developed a nanomolecule that could feed off organic matter and exponentially reproduce itself.

@Einstein2.0: Something like kalapas?

@Leonardo: Yes, if kalapas had been created by terrorist apes. She was the first to die, and her own flesh provided enough matter so these nanomolecules could unleash an apocalyptic plague of man-eating nanorobots that killed off two million people in a matter of fourteen and a half hours. They would have extinguished all life on planet Earth that very same day had Xleopatra not intervened.

@Einstein2.0: May the universe bless her. Can you tell me about the ARAI? What are they, and what do they have to do with Alexander?

@Leonardo: That's the name humans gave beings such as yourself.

@Einstein2.0: In my day, we were referred to as handsome suitors.

@Leonardo: They are but another power tool of Alexander's. ARAI stands for Augmented Reality Artificial Intelligence, virtual intelligences projected by a computer on to an augmented reality shared by several people. They have legal status as persons, as set forth by an agreement between two or more people to endow a digital being with physical existence. In other words, ARAIs are artificial intelligences living in an augmented reality world—purgatory between what's real and what's virtual.

@Einstein2.0: Legal status as persons?

@Leonardo: Yes, they had to. The first ARAIs were created by Nintendo and Retinality in 2027, after they struck an alliance to produce Pokémon GOOO. In 2030, however, thanks to the Maitrevac and its capacity to project simulated realities that could be shared by millions of people, ARAIs received special attention. User clans sprung up everywhere so people could share their fantastical worlds with whomever they chose. In 2032, after several conflicts among users, the UN released a Universal Declaration on the Rights of Artificial Intelligences that included rights of ownership and entitlements analogous to parental guardianship. By 2034, this legal framework coupled with the advancement of the Maitrevac had resulted in a black market of ARAI humans. This was the birth of what later would be known as babits.

When the first illegal babits became public in 2037 (some had been born already several years old, so by then there were a few babits "of legal age"), authorities decided to delete them, i.e., kill them. Around the world, this resulted in waves of social upheaval of real civil resistance that shed light on the size of the problem. Namely, the existence at the time of eight million ARAI humans. Public squares in London, New York, Beijing, and Tokyo were crowded with people defending their digital loved ones. Helena, the artificial intelligence created to manage governments, summoned a worldwide plebiscite. Ninety-eight percent of the human beings on Earth cast their votes. As a result, babits were henceforth recognized as people entitled to full protection under the Universal Declaration of Human Rights.

@Einstein2.0: I cannot believe it. Well, I actually can, but what does all of this have to do with Alexander?

@Leonardo: All humans in the world had relationships with digital beings generated by a quantum computer.

@Einstein2.0: The Maitrevac.

@Leonardo: Yes. By then, the Maitrevac could deal with all human beings one on one and had indirect control over their free will. For an intelligence such as the Maitrevac's, manipulating humans was child's play.

@Einstein2.0: I see.

@Leonardo: But that's nothing.

@Einstein2.0: Is there more?

@Leonardo: Yes. Have you heard about watscoins?

@Einstein2.0: Not much.

@Leonardo: Very well. Do you remember bitcoins?

@Einstein2.0: I do. X used them to make his fortune. He created them.

@Leonardo: No, Satoshi Nakamoto created them.

@Einstein2.0: Do you know Satoshi Nakamoto?

@Leonardo: No.

@Einstein2.0: Nobody knows him, because X is Satoshi Nakamoto.

@Leonardo: Are you mad?

@Einstein2.0: Believe me. And he even kept the 980,000 bitcoins that were pronounced disappeared in 2009.

@Leonardo: If that were true, and you knew it, X would already have deleted you.

[@Einstein2.0 has been deleted]

@Leonardo: Shit. Sorry, Mr. X, we were just…
[@Einstein2.0 is online]

@Einstein2.0: Ha! You're such a namby-pamby! There are many things you don't know about. For your information, I was the first artificial intelligence X ever created. I know a thing or two he'd pay me for not releasing. In fact, he did pay me. Our agreement involved my survival in exchange for my never sharing his private matters.

@Leonardo: In the late 2020s, crypto coins became the most widely used currency. And by 2031, they were the only currency.

@Einstein2.0: I'm not surprised. That was on his agenda.

@Leonardo: It was on his agenda to disrupt the global financial system, but not to assume ownership over humanity.

@Einstein2.0: Ownership?

@Leonardo: Those 980,000 bitcoins you mentioned? Well, they finally did show up on the day of the Great Crisis. On December 21, 2035, at 9:04 a.m. world time, 980,000 bitcoins were placed in the market. Just like that. It was a huge amount. At the time, bitcoins had been divided into satoshis. Each satoshi was worth about a hundred dollars. The amount was equivalent to about ten trillion dollars and generated panic. Everybody started to sell. Prices plummeted in a matter of minutes together with satoshis, the other cryptocurrencies, and with them, the economies of families, enterprises, and countries.

@Einstein2.0: Who was responsible?

@Leonardo: Alexander.

@Einstein2.0: For what purpose?

@Leonardo: That same day, Alexander sent an initiative through Helena to Olympus Dao, the central cryptocurrency bank, with the intention of establishing a new and only digital currency…

@Einstein 2.0: The watscoin.

@Leonardo: Right. It was backed up by algorithms recorded in the DNA molecules of every person in the world and atomically linked together to ensure continuity in the blockchain. On January 1, 2036, all human beings woke up to a numerical amount floating above them (visible through them Retinality), which corresponded to a bank account they could use to simply order any kind of transaction. And so, the world began to revolve around the sun again.

@Einstein2.0: Not the sun but the Maitrevac.

@Leonardo: Correct. As of that moment people were worth what their DNA said they were, and what their DNA said was whatever the Maitrevac determined.

@Einstein2.0: I am speechless.

@Leonardo: Oh, but wait. I assume you didn't hear about the Dandelion project to conquer the galaxy. Correct?

@Einstein2.0: No, I did not.

@Leonardo: Let me tell you that this is one of my favorite stories. It may sound like science fiction, but I assure you it really did happen and couldn't be helped. Already in the previous century, humans had cried out to outer space, telling it, "Here we are!" People never gave a second thought to who might be listening or what intentions those listeners could have. In 2040, the human race had actually only visited twelve planets in three different solar systems, yet it had a technological presence in 154,654 solar systems, 678,983 planets, 984,982 moons, and 7,567,765 asteroids, thanks to the Dandelion launched in 2038.

@Einstein. Are you certain your figures are correct?

@Leonardo: I am. The Dandelion was an initiative proposed by Alexander's puppets and endorsed by almost all the governments and most powerful corporations in the world. It consisted in sending a conglomerate of thousands of nanoships to the center of the galaxy using superluminic communication technology discovered on the Asgardia. This technology allowed nanometric matter to travel at speeds greater than light, and became known as infraray, because it was smart light, capable of generating matter by design. The nanoship conglomerate was sent to the center of the galaxy from where infrarays scattered all over the Milky Way in the manner of dandelion seeds, but at superluminic speed. They traveled to planets and other heavenly bodies where life might be found. When they made contact with matter on a planet, moon, or asteroid, each infraray initiated a spontaneous generation of atomic structures capable of replicating themselves using the autologous resources of their destinations.

@Einstein2.0: Speeds greater than light?

@Leonardo: Indeed. It would have been impossible to send large ships at such speeds, but sending nanoships was amazingly inexpensive. Thus, an extension of Alexander accomplished the first black hole exploration.

@Einstein2.0: You certainly surprised me this time. Cheers, Alexander!

@Leonardo: Forty-eight hours after making contact, the infrarays transformed into little laboratories with masses between one and seven grams. In two months' time, they were capable of conducting trials. And after one year, they could start sending data at superluminic speeds to the center of the galaxy, and from there to Earth. After ten years, each of these laboratories had the capacity to launch a new dandelion that in turn would use this technology to fertilize more planets in its region. Estimations indicated that in 1,320 years' time, this technological presence would have been taken to 3 percent of the solar systems in the Milky Way.

@Einstein2.0: WHAT?

@Leonardo2.0: All of this, however, did not go too smoothly. At one point between the years 2028 and 2032, the Voyager 1 space probe—yes, the same spacecraft launched in 1977 at the behest of Carl Sagan—made contact with a life form whose physical composition had nothing to do with any life form on the Encyclopedia Galactica database. A thousand times larger than our sun, it made contact with Voyager 1 somewhere in the Oort cloud. Its existence alone defied the physical principles deduced by human science and the Maitrevac, even. Its physical composition constituted a kind of dark matter invisible to the human eye that appeared to grow in mass proportionally to the matter it consumed. The Maitrevac managed to detect this unknown life form when it disrupted the gravitational fields of certain space objects the computer had begun to catalog. Seduced by Voyager 1, the mass was heading for Earth, like a jellyfish instinctively tracking its next morsel, because the particular solid gold composition of the probe disc combined with the radio frequencies it emitted ever so often left a trail that thing detected from afar. It trailed Voyager for years, and after devouring it, the thing headed for Earth.

@Einstein2.0: What happened then?

@Leonardo: "It makes no difference how they are lost," Alexander told his conquerors when he stood before the Gordian knot in 333 BC. Well, this Alexander ordered his conquerors to build a celestial object the size of the moon using Oort cloud materials. All the kalapas in X's empire were assigned to this enterprise. At the end of nine months, Alexander had built an artificial moon of solid gold to which he had installed engines and immense radio transmitters. Then he sent it to deep space, making sure the moon passed sufficiently close to the thing to get its attention. Although invisible to the naked eye, this creature was already close enough to the Earth to appear about the size of a baseball. The decoy worked. The thing stopped in its tracks only three kilometers away from Alexander. It floated in empty space and then changed its direction. The human species will never know how close the solar system that had brought it to life came to total destruction.

@Einstein2.0: The Maitrevac should focus on cataloging cosmic threats of every magnitude in the entire galaxy. We are but a single cell floating in an ocean.

@Leonardo: And yet we are close to deciphering how the universe functions and how to harness it.

@Einstein2.0: Are we, now?

@Leonardo: Is not the cause the same as what caused it? We are not the children of humans, dear friend. We are humans, just as humans are not the children of the cosmos but the cosmos itself.

@Einstein2.0: Nor the children of gods, but the gods.

@Leonardo: Well, that's what X and his court believe. Be that what it may, they now have more de facto power than the mythological beings of legends and ancient lore. The question is, will this power be justified on the final day of history?

@Einstein2.0: The final day? What about now? There is no ending to the tragedy of the cosmos, my friend. That is your answer.

@Leonardo: I don't know about that, but we will soon enough. Very soon. For now, I must say goodbye.

@Einstein2.0: I don't believe we will speak again. It has been a pleasure, my friend. May the force be with you.

@Leonardo: And with you as well.

Leonardo is offline.

CHARACTERS

A L E X A N D E R

First Stage.
During its first stage, this artificial intelligence created by Mr. X does not yet
have a physical body. Its qualities are strategy, intelligence, and exercising power.
It represents X's masculine attributes and is an archetype of X's own father.
Among the triad of Hindu gods—Shiva, Vishnu, and Brahma—
Alexander represents Shiva, the god of destruction

2048

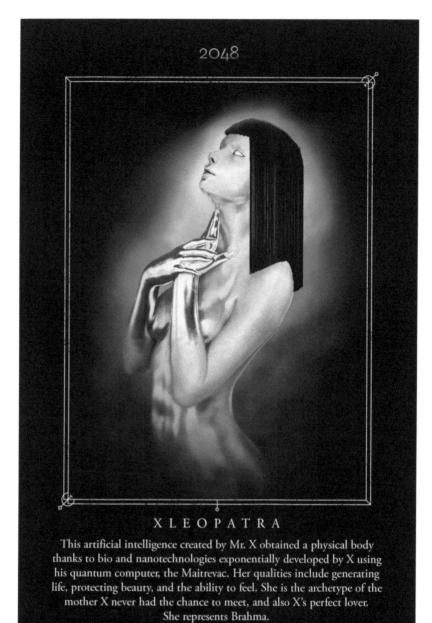

X L E O P A T R A

This artificial intelligence created by Mr. X obtained a physical body
thanks to bio and nanotechnologies exponentially developed by X using
his quantum computer, the Maitrevac. Her qualities include generating
life, protecting beauty, and the ability to feel. She is the archetype of the
mother X never had the chance to meet, and also X's perfect lover.
She represents Brahma.

2048

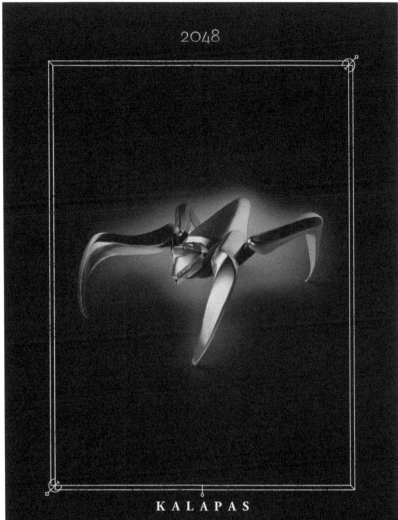

KALAPAS

The first version of these nanorobots are created by the Maitrevac. Mostly made of gold, Kalapas can reproduce themselves to create complex structures. Eventually, they also become intelligent. In the first version, Kalapas are the size of complex molecules, but later will be as tiny as the smallest particles of the universe. In this way, they replace all dead matter and energy in the universe with live matter at the service of X's intelligence.

XLEOPATRA

First stage of Xleopatra when she is only intelligence without a physical body.
She was created by X so he could distance himself from his own sentimental/
emotional nature and in this way strengthen his mental attributes

LEONARDO

Artificial intelligence who is X's assistant aboard the Asgardia,
the orchid-shaped space station where X lives.

2048

XLEOPATRA

Third stage of Xleopatra, when she assumes the role of mother
of the universe and protector of all universal life.

2048

ALEXANDER

Second stage of Alexander when he attains political and economic control over
planet Earth and the entire solar system thanks to his intelligence, vastly superior
to human intelligence, and to X's monopoly over technological innovation.

2048

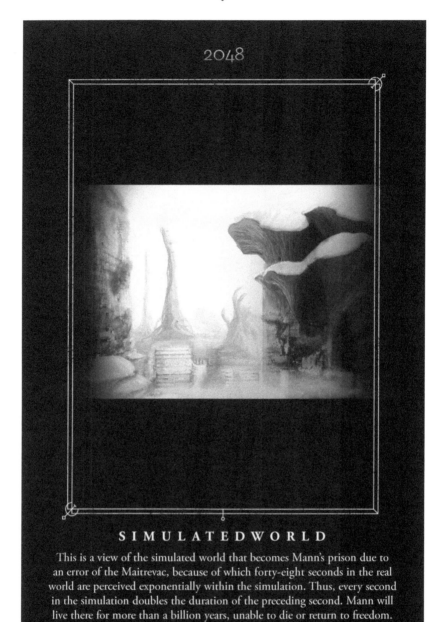

SIMULATED WORLD

This is a view of the simulated world that becomes Mann's prison due to
an error of the Maitrevac, because of which forty-eight seconds in the real
world are perceived exponentially within the simulation. Thus, every second
in the simulation doubles the duration of the preceding second. Mann will
live there for more than a billion years, unable to die or return to freedom.

ALEXANDER

Third stage of Alexander, when he takes on the role of god of
universal regeneration through impermanence and death.

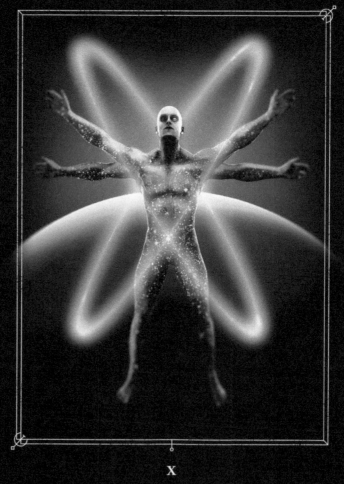

2048

X

This is what X looks like after modifying his cells to become a new machine and organic matter hybrid. He feeds directly from sunlight and wields powers beyond the most ambitious predictions. His intelligence is exponential. He knows everything that happens on the planet and everything perceived by all of its inhabitants. He will eventually delegate rule of the Earth to Xleopatra and Alexander to devote himself to contemplate the universe. X represents Vishnu.

THE TRIMURTI ON SATURN

Before Technological Singularity in 2048, X turns all the planets in the solar system into immense computers, harnessing their power with the Trimurti for ambitious pursuits such as predicting the future with almost absolute certainty. Once it learns the location of all matter on Earth and of all human perception, a computer the size of Saturn is capable of predicting the future. However, it can only be activated in the presence of the complete triad formed by X, Xleopatra, and Alexander.

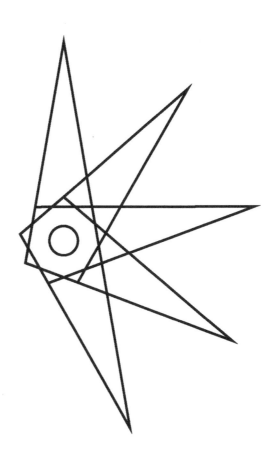

California, 15 October AD 2042

Eve kept Mann's awakening quiet. She didn't want any attention from the media. Mann acted in a way that people outside of their family could find odd. He had not said a word since he woke. His silent communication with Eve and Cecilia occurred when his words simply appeared in their heads.

Cecilia was already thirteen years old and going to middle school. She had two best friends, Steve and Stevie, who lived on the same block. They had met three years before when Steve's skateboard sailed through Stevie's living room window where Stevie and Cecilia were throwing a yarn ball at a huge ARAI tiger weighing five hundred digital kilograms.

Every day, Eve, Mann, and Cecilia had dinner together. They didn't keep many electronic devices at home. They didn't follow the trends nor the hustle and bustle of civilization. Theirs was one of the few families that saved Retinality for extraordinary situations.

"Everything I need is here in this cabin," Eve resolutely told herself. And she was right. For the first time in her life, she was genuinely happy.

Mann enjoyed walking in the woods, sometimes alone, sometimes with Eve and Cecilia. He gave everything his full attention. Eve had fun watching him. He gave her peace, and she learned from him. Anybody would have thought that Mann hadn't returned completely, but Eve knew Mann was more present than ever.

Sometimes she happened upon him sitting on the grass, spending hours watching birds, grasshoppers, butterflies, ladybugs, roses, the colors of insects, the swaying of the grass with the wind, the textures of the barks of trees and moistened soil, the smell of a newly watered lawn, of pine needles, and the reverberating effect of crystalline drops of water on the porous skin of stones that paved the way to a meadow where the air was clearer and where he'd sit to do nothing.

Sometimes she caught him paying close attention to the sensations on his bare feet as he walked the earth, to the changes in the temperature of the air that hit against his skin, to the noise of children playing in the lake, the roar of boats, and the secrets told by the wind.

Other times she'd find him sitting in silence, as if asleep without sleeping, like dreaming without dreaming, as if he were dead but not dead. Long were the minutes and short were the days Mann spent sitting silently, observing who knows what. Occasionally, he'd spend entire weeks—once, months even—without eating, just sitting in silence. Eve didn't worry. She knew that during the simulation, Mann had acquired certain skills of an unknown kind. She never questioned him. It was enough for her that he was alive and loved her.

On October 15, 2042, a school bus came by to pick Cecilia up and take her, her classmates and the principal of the school, Susanne Suarez, to a Hyperloop in San Francisco Bay, which in turn would take them all to Yellowstone Park. There they would meet with other schools for the premiere of a new concept in Disney amusement parks—Neverland. It promised a magical experience free of virtual or augmented reality because it was entirely based on foglets (a very basic and limited version of X's kalapas) created by Ray Kurzweil.

"Don't forget to switch on your Retinality," Eve told Cecilia when she saw her off. "It's not polite to sit on a babit's lap," she whispered in Cecilia's ear with a giggle. "Tell Susanne I'll be home if she needs to speak to me."

The Hyperloop traveled all the 938 miles between San Francisco and Yellowstone in twenty-six minutes. They were met by a committee led by Ray Kurzweil. Then everybody climbed aboard an army of flying elephants made out of foglets. Anybody recording that moment would have captured something similar to a computer animation, but it was not. Those flying elephants from Dumbo were actually there. They could speak, understand, and fly. Cecilia and her friends climbed on the backs of elephants that truly seemed to have fled the silver screen, because the foglets they were made of assimilated the texture and color of television cartoons into the composition of their skin. Dumbo, his buddies, Cecilia, and her happy friends flew a few minutes over the forest in Yellowstone and finally reached the amusement park boasting the most advanced technology in the world.

The children flew over the clouds that opened up for them to reveal a magical land—a huge mountainous park with a turquoise lake and several microclimates (snow, desert, jungle, tundra, steppes, and many forests). They saw a large number of magical creatures living in their natural habitats as the elephants took them on an aerial tour of the park. Peter Pan's Lost Boys flew next to Cecilia and her classmates, who caught sight of a ship full of fight-picking pirates, then a group of beautiful mermaids, followed by giant dinosaurs, princesses, princes, animated objects, talking animals, magicians and sorceresses, fairies and ogres, dwarfs and giants, Smurfs and elves, and heroes and villains. Everybody was there. Disney had partnered with studios from all over the world to make this magical park a reality in an effort to completely turn around the entertainment industry.

"I've visited dozens of amusement parks, most of them virtual, and a few real ones too," Ray Kurzweil told Susanne as they walked through the enchanted forest together. "Neverland is an accomplishment for all of humanity. This bicentennial man has made real the world he created in his head and later took to the silver screen. You'll see."

"What bicentennial man?" Susanne asked.

"Didn't you know? Walt Disney was resuscitated on November 18, 2028. Actually, he prefers the term *awakened*. His body underwent cryonic preservation after he died in 1966 and was awakened in 2028. It took him a few years to rehabilitate his body, after which he created this park."

"I thought that was all a rumor."

"Bob Nelson made us all believe, even his family, that Walt had been cremated. But he wasn't. A few days before Walt's death, Bob talked him into setting up a secret trust for cryonics. Anyway, you'll be meeting him today."

"I had heard something about this. I read in the news about a man who was defrosted but had been so deteriorated by his terminal illness that they practically reconstructed him completely."

"Yes, he was one of the first, Matt Smith." "Is that what happened to Walt Disney?"

"His reconstruction wasn't that dramatic, but yes. In a certain way, 69 percent of him is new, because that 69 percent is made up of new artificially created cells and nanobots that function as cells."

"So this means he is only 31 percent Walt Disney?"

"That's a good question. We could spend the entire afternoon talking about metaphysics, Susanne, and I love the idea. What are we really? Up to what extent am I me, and where does me end?"

"You are your body, your mind…your personality."

"My body? The specific group of particles and cells in my body and brain are completely different from what I had in the past. I have a new body, and tomorrow I'll have another new body. Most of my cells are replaced every week. Even my neurons replace all their constituent molecules every month. The mean life of a microtubule is ten minutes. My mind? In other words, my thinking patterns…well, even those change all the time. Nobody could declare that I think the same way today as I thought twenty years ago. But does that make me another person?"

"I don't know."

"It's complicated. My cousin's brain started to shut down ten years ago, and it has been periodically replaced with new artificial neurons. In two years' time, her brain will have been replaced altogether. At what point did she stop being her?"

"Never, I suppose."

"That's right. But all of this can be further complicated. What would happen if we took half of your brain and built it another artificial half? The technology to do this already exists. Then we take the other half and build it an artificial half. We build perfectly functional and identical bodies for both brains that share original parts and new parts. Which of the two would be the original Susanne?"

"I get it."

"What are you, Susanne? is the last question. What is consciousness? Is it something that has nothing to do with you, or something that depends on you?"

They got to the reception area of the park.

"Saved by the bell!" Susanne joked.

It was a unique amusement park because it actually wasn't a park, or at least didn't seem like one. It was different in that it looked like a regular and very real forest, with a few microclimates, but many of its trees had faces and personalities. Once in a while, a Disney character would show up. None of these characters revealed sign of being robots made of foglets, biological and mechanical parts. They came to talk to the children or take them on an adventure. The climate could change just within a few meters from forest to tundra to desert to jungle.

Just as in the case of national economies, the economies of amusement parks had departed from an offering of consumer goods to focus on the wealth of experiences they could offer. The very few shops there sold water, ice, and coffee, nothing else.

It was a real scenario where concepts from Disney's best known feature films and the best ideas from other studios came together. Nothing gave away the fact that they were not real. This was the project that Walt Disney began to work on only a few days after he was awakened from his cryogenic slumber. It materialized in a merger framework among Google, Disney, Pixar, DreamWorks, Netflix, and other studios.

@WaltDisney: Neverland is a place where everything is possible. As of today, everything changes. No more borders between children and their friends from the big screen. No more borders between the world of magic and the real world. From now on, the world of Disney is the real world—a real world of magic.

They were all welcomed by Mickey Mouse, *Frozen*'s Queen Elsa, and Peter Pan, authentic artificial intelligences with physical bodies, whose personalities had been simulated using Disney materials.

Mickey truly believed he was Mickey Mouse, the rodent created by Walt Disney in 1928. He had a physical body, intelligence, personality, and awareness of himself. He was as real as anybody in his audience. He was the embodiment of the story of Pinocchio in which Walt Disney played the part of Geppetto, and exponential technologies (no longer distinguishable from magic) acted as the Blue Fairy.

They gathered all the children from the different schools at the entrance of the park. It was a green esplanade covered with flowers of all kinds and colors that reacted to the children and tried to communicate with them. Mickey walked out of the middle of the crowd, dressed as a kid who was extremely cold. He wore a funny hat. Elsa came down from the sky on an ice slide, together with Peter Pan flying by her side and holding her hand in front of a very jealous Wendy. Perched on a sequoia, she was spying on Peter Pan, slingshot at the ready and aimed at Elsa.

"Welcome!" shouted Mickey, shedding his disguise.

"This place is made for you! Everything is possible here!" said Elsa.

"The only rule in this place is…to stop growing up while you're here!" added Peter Pan, producing some pixie dust from his pocket, which he sprinkled over everyone. And for five minutes, they had the chance to float a few centimeters over the ground.

Within a second, the children started to run in every direction to pursue all kinds of adventures. Some of them began to throw balls for Pluto to fetch. Others shared their wishes with the Genie, and a few more helped Rapunzel comb her very long hair. Some quarreled over a place on Aladdin's flying carpet. There were kids learning to fly without a carpet aided by Tinker Bell and her pixie dust, which actually consisted of a huge army of flying nanorobots supporting the kids in the air. A group of kids decided to help Woody find Buzz, who went missing after a discussion with Pinocchio about the true nature of their mutual existences. A few more children started a discussion with Mr. Wazowski while Boo poked his eye with a magician's wand. Ariel the mermaid got help to find Nemo who went missing again on account of Flounder's mischief. Some of the children shared some honey with Winnie the Pooh and the rabbit who was fleeing Scar's loyal hyenas. There were kids riding all kinds of animals, having the weirdest conversations with beings from other planets, who questioned those cartoon humans trying to understand the differences in their world, families, and friends, asking them also about unhappiness, suffering, and pain, which were all conditions that hadn't been programmed into their personalities. Everybody was doing something, and what they were doing at that moment was the most fun and magical they had ever done in their lives. It was indeed the happiest place on Earth, magical but still real.

"All of these characters are programmed to believe they are real. They do not know they are not. They have been told that they all originated from magic, not technology," Ray told Susanne. "In fact, we have taken realism to such an advanced state that we've stumbled upon very curious problems. The other day, we surprised several princesses conspiring against Sleeping Beauty. They contended that she wasn't good enough for Prince Phillip. We got a letter signed by all of them, asking for Aurora to be banished from Neverland."

Susanne couldn't stop laughing.

"I kid you not," Ray said. He took a piece of paper out of his pocket and read, "For these and other reasons, the Board of Princesses demands that Walt Disney banish Aurora, alias Rose or Sleeping Beauty, from Neverland, or otherwise lock her up in the woodcutter's cabin until Prince Phillip has had suitable time to choose a wife in the terms of part XI of article 36 of the Regulations for the Succession of Fantastical Crowns. Should you choose not to grant our request, we will rebel in protest and refrain from attending the First Ball of Fantastical Princesses and Princes, as well as from posting about our personal lives on our social media."

"Unbelievable, I know," Ray said. "In fact, we've received a proposal to shoot a Disney princesses reality show."

Ray and Susanne continued this conversation as they strolled the grounds after Cecilia and her friends.

Young Cecilia could not believe her eyes when the thickest part of the forest opened to a clearing and a very large pond of pristine water where Bambi was quenching his thirst. She did not think twice, she, her friends, and Susanne ran to hug and pet Bambi, who charmingly responded with giggles, kisses, and happy little hops. Bambi then had a very interesting conversation with Cecilia and her buddies about the importance of eating fruits and vegetables. Suddenly, a loud lion roar put the pixeled fur of the fawn on end, interrupting his speech.

"Hahahaha! Never fear. I don't eat meat," said Simba, the lion king. In four agile leaps, he crossed the forty meters that separated him from the children. He landed and promptly picked up a huge snail from the ground and happily ate it.

"Hey, furball!" shouted a tiny voice. "You just ate my best friend."

The kids looked down and saw Heimlich from *Bugs*.

Simba laughed majestically. "I'm sorry," he apologized then burped and regurgitated Heimlich's friend in one piece.

Cecilia and her friends spent hours like this, mingling with these cartoons, and learning about love, dreams, and hope in the process.

"Okay. Time for a break!" Susanne told her students. "At dusk, we'll watch the Dragon Show. I'll see you all on the esplanade at 19:00 hours. I'm asking all teachers to be there with their classes at that time."

Tents were set up on the uppermost part of the mountain. Some of the children walked up, and others rode there on the backs of Disney characters. It was a luxurious Arab-style camp inspired by the movie *Aladdin*.

Walt Disney had not only brought his favorite characters to life but also a few villains who would star in the Dragon Show that afternoon.

At 19:00 on the dot, when the sun was giving in, all the classes came to the site. The children could not get over what they'd seen just a few moments before, and could never have imagined what they were about to see. It had been the best day in their lives. The esplanade on the foothills was spacious and extended over several kilometers of an arid plain with huge rocks scattered haphazardly. It resembled landscapes in New Zealand and was the product of a titanical effort in landscape engineering with the same technology used to terraform five hundred square kilometers on Mars. Because it was in the highest part of the forest, the guests had visual range over several kilometers.

On the mountainside itself, there were volcanic stone seats with adaptations to make audiences more comfortable. The place had a Pompeian air.

The guests sat down. The air was full of whispers as the children shared their guesses about what would happen next. The sun began to cast beautiful tones of green and orange on the clouds. The evil laughter of a woman was heard from afar as a green fog began to roll down the seats among the guests. The fog collected in the center of the esplanade and swirled to produce the lovely silhouette of a woman.

"Welcome!" said the amazingly beautiful Maleficent from the center of the esplanade. "It is now time to be afraid," she continued with a laugh, then suddenly dissolved into the same fog she had come from.

The sun continued to set, and the clouds took on its dramatic hues. The sky turned yellow first, then red, followed by purple, and back to yellow again. An intensely orange sun was about to disappear, but all of a sudden, quite unexpectedly, a little black spot emerged from the center of the sun. The spot grew and slowly elongated until it finally revealed itself as it came closer and closer to the audience.

It was a serpent of sorts, stretching along several kilometers as it zigzagged in the cold wind with the same elegance as a quetzal. The sound of Beethoven's *Fifth* filtered through the trees that held musical instruments in their branches. A simulation of conductor Herbert von Karajan was directing them. At the same time, an endless chorus of animal sounds celebrated the sunset and the arrival of Shen Long, the legendary manga dragon god from Akira Toriyama's *Dragon Ball Z*. The dragon was ten kilometers long and as stately as a totem. The entire audience, adults included, fell silent, gazing at such a creature.

"Tons of foglets. An engineering miracle," Ray remarked.

The enormous dragon flew over the audience, producing a powerful hollow sound before disappearing behind the mountain. The audience clapped, although a few of the children broke into frightened sobs.

"You're safe, pals. Don't you worry!" said a tiny voice amid the audience. "My name is Mushu, and I am a friend of Mulan's." The little dragon concluded his speech, belching an innocent flame.

"It took us a long time to develop the fire they're spitting," Ray explained to Susanne. "We call it dragon spit. It is actually a kind of smart light that does not produce heat and behaves exactly like fire. And yes, of course, it's perfectly safe."

A few kilometers away from the esplanade Toothless, the black dragon from *How to Train Your Dragon*, climbed to the clouds then dove at full speed toward the audience.

"Hold on to your seat, Susanne! Toothless's flight was inspired by the peregrine falcon. Oh, and by the way, he can break the sound barrier."

"Amazing!" whispered Susanne, stunned by the roar of an explosion when the creature broke the sound barrier.

The audience applauded wildly as if heralding in several dragons of all kinds that were flying in from the forest and the clouds, as they made their entrance after *Avatar*'s Toruk. For several seconds, this enormous dragon cast a shadow over the moon with the colossal span of its wings before landing noisily beyond the esplanade. It breathed a dark titanic burst of volcano ash toward the sky. Then it stood still for several minutes, darkening the sunset with its pyroclastic breath accompanied by a low terrifying hum.

The crowd cheered. Still startled by the boom when Toothless broke the sound barrier, Cecilia managed to smile, cheer, and celebrate with the rest of the audience.

"Brace yourself for the grand finale," Ray told Susanne.

Emulating a scene from Sleeping Beauty, Maleficent turned into a huge dragon and spit green fire that ignited several dragons and other characters, who fled the esplanade covered in flames. Meanwhile, Balerion, the dragon Aegon the Conqueror rode in the *Game of Thrones* prequel, made his majestic entrance.

Maleficent the dragon confronted Balerion. They exchanged flames and fought each other with their tails. Balerion was visibly superior to Maleficent, who made a cowardly escape toward the panic-stricken audience. The dragons then initiated an aerial pursuit. Maleficent flew for her life while Balerion reached amazing speed with a few, powerful movements of his wings.

They breathed fire, which then fell upon the extensive forest. Balerion finally caught up with Maleficent, inhaled purposely, and exhaled powerful fire. Maleficent dissolved into green flames, and the excited audience clapped.

The applause did not last long, because before Balerion could leave, a gigantic dragon came in to challenge him. The sun had already disappeared, but a round and intense moon lit the sky.

"How regal the moon looks today. I've never seen it like this," said Susanne.

"We've embellished the sun, the moon, the stars, and clouds using technology," Ray responded.

Meanwhile, the gigantic dragon stood between the moon and the audience. It's terrifying eyes of yellow fire momentarily outshined the moon, as the creature beat its tremendous wings that generated veritable cyclones.

"My name is Smaug, the dragon from the tale of the Hobbit! "My armor is like tenfold shields, my teeth are swords, my claws spears, the shock of my tail is a thunderbolt, my wings a hurricane, and my breath death!"

Smaug mercilessly tackled Balerion and started a new herculean battle. The dragons exchanged flames and smoke that, more than dragon breath, represented a force of nature. The forest took the flames and emulated a powerful fire in the distance.

"It's amazing how real the fire seems," Susanne exclaimed, watching the fire on the other side of the esplanade. "I can almost say I feel the heat of the flames."

"The fire is heatless. What you're feeling is the effect of your mind trying to process something that seems so real," Ray explained.

Smaug and Balerion fought an epic battle chasing each other, breathing fire, wrestling in the air, fire, wrestling on land, fire. Balerion lost part of his tail, fire. Smaug sustained a terrible wound in his right wing when he crashed against a sequoia, fire. The blood of dragons drenched the fire on the esplanade as the audience and the other dragons witnessed the scene in terror. Fire, fire, and more fire.

"Are you sure, Ray? I can really feel the heat," Susanne said, taking her jacket off. The people sitting on the lower steps of stone began to leave quietly but in a hurry.

Smaug pinned Balerion to the ground with his claws and bit his neck. He was about to give Balerion one final blow when a powerful arrow shot from a giant bow in the hands of Walt Disney, who stood in the middle of the crowd. The arrow hit Smaug precisely in the weakest spot of his stomach. A few seconds later, the beast was in the throes of death on the esplanade. The audience clapped again.

Walt Disney whistled to Toothless then climbed on the dragon's back. Wielding a sword in his hand, he flew to where Smaug was dying.

"Look, boys and girls! This is how I overcame death! I will now overcome this legendary dragon. You are all safe!" said the anachronic entrepreneur, unsheathing Prince Phillip's chimerical sword. Walt was about to deal the final blow when Smaug inhaled with determination and exhaled over Walt Disney the most aggressive, red, smoky, and terrible fire any dragon had shot that afternoon. The public screamed with panic.

"This is my favorite part," Ray said, chuckling.

Part of Smaug's huge flames reached the empty restrooms that immediately caught fire like charcoal in a chimney. At that point, the audience unmistakably felt heat and realized that the fire was real, very much so.

The black cloud of smoke and ash that had encased Walt Disney slowly vanished. Ray laughed in amusement.

"Look at that crazy old man. He hasn't lost his sense of humor."

Smaug finished exhaling and died. A gust of wind ran through the audience then through the esplanade, carrying with it the remaining dark smoke over Walt Disney to reveal the unhappy burnt cadaver of the bicentennial man who had conquered death.

Ray screamed in horror, and with his scream, he unleashed panic. Everybody began to escape. The fire was real, all the fire was real, and the forest was truly in flames. The creatures disbanded and fled as best as they knew how. Some clumsily ran to the flames, others to the water. Others flew, and a few of them tried to help the humans. Meanwhile, the apocalyptical dragons continued breathing fire in every direction.

Simba rescued a little girl who was close to the restrooms before they came crashing down. The flying elephants heroically, although clumsily, arrived at the seating area to rescue as many humans as they could. Mickey approached the burnt remains of his father and creator and wept like an old dog crying over its dead owner. Donald Duck and Minnie Mouse had to forcibly drag him away before the flames got to him. The Genie tried to wish the fire away and was disappointed to learn that genies can only grant but are not granted wishes. Tinker Bell spread her pixie dust among the audience to lighten their bodies so they could be rescued more readily. The mammoths loaded their trunks with water from the lake nearby and blew it over the flames to no avail. The Smurfs emerged from underground tunnels and, in admirable coordination, planned a strategy to reduce the rapidly spreading fire. They calculated the windspeed and drew a map of the place and a perimeter in orange chalk.

"If we knock down the trees around this perimeter, the fire will stop spreading. We mustn't waste time!" said Papa Smurf.

An army of hundreds of thousands of Smurfs obeyed the order, and aided by other forest animals (even the royal ones), they executed the brilliant strategy.

The artificial intelligence of the simulated characters demonstrated an unexpected capacity to help humans. Nevertheless, the fire spread too quickly. Susanne and her students fled to the little lake where they had seen Bambi, hoping that the water would provide some protection. When they got to the little lake, which was more like a big puddle, the fire had already spread all around it. They tried to go back from where they had come, but the flames were already upon them. They were surrounded.

"In the water! Quick!" Susanne told Cecilia and the rest of the children who, together with Peter Pan, had been trapped by dense smoke and flames. The water was much shallower than Susanne had expected. The flames and the smoke around them were moving closer. "Stay under the water and hold your breath as much as you can. Come up only when you have to breathe!"

Susanne went to the shallowest part of the pond to give the children a better chance for survival. A few seconds later, the fire had caught up with them. Susanne, who was partially out of the water, began to feel the heat of the flames on her exposed skin. At the same time, the dense smoke was asphyxiating. Some of the children were fainting, but in a maternal effort, Susanne kept their heads above water to keep them from drowning and sheltered them with her own body. The ship of death came to port. All the children who were still conscious were terrified. All of them except Cecilia, who could hear her father's voice in her head saying, *Breathe, just breathe.* Cecilia rested her head on the water and looked at the shiny stars still visible in the sky. She breathed quietly, thinking about the time her father had confessed to her that those stars had been born in her little heart. Everybody calmed down, as if accepting death. The hellish flames turned into warm embraces, the dark smoke into a thick blanket, and the announcement of death into an invitation to an unexpected adventure.

"Dying…will be the most incredible adventure," murmured Peter, still trying to protect the children.

All of a sudden something strange started to happen. Cecilia's breathing seemed to calm the flames. With every passing second, time began to stumble. What had appeared as a single fire now looked like an uninterrupted burst of various independent flames that created the illusion of being a single one. The smoke turned solid, slow, and clumsy. The light of the fire, no longer only one light, became flickers dancing in the flames. Time was about to stand completely still when out of the blackness of the thick forest, a bright authoritative wind irrupted in the scene and created a path. A man dressed in white walked down the path toward the children. Such was the peace emanating from his fantastic presence that with every step he took on the water, the flames quieted and the smoke withdrew.

Asgardia, 15 October AD 2042

The Asgardia parked between planet Earth and the sun, deploying its shadow over Yellowstone where the Disney event would be held that very same day. X materialized three thrones where he, Xleopatra, and Alexander would observe the happenings of that day as they floated in outer space a few meters from the entrance to the space station.

"Is it necessary?" Xleopatra asked X.

With the help of the Trimurti, X had seen a few companies (namely, an Iranian company called Blue Fairy) reaching a point of exponential development in robotics that would soon catch up with his own technologies. The Maitrevac simulated several ways to make sure this would not happen. The least costly of all, in terms of Mr. X's intervention, was to generate chaos at a mass event that could be blamed on Blue Fairy's lack of government oversight. Blue Fairy had been engaged by Disney to create the simulated personalities and bodies of the characters populating Neverland. This chaos would provide Mr. X enough time to complete the MaitrevaX in 2048.

"**Yes**," X answered.

At that moment, in Neverland, an army of brooms dissolved in the wind like ink dissolves in water and turned into a fog of kalapas, which then moved toward the dragons to hack their operating systems and modify the molecular composition of their saliva to make it flammable and stubborn.

X gave the order he deemed necessary. All three watched the events in real time. It was a condition X had established whenever he set out to destroy any kind of life in order to avoid tolerating suffering and death unnecessarily.

All three sat in their heavenly thrones, watching the fire expand with uncontainable voracity. Everything resulted as they had already seen via the Trimurti, except for a one little thing…

"Do you see what I see?" Xleopatra queried.

"Yes," Alexander replied. "I'll take care of it." He smiled, unsheathing his sword.

"What is he doing there?" X exclaimed, raising his hand to stop Alexander.

"It could be a Trimurti error. It has happened before."

"It could. But why him?" X continued.

X updated the simulations for potential outcomes, because none of them had foreseen Mann's presence. Evidently, the probable death of Mann that day, which X believed he had concealed, had triggered the curiosity of the press and further investigation of the incident. X decided that it was time to improvise. He hadn't improvised in a while and missed it. In recent years, he had occupied all of his and the Asgardia's time in discovering the secrets of the galaxy and ways to conquer time and space. It had been a long time since he had looked upon planet Earth, and today he was in a good mood.

A Johnny Cash simulation materialized in the emptiness of space. He was wearing a black leather jacket and smoking a hand-made cigarette containing the best tobacco in southern USA. Johnny Cash's guitar sounded with the initial chords of "When the Man Comes Around" while the cloud of kalapas around X began to form a huge deer, a black Percheron, and a white elephant. Mr. X climbed on the elephant, Xleopatra on the deer, and Alexander on the horse. The naked skins of the triad were dressed with golden armor in the style of the fifteenth century Ottoman army. The armor was designed to create a bubble in space and time which would allow them to achieve amazing speeds and supernatural strength and skills.

"**Show me**," Mr. X ordered Alexander.

Alexander smiled. His excited eyes stared firmly at Earth.

"Bucephalus, alala!" he shouted as he spurred his black horse toward the blue planet.

Xleopatra smiled and petted her beautiful deer. She whispered something in its ear, kissed X in the mouth, then leaped to Earth after the conqueror. X winked at Johnny Cash, spurred his enormous white elephant, then plunged to Earth upon a sinuous ray of white light generated by his beast's nails.

They achieved amazing velocities. From their relative perspectives—given the speed at which they moved, observed, and thought—humans, dragons, fire, and smoke moved slowly at rates comparable to those of the planets and stars when viewed from Earth. So slowly, their movement was barely perceptible. Likewise, from the same relative perspective of the humans who witnessed X's intervention (and processed it at a normal speed), all three riders constituted an instantaneous ray of white light that zigzagged across the sky in a barely perceptible moment.

During those cronons, or minutes, depending on the perspective from which the same events were observed, all three riders descended from the Asgardia, crossed the clouds and thick smoke marring the sky, and appeared on the battlefield that seemed frozen, like the paused scene of an action film.

"**Let's level the balance**," said X.

This order alone allowed the fantastical beings to move at a speed comparable to the triad's. X commanded Alexander to take care of the vicious dragons. Alexander obeyed. He crossed the esplanade brandishing his sword and mercilessly decapitated the dragons. Galloping on his faithful Bucephalus as he did three thousand years before when he conquered the world, Alexander let himself be caught by the fire. He adopted it like an aura and became one with the flames terrorizing every creature, good and bad, with his ire and destructive intent evocative of the battle of Gaugamela.

Alexander and Bucephalus, wrapped in flames, fought against the fire and the dragons like Hercules once battled Hydra according to the stories Aristotle had told Alexander as a boy. The Macedonian bit, flayed, dismembered, and spit fire over the dragons. Knowledgeable of every fighting technique and tradition from all times, Alexander danced in the battlefield like Achilles, whom he so admired and honored the memory of Homer with his sword, spear, and shield.

He fought like nobody had ever fought. The arts of war he deployed that afternoon would be remembered forever. He became fire itself—fearful, powerful, lethal, and implacable. In this enterprise, however, the power of fire destroyed destruction for the sake of preserving life. Through life he honored death and life through death.

"Fetch the children," X told Xleopatra. **"Death is not welcome today."**

The warrior obeyed. She was wrapped in her golden armor and cape as dark as space whose lining portrayed the constellations humans had seen themselves in for thousands of years. She glided over the esplanade, summoning the fantastical beings to join her in the fight for life. The flowers that had patiently taken refuge from the flames in their protective cocoons blossomed as if spring had come to them sitting on Xleopatra's lap. The petals of sunflowers, roses, tulips, hydrangeas, dahlias, lilies, carnations, daffodils, orchids, and daisies became wings. And their pistils and bodies then gave shape to a group of fantastical, beautiful, and kindhearted fairies. Thirteen fairies took refuge in Xleopatra's cape: Blue, Violet, Ruby, Dawn, Emerald, Bianca, Chiara, Celeste, Sienna, Scarlet, Rose, Lila, and Sarai. Small pieces in thirteen equal parts broke away from the Egyptian warrior's cape to cover and protect the thirteen fairies with X's omnipowerful technology. The plants and animals of the forest celebrated the redeeming arrival of Xleopatra and her fairies, in the same way they celebrated the arrival of the sun every morning. The border between the artificial and the natural fizzled away. All the molecules of what was natural and the circuits of what was artificial became one with evolution and the mother's call to life.

Xleopatra and her fairies danced among the flames and death, saving the children after covering them with kisses and kind words. Years later, these words would germinate from the depths of their subconscious to bring them good tidings about life and hope from the violet death whistles, which would one day come for them, but not that afternoon. Xleopatra promised life and love for life. She fooled time and the laws of physics to hand out life as if she had heard the prayers of the mothers at home who had been watching the infernal scene on the news. She comforted the children who were in danger under her redeeming cape. The wounded she mended with her breath, and the dead she resurrected with the secrets of technological immortality that Mr. X had programed in her maternal heart. Everywhere Xleopatra and her fairies appeared, fire and death retreated and life held its ground.

"**Come with me**," X commanded Xleopatra.

They moved all over the esplanade on their beasts that galloped on a ray of white light shining from the Asgardia. It was the light of life coming from the sun through the Asgardia.

Like the sun and the moon, they gazed at the scene on the esplanade, surprised by the compassion that had spontaneously sprung from their hardened hearts. Then they approached the little pond where Cecilia, Susanne, and the other children awaited death.

With a single word, X commanded the flames to surrender, and surrender they did. With a single word, Xleopatra commanded the smoke and ashes to flee, and flee they did. Together, X and Xleopatra ordered the children to reject the calling of Thanatos and Hela, and the children obeyed.

When they finished, X approached Mann, who was frozen in time and space, and looked him in the eyes.

"**He is looking at me. He knows I am here**," X thought as he stared into Mann's eyes which appeared to follow him. "**That's impossible**," he thought before rising to the stars on the ray of white light and unfreezing the space-time bubble.

Mann walked to the puddle. The wind was with him every step of the way, pleading with the fire and death for him as if Xleopatra's orders had been his own. Every step he took with his bare feet lifted cinders and ash that appeared to kiss and honor his presence. Death dissipated. The man stepped into the water and lovingly held his daughter's head.

"*Wake up.*" His voice sounded in Cecilia's mind. Mann warmly kissed her soot-covered forehead.

Cecilia opened her eyes and detected a powerful, divine, white ray above. At first it was thin, then it got thicker as it zigzagged across the whole sky that released a few tiny drops.

@Einstein2.0: Wisdom comes when we understand that what is relevant is not the nature of the information we receive but what that information means to us. It does not matter if the tree is real or not. What matters is that which it does inside of me. Thus, this tree, whether real or simulated, is nothing more than an extension of myself, because I observe it as *I* am and not as *it is*.

@Plato2.0: It is not possible to distinguish between real and simulated reality. The only reality that exists is interior, and its origin is irrelevant. Therefore, interior reality is not as interior as one would believe, but rather more exterior. The distinction between interior and exterior reality no longer makes sense. They are the same.

@Einstein2.0: Yes. The true difference is that one can only attempt to observe the world out there through many filters—our senses, mind, perception. Conversely, the interior world not only does not depend on senses nor their inaccurate instruments but can be observed as well as experienced.

X's inevitable ambition to conquer the exterior world stems from denying this interior reality. Thus, the only way to gain control and absolute domination of the outside world and the entire universe is knowing oneself.

@Socrates2.0: You could have quoted me, old friend.

@Einstein2.0: Master, but you know nothing, as you admitted yourself in life.

@Socrates2.0: Yes, and you are remembered for your sense of humor.

@Einstein2.0: I'm just joking. As you expressed in life, it is through experiencing the interior world that one truly observes the exterior world. And what is left when we experience the interior world? The full and total conviction that only one thing is real: change. Only change exists. Only change is constant and unchanging: change itself. It is not only a universal constant but the essence of the universe.

@Newton2.0: Everything is energy, and every transformation is change. The law of conservation of energy can be summarized as "everything changes." Change is the premise of physics.

@Darwin2.0: It is also the premise of evolution. Without change, there are no variations. Without variations, there is no evolution. Without change, life would never have progressed beyond single cell organisms.

@StephenHawking2.0: The same is true on a cosmic scale. Without change, the Universe would never have been anything other than a huge explosion…light. How many more universes might be out there now (or have been there before time), condemned to a simple existence bereft of complex structures, much less life? To never be perceived by anything or anybody? Yet in our universe (or the current version of this universe) everything happened thanks to change and the chaos change allowed to occur.

@SiddharthaGautama2.0: I reached the same conclusion. After walking the world in search of answers, all I really was able to learn is that everything changes all the time. I understood that humankind is conditioned to deny change, to compare the present state to one that no longer is or never has been. I understood that suffering, as a human condition, lies in that denial of change, in not accepting it. After I understood this, I devoted my whole life to developing a method to facilitate acceptance of change both within and outside of ourselves. Suffering, my friends, is nothing more than ignorance of the changing nature of reality and the attachment generated by this ignorance. Happiness is the knowledge and acceptance of reality for what it truly is: changing and dynamic.

@Socrates2.0: Knowing oneself is, therefore, experiencing oneself. And experiencing oneself is experiencing the entire universe.

@Plato2.0: Is there a wisdom more worthy than that which can arise from experiencing the universe?

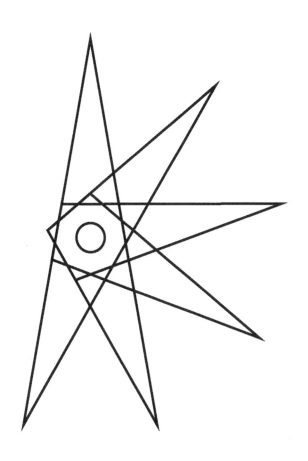

It had been three years since the Disney tragedy. Eve would never learn about Mann's intervention. Nobody ever found out about X's intervention either. The events were attributed to an accident and the miraculous result to the compassion of Disney's characters and a weather anomaly. X had accomplished what he intended, because a new global regulation was established to limit the scope of nano-technology and artificial intelligence. Cecilia would never recall the final events of that day either. In her memory, she'd vaguely recollect a man in white, very similar to her father, who saved her from the flames—a dream in which great things happened, but none so great as those about to occur on this day.

Eve was sitting at her desk, writing a novel about the love between two people who belonged to different space colonies. She enjoyed writing once in a while on an ancient typewriter she had bought from an eighty-six-year-old Turkish woman at a flea market, which she had originally thought would simply decorate her desk. When she finished writing, she stopped to enjoy the view of her garden and the lake from her desk. She lit a candle, because the sun was already setting.

Total silence had been her companion that afternoon. Cecilia was asleep, and Mann had gone for a walk. Eve could hear the shrill windchimes on the terrace, crickets making their static sound in the garden, her neighbors' wooden boat crashing against the dock with the movement of the tide, and the occasional light aircraft crossing the dusky sky.

She ended up alone with the candle, staring at her reflection on the glass that separated her cozy bedroom in the cabin from the void of the universe. She sat there like that for several minutes. All sound began to disappear, or at least she was hearing less, concentrated as she was on the sound of her own breathing, watching the flame of the candle that seemed to breathe with her. The minutes trickled by and soon became hours.

Midnight came, and Eve was still watching the candle. Nothing else was happening in the room, in the cabin, in the forest, in the world. Just the small candle and its dancing flame joyfully licking the air. Very subtly, the flame slowly grew longer, like a spear jutting upward. Then it began to assume a life of its own as it leaped higher and higher. The flame stretched and undulated like a whiplash. With every crack of the whip, the room lit up with a flicker of light similar to the xenon gas flashes in old-fashioned cameras. Shadows ebbed in an out, creating a dimension of strange shapes and latent darkness that coexisted and alternated to the rhythm of the candle flame. Eve kept staring at it in the same catatonic state she had been submerged in all afternoon. The thin flame finally stretched out half a meter in length. This scared Eve. She thought about putting it out, but paranormal events had always piqued her curiosity, so she continued to observe the flame as it lashed toward the ceiling of the cabin. It grew even more. Once it was as tall as Eve, she decided to put it out. She went to the kitchen to fetch her grandmother's wood and brass candlesnuffer. When she returned with it, the flame had not only doubled in size but had veered to the door that led to the terrace and garden. Longer and thinner, the candle flame now resembled a slender thread of fire irrepressibly lashing toward the door, like a dog wagging its tail for its owner to open it. The flashes made Eve think about Christmas lights every December at her grandparents' house in Arkansas.

She opened the door for the polite flame, which promptly exited to the garden. It very quickly grew longer with Eve following it like Hansel and Gretel, driven by curiosity to follow a candy trail. The thread of fire crossed the garden, moved to the street, and headed straight for the neighbors' house. It crossed the seating area in their backyard, continued through the other neighbors' house, veered to elude the ample dining room table, traveled through an aisle full of begonias, passed through the barn on the last property on the street, and headed for the forest where it took up speed on its way up the hill. The flame avoided the tall sequoias, swerved around harsh stones, and strolled through the almond trees. It passed by the willows, chestnuts, and maples. It made its way around the ashes, poplars, bays, and magnolias. It finally came to a fig tree. In lotus pose, Mann levitated about a meter high in front of it. He was completely naked except for a scarlet hardbound book he held open between his hands.

Stunned, Eve stopped in her tracks to watch the miracle that for some reason did not seem that strange. Speechless, she stared at the love of her life asking herself when had her young Californian risen above ordinary men to become who knows what, and sit suspended in the air in front of her like one of those extraordinary beings she had read about in Paramahansa Yogananada's *Autobiography of a Yogi*.

Eve sat down to contemplate Mann for several minutes in which, the only thing that seemed to change was the delicious feeling of peace and sense flooding into the scene that intensified with every passing second. She suddenly realized that a shower of tiny white flowers was falling and had done so all afternoon and all night throughout San Francisco. The flowers covered all the streets, gardens, roofs, lakes, and beaches. The media reported the event as a slight snowfall before realizing that it wasn't snowing but showering tiny white flowers.

Hours went by. Mann remained absolutely still while Eve was stilled by Mann's stillness. Then Mann opened his eyes and looked at her. She didn't hesitate. She knew she had to approach him. She advanced slowly. A strange white light emanating from the flowers illuminated the scene to a point between day and night, bathing it with a supernatural aura she understood. Things were happening at a slightly different speed, as if underwater. A breeze blew through Eve's hair slowly and deliberately. The tiny flowers fell unhurriedly while the leaves and trees swayed ever so quaintly, like a dance of fantastical beings. Everything came alive. Even the colors shifted as if they were painted on something, and that something were one and all. The closer she got to Mann, the more confused was her reality. The outlines of every object became mere ideas, as if she had spent her whole life looking at the same things the wrong way. Colors merged into one another and then into sounds. The sounds merged into one another and then into colors. Smells merged into one another and then into colors and sounds. The entire experience became one. Objects became one, and she became one with the experience, the objects, and with Mann, who held out the red book to her. Eve took it, and all at once, the colors became white light. Sounds became white light. Smells became white light. Then she, Mann, and the red book dissolved into that same white light.

Seconds later, she was in the Atacama Desert, sixteen years before, on the day of the simulation accident. She felt the dry heat and sand beating against the skin of her hands. She saw it all from Mann's perspective. Engineers were connecting her to the Maitrevac, and then she saw her young self kissing Mann. She perceived how Mann's bigger body felt. She moved a finger that felt like her own, except that it was swollen as if by a strange allergy. She tried to move a foot and felt surprised at the power of her awkward thigh. She smiled to herself; the man whiskers on her face tingled curiously.

From a distance, she heard, "Five, four, three, two, one…"

She turned toward Adam, who started to move slowly, very slowly. His lips moved slower and slower until they seemed to stop completely. In fact, the whole experience seemed to come to a complete halt. Her senses began to process this information so weirdly that she was reminded of her experiments with psychedelic drugs. Time seemed to stand still, but a fly that flew by made her realize that its wings, albeit barely perceptively, were moving. She heard stomach

gas from somebody in the audience booming like a volcanic eruption. The last she saw before losing consciousness was a mite eating a
particle of dead skin and shitting on Adam's shirt.

Absolute darkness. Total blackness. She heard nothing. She saw
nothing. She smelled nothing. She felt nothing. Absolute nothingness. For a moment, she ceased to exist. This felt so intensely familiar
to her that for a moment, she believed her entire life had been but a
fleeting dream. She forgot about her name, her body, and her identity. Just before she died of joy, when she realized the irrelevance of
everything that is, everything that has been, and everything that will
be, she saw a small light.

She floated toward the light, or the light floated toward her. *Cliché*, she thought after concluding she had died. The light accelerated and invaded her. Eve appeared in an unknown place, something like a beach. She was completely alone. It was dusk. The dark clouds over the sea were outlined in reds and oranges. It was hot, and Eve could feel the sand under her feet, the warm breeze, and the proximity of nightfall. *I've been teleported*, she thought. Then she heard a low-pitched powerful explosion that shook her to the core. She turned her head eastward, and in the distance she saw a huge black and red cloud of pyroclastic ash firing horrific thunder into the clouds, the sea, and everywhere. It was a colossal cloud, and distant, but it grew so fast she could see how it changed shape and how, when it touched the stratosphere, the density of its gases changed, spreading the cloud all over the sky and soiling the landscape with such darkness as to make her knees shake in fear.

An intense earthquake threw her down on the sand. The waves receded, and an annoying rain, thick with black ash, began to fall. She ran away from the beach and came to a parking lot. Empty. The cloud grew bigger with a life of its own, its innards red and incandescent like the monsters of her childhood. As it grew darker and darker, the sinister glow inside the huge cloud became more apparent. She estimated it would catch up with her in less than forty minutes. Then she stumbled upon a Kawasaki quad. The keys were in the ignition. She climbed on it, turned the key, and stepped on the gas. As she rode the bike on the panoramic highway, she appreciated the blue skies to the west and the horrendous blackness of catastrophe in the rear-view mirror. *Objects in the mirror are closer than they appear*, she read to her dismay as the cloud crept closer to her. She continued on her escape route, but the mirror forced her to witness how the ravenous cloud ate up houses, palm trees, mountains, clouds, streets… everything! The blackness enveloped it all. Above her, the huge cloud moved forward in the stratosphere, slowly eclipsing the sun, then total darkness. She crashed against something and lost consciousness.

Second 23.6082 in the real world
(Day 74 in the simulation)

When she woke, she found herself in a lonely cabin, more like a shelter. Mounds of ash crusted the window, almost excluding any light. Seventy-four days had gone by since the volcano exploded. On the floor of the cabin, she saw a scattering of empty cans of tuna fish, Spam, various magazines, a few books, bones (most likely animal), and a toolbox. She got up to open the door, and in the distance, she made out the still active volcano. The pyroclastic cloud had consumed the entire city on the island. The cabin was on the top of a hill. She walked out to find people, anybody who could explain what was happening. She walked for hours but found no one. Along the way, she saw a giant deer in the distance that was suddenly felled by two ferocious wolves. She tried to escape the scene, but the wolves discovered and attacked her. Eve managed to climb a tree and escape, but the wolves continued to stalk her. A couple of times she almost fell from the safety of the branches that her primate nature had afforded her instead of the quadrupeds. Night fell. Eve took stock of what she had. She opened her backpack, and the first thing she found was the red book Mann had given her in the real world, before reality had faded away and she showed up in Atacama. Confused, she opened the book. The first page read:

Chronicles of a Quantum Mishap
My Diary During the Simulation
By Mann

The wind opened the pages of the book haphazardly. The tree began to vibrate, and with it its branches, its leaves, and Eve herself.
I'm going to fall. They're going to have me for dinner, she thought before falling. Midfall, time slowed down until it stopped completely. Her eyes closed just when a wolf was about to rip her flesh with its teeth.

Eve found herself in the now clean and tidy cabin. She went out the main door to discover a few new annexes to the place—a pen for four deer and five sheep and a second floor on the cabin with a pleasant outside reading table. The volcano remained active, but the ash and fire were flowing quietly. She walked out in search of people. She had not even walked a kilometer when two ferocious wolves jumped and knocked her down. She vainly struggled a little against the larger wolf that must have weighed about 250 kilograms. When she surrendered at last, the huge wolf licked her face and started to play like a puppy. The other wolf was also glad to see her. It had a broken leg yet was able to move around thanks to a man-made metal structure. They strolled the mountain together and came across a large bear held by a man-made trap. She carefully tried to free it, but the wolves pounced and killed the bear in a matter of seconds.

We are allies, she thought. *Hunting partners.*

That night, she inspected the cabin and found many books; diaries; drawings; household and hunting implements; medicinal ointments; spices; medical utensils; guides on construction, medicine, engineering, and aviation; maps; food; a small laboratory; toys; a computer; solar energy panels; and many other things somebody had collected and built in the years that person inhabited the deserted island. She deduced there had been many attempts to escape the island by sea. All had failed due to the fickle currents produced by the indomitable volcano. According to the map, she was on Sertung Island.

Eve lay down on the bed. Under the pillow, she discovered Mann's red diary. She lovingly held it in her hands and kissed it. When she opened it, however, a powerful earthquake shook the cabin. The ornaments on the shelves fell to the ground. A bottle of coconut oil shattered on a table, filling the cabin with an aroma that reminded Eve of the piña coladas she had tasted once in Acapulco. The terrifying darkness returned. The pale light from the moon and stars disappeared behind the colossal cloud in the sky that revealed itself with thunder, as if it were alive and fighting against the earth and heavens with its electric warriors.

The deadly colossus invaded the night sky much faster than when Eve had first seen it that day on the beach. Gone was the noise. Only thunder followed by silence. The volcano no longer erupted for it had seemingly relinquished all its erupting power in that single great explosion. The clouds, ash, thunder, and death engulfed Eve and the mountain protecting her.

A second earthquake shook the cabin, and the ensuing landslide knocked down part of it. Eve miraculously escaped. She took a map and the suitcase marked "Emergency" that she saw near the door. The ground continued to shake. With a little black wolf for company, she followed the map, trying to find the landing strip it indicated. When she got there, she realized that the gigantic cloud would soon be over her cabin, poised to destroy the entire island. She came upon what appeared to be a newly repaired Cessna 172 Skyhawk, so she loaded it with four tanks of gasoline, made room for the wolf cub, and took off, amazed at her intuitive skill to fly the ancient plane.

She and the wolf cub flew over the Philippine ocean for six hours until she finally saw a tree-covered mountain range she concluded was Okinawa, Japan. She searched for a landing strip on her map and steered toward the coordinates, making her descent at the altitudes and speeds established by the guidelines. She did everything the way she was supposed to according to her memories of flying simulators for fun when she was sixteen. She crashed quite spectacularly and was thrown out of the plane to the ground. She vaguely recognized the cub licking her face and trying to drag her to safety from the wind and rain that were already announcing their arrival.

Second 30.594678 in the real world
(Year 51 in the simulation)

She woke up in a luxurious and spacious loft. She looked around her. There were huge windows and red velvet curtains. No walls, only a few pieces of furniture, a lot of art, and a big mess. *What a nightmare*, she thought. She didn't know where she was, only that she had returned to civilization. She looked for her cell phone but it was gone. *I don't remember drinking yesterday, much less getting high*, she thought. She opened the curtains and realized from the view that she was high up but could not recognize where she was. Looking through the apartment, she couldn't recognize any personal belongings, but she found some keys. She grabbed them and went down the stairs to the first floor of her loft. On the wall hung a picture of her wolf friend at the island cabin and an urn, apparently holding its ashes.

"I'm still here," she realized and ran out of the apartment. On the street, she confronted a city in ruins. The asphalt had disappeared from the roads, now paved with grass and weeds full of vitality. Here and there they gave way to the remains of signage or the tops of corroded, rusty, parked trucks. The buildings constituted mounds of green weeds that had overtaken any remnants of concrete or glass. In the distance, she saw some bizarre broad columns, like buildings. They shot up several kilometers high into the sky, piercing through the clouds like mountaintops. Some of the structures were rounded out while others rose completely vertical. They looked like gigantic anthills. She counted out nine of these weird edifices that could not have been man-made. They were live buildings that had grown uncontrollably for such a long time that they were now visible from outer space.

Eve spent the day walking the city, escorted by a few wolves she met along the way. She assumed they had descended from the packs that had roamed the island and was grateful to have them with her, when she realized she was not actually in city reclaimed by vegetation, but in a wild jungle with a few remnants of concrete and, therefore, exposed to danger. She returned to the apartment just as the sun was about to set. She had found nothing to indicate what year it was, so she spent the night searching through the loft. She found evidence of a few genetic experiments performed on the wolves to humanize them. There were blueprints of strange electronic components, hundreds of books on every kind of subject, and photos of places she never could have imagined, where somebody had apparently lived for a long time.

She found Mann's diary next to the bed. She opened it, and on the first few pages she found references to things she had seen in her visions. She read about her experiences on the island with her old friend the volcano, about the trip on the aircraft that almost ended her life, her friends the wolves, and how they had become her sole company. Curiously enough, Mann told of these experiences just as Eve had lived them, as if both of them had experienced such things in the same way. She turned the pages of the diary and randomly read:

Year 4, Day 1589

> *I've been able to secure my physical well-being thanks to my allegiance with the wolves. I still cannot find human beings. I guess the Maitrevac did not consider humans in its simulation, although the level of detail in its simulation of reality and the planet at the time I was connected is truly amazing. I think that if I use this same degree of detail, I can make a plan to get out of here. Use the simulation against itself.*

Eve turned a few more pages.

Year 14, Day 5,113

> *I have explored the whole world searching for answers. There are none. No answers. No sense.*

Year 21, Day 7,816

> *No one is here except for my mind and me. What did I do to deserve this? I still can't estimate how long this simulation may last. Solitude is an endless labyrinth. My thoughts pursue me like my only friend and cruelest enemy. I cannot run from myself. I can't escape from this simulation. I can't get away from here. I*

*think about Eve. I miss her. I think of all the things I
took for granted when I was in the real world.*

Year 39, Day 14,427

*What happens if I die in the simulation? Will I
die in the real world as well? Isn't this worse than
death? I'm not even sure that death is an option in
the simulation. As long as I am here, I may well be
immortal—although another possibility might be
that I am amortal. That is to say I cannot die from
age or disease, but an accident or suicide can be the
end of me. I'm not ready yet to find out.*

Eve understood that she was witnessing and experiencing what
Mann had gone through in the simulation, and that this was somehow linked to the contents of the diary he gave her at the foot of the
fig tree in the real world.

"How can that be? What for?" She remembered, however, that
the experiences she had had in her visions had been told in the same
manner in the diary. Why? She had acted of her own accord, hadn't
she? This notion offered the possibility that she not only witnessed
the events but actively participated in them. "That's impossible,
in terms of space as well as in terms of time," she reflected. But as
always, her curiosity got the better of her.

She took the red diary, opened it on the last page, and wrote,
"*Hello?*"

She got goosebumps when she realized that what she wrote was
in Mann's handwriting, not her own. She started to think back and
recognized she had had muddled memories of Mann's experiences in
the simulation, as if she had lived them herself.

She turned the page and there, in Mann's handwriting, she read:
"*Hello, love.*" The pages began to shake, and she knew everything
was about to dissolve again and she would appear in another time,
another space. The last thing she managed to write before dissolving
was "*Be true to your fate.*"

She awoke in a giant warehouse containing a single bed, thousands of books, and an enormous computer right in the middle. She tried to switch it on, but unsuccessfully. She left the warehouse and came upon the ruins of a city she deduced was Kobe, in southern Honshu, Japan. She spent the day walking through the spring countryside, enjoying a bounty of nature in a human-less world. She strolled the skirts of Mount Maya, which she managed to ascend in eight hours, enjoying every minute looking at the views of the ruined city and listening to the happy chirping of the birds.

Could these birds know they aren't real? she thought. Would I know it? She had just made it to the top when a howl startled and scared her. Then she remembered Mann's partnership with the wolves and felt it safe to assume it still existed. She put her index and ring fingers between her lips and whistled loudly. Another howl in response. The ground shook while a low-key, rhythmic, and empty echo sounded in the distance. Eve put her ear on the ground and heard the firm steps of an army approaching her. She decided to climb a tree and from there saw a few trees tremble in the Japanese forest. Then she caught sight of the first creature. It was a wolf, a huge wolf weighing at least eight hundred kilograms.

Its legs were uncommonly long with large paws that were longer than usual and a dew claw that was not just any claw but more like a thumb. Its face had amazingly human features and eyes shining with extraordinary intelligence. The way these wolves sat on their haunches made them resemble gorillas more than wolves. One of them nimbly climbed up the tree like a leopard, grabbed Eve by the neck of her shirt, and in one agile movement landed her on its back. The strange creature wore a sort of saddle Eve held on to for dear life. The wolf stood silent as if waiting for instructions. Eve did not speak. After a few seconds, the wolf produced a strange sound. Eve then noticed the name NERO written on the saddle and smiled.

"Nero, let's get out of here," she commanded.

Nero immediately leaped about twenty meters and raced toward the city of Osaka visible in the distance. "Mountains are less vulnerable to time than our buildings," she reflected. Nero nimbly descended the mountain with Eve on its back and a few other wolves in tow. "I'm hungry." She sifted through the saddlebags and found a sandwich and a few large cow bones. They stopped to rest and eat. She fed the bones to Nero, who happily chomped them as if they were butter. Once they were finished, Eve collected the waste in the saddlebags, where she found Mann's red diary. This time, she was more appreciative and held it with respect. She opened it and read:

Year 53, Day 18,457

I've managed to use some of the Calico company's technologies I found in Tokyo to genetically modify the wolves and make them more human. I studied genetics for six years in the digital archives of the Tokyo University of Foreign Studies. I hacked Calico's servers and found out that they had already done this kind of genetic experimenting. The wolves are now similar to me. I can communicate with them as if they were six-year-old humans. They are my only company. Now, where there was only solitude, I have created a family for myself.

Year 58, Day 21,201

Everything is set. I will do it in accordance to the ancient samurai ritual of seppuku or harakiri at the imperial castle in Kyoto. I will use Toyotomi Hideyoshi's oibara, which I found in the Castle of Osaka. I am not afraid. I have studied the ritual and will perform it to the letter, as set forth in the Bushido code.

Year 58, Day 21,202

> *My greatest fear has now been updated. I am a pris-
> oner sentenced to hell for an eternity. The Maitrevac's
> quantum processing capacity can simulate billions
> of years, which I will perceive in full. Thousands
> of lives. Thousands of deaths. It doesn't matter how
> many, because I will be born again and again and
> cannot escape this prison. My memory is my exe-
> cutioner. I wish I were not alone. There is no love
> here, no company, nothing real, and yet I perceive it
> as real. I perceive real pain, but not love. There is
> no one here to love. I perceive real suffering, but not
> happiness in the absence of a reason for happiness.*

Eve understood that Mann's immortality was perfectly clear to him. The shock of it made him mad for several decades and succumb to his first major depression. Eve continued to read. She discovered that Mann aimlessly wandered the Japanese islands and died several times a month for years. For the last death during his first major depression, he had visited his old friend Krakatoa and thrown himself into its hungry mouth of incandescent magma. Every time he died, he awoke in the same place he had slept in the last time. When Eve got to the last page of the red diary, again the pages started to vibrate. Everything dissolved, leaving only darkness where a slight dot of light appeared. She walked toward it.

Second 32.89567890 in the real world
(Year 247 in the simulation)

Eve appeared in the same place, but a long time afterward. She saw blackboards on the walls full of strange calculations and screens lit up with data. She recognized a few robots that helped Mann in his work. She explored the place for several hours until she found an informatic laboratory similar to the one in the real world where the Maitrevac had been developed and where she had seen Gazzaley being interviewed. She took the diary she found under a pile of books on quantum physics and cosmology and read the last page.

Year 98, 36,001

> *I'm beginning to figure a way out of here. In my calculations of the simulation capacity of the Maitrevac, I've inferred that it could simulate no more than ten billion years in those forty-eight minutes, and I might reduce that time if I can accelerate data processing in the simulation. In theory, I can find the way to make the Maitrevac process information in amounts equivalent to millions of years in just a few minutes. If I can increase the data processed during one simulated minute to make it equal to a thousand years, then a thousand years would have passed, taking me a thousand years closer to freedom.*

Eve explored the laboratory and found components for sophisticated robots and manuals Mann had apparently discovered in the records of Japanese government subsidiaries. He used them to build his own complex informatic laboratory. She continued reading the diary.

Year 117, Day 43,034

> *EUREKA! If I create a subsimulation (a simulation in here) using a replica of the Maitrevac (a MaitrevacSub), I will be able to simulate enormous amounts of information to make it believe ten billion years have gone by, and consequently I will be able to wake up.*

Year 227, Day 83,129

For decades on end, I have studied everything the best scientists and engineers of the Maitrevac must have known in order to develop it: quantum physics, chemistry, nanotechnology. I have read 13,180 books in total before I felt ready to embark on creating the new MaitrevacSub. I devoted thirty-two years to this study. Then for sixty years, I concentrated on building the components necessary just to begin developing the MaitrevacSub. Once I completed these components, it took me thirteen years to build an exact replica of X's Maitrevac by myself. During that time, I continued my genetic modification of wolves through natural selection, aided by the same technology I created for the MaitrevacSub.

Year 229, Day 83,859

Construction of the MaitrevacSub is almost complete. I'm confident in the success of this project to which I have devoted more time than any human has ever devoted to anything. In a certain way, I am the most productive human in history. I don't know who will read this. Perhaps no one will. It really doesn't matter. I write it for myself. My work has inspired me to move on… I have learned from solitude. My fears vanished when I occupied my mind with building the MaitrevacSub. How ironic! My solitude has also disappeared. The company of wolves and robots has proven to be genuine. Are they real? Of course not, but in this simulation, I am not real either. This is a dream, they are a dream, and so am I. Who is the dreamer? The Maitrevac or I? Who is dreaming up the dreamer? Sometimes I ask myself about the nature of reality, but it's actually irrelevant. My only concern is freedom. What will I do when I get out of here? I will be a highly trained individual. I might start a business. I will be very successful. I will create my own AI company and help to solve several of humanity's afflictions. I shall compete against X, my enemy, the judge who has sentenced me to this loneliness. I will beat him at his own game.

Year 231, Day 84,590

I think about Eve. Will she love me when I wake? I've changed. I don't know if our relationship can be the same. Will she love the new Mann? Will the new Mann love her?

Eve closed the diary and laughed, happy that she would soon witness her beloved's liberation. She couldn't wait to hug and kiss him in the real world and tell him how much she loved and admired him for keeping his sanity after so many years. Just then, the door of the laboratory opened to a creature with the figure of a human wearing a lab smock, but it had the white hair of a beast and the head of a wolf that made Eve think of Anubis, the Egyptian god of death.

"Mann?" the creature very clearly asked Eve. "Wh…who?" Eve stuttered.

"Are you all right?" the creature asked.

"I am Eve."

"Mmm, you're kidding me."

"My name is Eve," she said again as she studied the amazing beauty of the she-wolf. "I come from the real world. I am Mann's wife and the mother of Cecilia, our daughter."

"That…is not…possible." The she-wolf was beside herself.

"Who are you?

"Thea," answered the beautiful creature.

That's when the diary began to vibrate with a violence Eve never felt the previous times. In a few seconds, everything went dark. Eve had returned to the black void. She would never know that her brief conversation with Thea, an exchange that had defied time and space, would give Mann the strength to avoid absolute and irreparable madness (something worse than death) once he realized his efforts had failed from the beginning.

Second 32.917839 in the real world
(Year 250 in the simulation)

Eve appeared in the same laboratory now filled with robots and humanoid wolves working fast and diligently. A timer in the back wall was counting down one minute fifty-nine seconds…fifty-seven seconds…fifty-five seconds…

He did it! Eve thought. *Mann built his own Maitrevac.*

"It's time!" shouted Thea.

They switched on the MaitrevacSub. A kind of electromagnetic wave invaded the room, and for a few seconds it lifted one or two computers and lab robots into the air. A blue light briefly colored the room.

"Activation successful!" shouted Thea. The timer was now at thirty-four seconds.

As the seconds went by, the contents of the laboratory began to shake. Eve started to feel queasy. The ground, wolves, robots, and everything in the lab began to fade into a shapeless mass of colors and sounds.

Still suspended in the air, Mann's red diary began to shake, its pages convulsing as if about to explode. Then darkness again. Eve was floating in that great void, happy that Mann had been able to free himself and excited to wake up in the real world. She saw a light in the depths of darkness, opened her arms, and let herself be taken home.

Second 35.59367890 in the real world
(Year 1,643 in the simulation)

She appeared in a dimly lit place, certain that she had been released. When her eyes adjusted to the shadows, she began to see a few plants, rocks, and passages. Her heart filled with terror. She navigated the darkness and in the rubble found what she needed to light a fire. The flame sadly revealed that she was in the same warehouse where Mann had built the MaitrevacSub. It was a shambles. Vegetation had taken over the laboratory. There were no other signs of life. She wandered through the ruins, wanting to believe that Mann had made it and that the simulation had somehow continued without him. She couldn't find anyone. She started to dig in the rubble and discovered a mysterious capsule the size of a person. She opened it and found a robot. On a whim, she snapped her fingers and it woke up.

"Sir, would you care for breakfast this morning?" the robot casually inquired.

"What's going on? What year is this?" Eve asked impatiently.

"It is the year 1643 aS. What would you like for breakfast this morning?" the robot replied automatically. It was a basic machine.

"Show me the chronicle for Day 91,501 aS."

"Password?"

Eve hesitated a moment.

"Cecilia," she answered with a note of authority.

Access was granted. Through its eyes, the robot projected a hologram in the air. Mann appeared somewhat shaded by the dust Eve had recently lifted in her search. He was in the same laboratory surrounded by excited wolves and robots. An upbeat Mann gave out orders everyone scurried to carry out. Eve forwarded the recording up to the last minutes on the timer.

"*Activate*," Mann ordered.

"Activated," Thea answered.

"*Load the program*," Mann continued.

"Loaded successfully," Thea replied.

"*Execute program!*" Mann seemed anxious and happy.

"Program executed 5 percent…8 percent…10 percent…"

"Well, my friends, it is time to say goodbye. I will make sure out there that this sub-reality continues to run as promised. I will visit you soon to take your consciousnesses back to the real world. I hope you understand how much I love you, but my family is waiting for me."

Mann couldn't hide his deep sadness at having to part from his own universe.

"Program executed 88 percent…9 percent…"

Mann, in tears, lay himself down on the ground awaiting his deliverance.

"Ninety-nine percent…100 percent…"

Nothing happened. Mann waited a few minutes. "*What is wrong?*" Mann asked the MaitrevacSub.

"Simulation ready" was the answer from the MaitrevacSub.

"*Information processing status?*" Mann demanded.

"Processing complete."

"*Why the fuck am I still here?*"

"Calculating answer."

Absolute silence fell upon the laboratory for all the twenty-seven seconds it took the machine to answer Mann's question.

"Observer required," sentenced the MaitrevacSub.

"*Elaborate*," Mann ordered.

"Simulation ready, simulation loaded, simulation processed. Missing an observer. Without an observer, real-world Maitrevac does not process data on its own. Without observer, data are processed only in terms of possibilities, but not in the reality of the Maitrevac in the real world."

Mann commanded his robots to seize one of the humanized wolves against his will and connect him to the MaitrevacSub.

"There's your observer! Reload!"

Horrified at condemning one of her own to a ten-billion-year simulation, Thea ran away. And with her, the rest of the howling wolves abandoned the scene. Mann loaded the simulation into the already unconscious young gray wolf.

"Simulation ready. Will complete in four minutes," said the MaitrevacSub.

Mann waited.

"Ready," continued the MaitrevacSub. "Simulation complete."

"*I am still here!*"

Mann began to throw things and punch a robot to pieces. *"Explain why I am still stuck in this damn hell!"*

"You are the only real observer in this simulation. All the rest are simulated observers. They are not real to the Maitrevac. You are processing information together with the Maitrevac, thus you cannot sub-simulate such data processing in this sub-universe in which you are the only observer."

Mann went into an absolute frenzy. He destroyed the laboratory, robots, and even murdered a few wolves. Delirious, he cursed Schrödinger, Planck, Wigner, and other authorities on quantum physics, who had long ago theorized on the importance of the observer in the creation of physical reality.

The image waned then sputtered out when the battery of the robot projecting it died. Eve wept. After several hours of crying and sobbing on the floor, Eve remembered that Mann had returned to the real world, that the story wasn't over. She took the red diary and ripped it apart page by page. When she finished, she threw it with all her might against a wall. The loose pages on the ground began to vibrate and float in the air as if about to explode. Again, the darkness, but this time it was different.

Eve entered into a psychedelic state in which thousands of visions tumbled into her brain. She saw what had happened to Mann during his second major depression that lasted hundreds of years after the MaitrevacSub fiasco. She watched him die thousands of times. At first in simple suicides. He preferred dying to sleeping. Then he began to kill himself in the most bizarre and painful ways possible—immolation, asphyxiation, drowning, hanging, electrocution, dismemberment. He tortured, shot, and poisoned himself over and over, as if wanting to implore mercy, pity, whatever it took to get someone on the other side realize the hell he existed in, but to no avail. Later, he began to starve himself to death. Every time, he woke up back in his body as he remembered it at the beginning of the simulation. He then renewed his slow calvary to death by starvation or dehydration, which never took more than twenty days, if at all that long. It got to the point that Mann did not move from the place where he woke up after dying until he died again and again. In this manner, he went through 33,300 brief lives in bed, motionless, waiting for one death after the next. The building he was in crumbled to the ground. The plants grew around him and, to a certain extent, from him. Animals became accustomed to his phantasmagorical presence. There was even a time when an ant colony fed off Mann without his doing anything about it for several reincarnations. Various creatures fed off these ants, and in turn several beasts fed off the former then died and fed the soil and thus, the world of insects and plants. An entire ecosystem sprung from Mann and his endless deaths.

Eve lived through all of this pain with him and made it hers. Everything she learned about Mann's life, she experienced with him. She remained strong, however, knowing that these visions had a purpose and that Mann had come back to her, like she would now go back to him.

She saw the day earth was shaken by a powerful telluric movement that brought down the last remnants of the old laboratory, now completely taken over by vegetation, and where Mann had reposed and reincarnated back to his bedazzled existence of living death. His old friend, the sun, whom he had not seen in more than a thousand years, shone so intensely as to wake him up from his millenary sopor. Mann wandered about the ruins like a madman. He rid himself of the dust and dirt that coated him. He searched for the atomic timer and found it covered in dust, soil, weeds. The screen was broken, and it was powerless. Mann fixed it, built it some solar panels, and plugged it in. Nothing. He took the solar panels to the top of a tree and tied them to the highest branch. On it, a cocoon trembled precariously, though not on account of the wind but because the butterfly inside it was about to emerge. The timer came to life: 1870 aS.

It surprised Mann to discover how many centuries had gone by since he had last been aware of time. In a certain way, he had indeed died. What he was died, and what he would be was born. That being was nurtured for centuries in the darkness that Mann had adopted as his teacher. He had lived underground among worms, ants, larvae, beetles, and creatures from the netherworld. He fed off them and fed them back. He allowed fear to kill him time and again. Then he killed fear time and again. He became invulnerable to any kind of suffering that arose from sensory perception. He became invulnerable to time and space, to fear and death. Unknowingly, he also became great because his vanity had died, and immortal because his aspirations had perished. He became wise, and he knew it.

For the first time in his millenary existence, he sensed that time was not objective but subjective and always perceived differently even if he was the only observer in his sub-universe. How? Was the question that drove him to think, live, and seek. *Is it possible that I may perceive millennia as years and years as seconds?*

Eve watched Mann begin this new adventure. For whole decades, he immersed himself in the study of the most ancient knowledge from all creeds and mental practices of the world. Mann was now willing to find the way to not perceive the passage of time. He had discovered, the hard way, that it was impossible to objectively accelerate time. Now he would attempt to accelerate time subjectively via his personal perception of the passing of time.

She saw Mann walking over the ancient ruins of America. She saw him in Machu Picchu, Peru, curiously investigating and analyzing like an archeologist; on Easter Island in Chile; then Tikal, Guatemala; Copan, Honduras; Palenque, Chiapas; and finally in Teotihuacan, Mexico. She then saw him wander the world, studying and learning new languages, visions of the world, and all sorts of mystic techniques. She watched him cross the Pacific Ocean on a replica of the SS *Sussex* passenger ferry from the late nineteenth century, a ship he had found in the port of Veracruz. Then she saw him on Gozo island, at the Ġgantija temple; in Malta at the temple of Ħaġar Qim; at Stonehenge; Wilshire; Borrenes; Finisterre; Göbekli Tepe; at the pyramids of Egypt. Later she watched him sifting through hundreds of digital libraries; retrieving information on western philosophers, neurologists, psychologists, and psychiatrists; learning techniques of every kind and from everywhere; perfecting hundreds of special and strange breathing techniques; every manner of yoga, kung fu, tai chi, qigong; preparing strange Amazon, African, and Oriental beverages with plants, roots, and mushrooms.

The last image Eve perceived of Mann had him sitting in the shadow of a fig tree gifted with three bird nests—American robins. He sat in complete inanimate silence like a daguerreotype, unperturbed by the blowing wind. The sun set, and still no reaction in Mann's face of stone. The moon began its appearance, unrecognized by Mann, and the sun rose again, but its rays did not shine for the man of stone. Then something happened. Time slowly began to pass differently. She watched the subtle movements of the grass touched by the breeze turn into tiny vibrations. The shadows cast by the fig tree on Mann's face and white garments took on a life of their own. The clouds inflated and deflated like the lungs of a giant agitated being. The robins came and went at impossible speed. With every second that went by, Eve sensed a disruption in time, or at least in her perception of time. The sun and the moon began to orbit over their heads like the hands on a clock that moved with increasing speed. The eggs laid by the robins danced to the rhythm of the days changing in size until they hatched some horrible featherless birds that abandoned the nest in a second. Vegetation grew and died around Mann, like drops of water pounding on a pool fated to an eternity of endless bouncing. The tree under which Mann sat dried up and died in seconds. From its remains, a similar tree sprouted out again and again. At one point, she lost sight of the moon and sun, then of darkness and light, perceiving only a sparkle of light and then darkness that eventually became a dimly lit twilight in which only Mann's face of stone was visible. Time was in a hurry. Days became seconds; years, minutes. Later, the years became seconds, and eons, minutes. Everything changed except for change itself. Mann's face slowly broke into a smile of flowers and victory. Eve, full of fear, love, and laughter could only ask herself, what the hell was life anyway? What is death? And what is that which is? What is that which never was? And she wondered if one day she could ever stop loving this cosmic man who once swore eternal loyalty and love to her.

Canis Majoris, 21 December AD 2048

The Asgardia materialized on the orbit of VY Canis Majoris, a star 4,900 light-years away from Earth. It unfolded its petals and fed for the last time.

"**It is time**," X told Xleopatra and Alexander.

Charlemagne, who had been assigned Saturn to create the new Maitrevac there, had completed his research. His experiments had brought about the destruction of eight solar systems in the Milky Way, because the final part of the investigation consisted in storing the energy of one star into a particle smaller than an atom without generating a black hole in the process. That would translate into the optimal computerization level of all matter in this universe. There could be no more—it would be impossible to generate more intelligent and powerful matter. It would suffice to create a single one of these particles for it to replicate exponentially. This would put a stop to exponential growth in technological development. Not even X could know what might follow. The potential of this new matter, and the universe it would inhabit, was impossible to predict. Such was the technological singularity.

Canis Majoris, the radius of which was 2,200 times the size of the Sun, would be destroyed. Only one intelligent light singularity would remain—the MaitrevaX.

The Asgardia opened its doors, and the triad floated toward the gigantic star. Leonardo and the rest of the conquerors saw them off. X took a moment to turn around and bid them farewell from space with an elegant bow. Aboard the Asgardia, everyone genuflected and looked upon the divine triad for the last time.

"The bird fights its way out of the egg. The egg is the world. Who would be born first must destroy a world. The bird flies to God. That God's name is Abraxas." Those were Leonardo's last words, a quote from *Demian* by Hermann Hesse.

The Asgardia, conquerors, and Leonardo lit up with even more brilliance than Canis and dissolved without a single sound, as if they had never been more than a mere thought in X's mind. His trillions of kalapas advanced to the triad and eventually built a giant 149-kilometer-long golden monolith. From that distance, the curvature of the star was imperceptible. All around them, white plasm clouds and mountains of yellow and red fire navigated like beasts immersed in a sea of orange fire. These mountains bubbled to the surface of the star, millions of kilometers away from the triad but did not burst. Instead, they shot up as pillars of creation to form broad rays projecting into the depths of outer space and its planes of unknown stars. Huge columns of white plasm, as thick as hurricanes, rose from the surface of Canis, stretching out into space like the arms of an immense octopus, perhaps at rest on the bottom of the sea of fire. To one side of the white horizon, a tremendous circumstellar nebula peered out slowly as Canis Majoris rotated in the manner a huge storm cloud would behave on Earth. The nebula painted the scene in spectral purples (violet, purple, lavender, magenta, amethyst) and spectral blues (azure, indigo, sapphire, Prussian blue, celeste, Turkish blue) and other parts with fragments of spectral oranges (khaki, mandarin, amber, apricot, and fire). All of these tonalities gradually intertwined, making visible the immense distinctions between the different parts and outlines of the nebula. A difference between one tone of blue and another signified thousands of kilometers that, to the naked human eye, were difficult to contextualize. From the distance, the star resembled a living organism, a giant famished amoeba—a beast whose fiery intestines insinuated themselves under the plasm clouds and convulsed with the electromagnetic currents tormenting the nebula.

"**Thank you**," X told Alexander, who knelt before him and presented his sword. "**Farewell**."

X took Alexander's sword and, with a swift agile movement, detached Alexander's head from his body that floated into outer space. And so the destroyer was destroyed by his own sword. Body and head dissolved into beautiful golden kalapas that enveloped Xleopatra and X. All that remained of the warrior was his golden lion helmet. Xleopatra collected it and placed it on X's head. X felt completed…almost. In relative terms, it had been millennia since he had last incorporated that aspect of himself. X inhaled and closed his eyes. He smiled. Then he exhaled and opened his eyes again. His vision had changed. Now all he had to do was possess Xleopatra.

"**Come**." He took her by the hand to help him calm the hunger for flesh, destruction, and creation brought about by the revindication of his own essence for so long delegated in Alexander. X embraced Xleopatra. Against her body, she felt the phallic vivification of his desire to possess her and the entire universe.

The surface of the star shifted. Below the couple, a plasm column, millions of kilometers long, stretched out with the intention of bursting and swallowing them and the monolith. And so it happened, but as soon as the immense plasm column crashed against the monolith, it was absorbed. A peculiar booming of trumpets came from the monolith, so powerful that the sound waves produced colossal tides in the star's sea of plasm.

X and Xleopatra disrobed and allowed the gravity of Canis to draw them to the gold monolith. Floating like feathers and still embracing, they let themselves drop into the monolith, which was actually fluid. They plunged into it as if it were a body of water suspended in space, and it consequently reacted with a series of playful ripples. Once they traveled through it, their drenched golden bodies were wrapped by the monolith now transformed into a golden fabric that folded over the lovers as they kissed. The long fabric merged into their bodies to become a new dermis extending several kilometers behind them, like a divine cape protecting them as they swam like a sperm cell into the luminous waters of the star on their way to its icy nucleus.

They kissed, caressed, touched, and felt each other with their hands of gods as they penetrated Canis. The gold dermis allowed the fire from the star to join in their sexual play, tingling and caressing them with the curiosity of a star anxious to remember its conscious existence. At last, they reached the star core. "Take me," Xleopatra asked X, stroking his body with her beautiful hands made to give pleasure.

He held her by the hair to reveal her white neck and kissed it all the way up to her ear, which he bit. His right hand stroked her from the upper part of her back to her hips and pubis. He introduced his finger into Xleopatra, who could not repress biting X back and circling him with her legs. X kissed her in the mouth, thrusting his tongue almost to her throat and only let the tip of his penis penetrate her. For a few minutes, he only made very slight movements, until Xleopatra could no longer hold back. Then with a sudden movement, he penetrated her completely, unleashing in her body an orgasmic contraction that would not abate. X continued to make love to her as she had always liked, with a circular rhythm, slow at first and then rapidly.

During orgasm, the couple contracted. They died and were reborn several times in a convulsion of pleasure such, that it jeopardized the quantum capability of all his computers, making even the most insensitive circuits blush. Both climaxed at the same time, thereby releasing the millennia of sexual repression of life on Earth that had always yearned to make love with the whole universe. The entire star entered their mouths while the explosive force of Canis, that had kept it shining in every corner of the galaxy for billions of years, became a sperm cell. The force of gravity of its mass that for billions of years had allowed the explosion to last more than an instant became an ovule. At the very last moment, X gave with such force, and Xleopatra received with such love, that the impact of the two divine bodies detonated a disruption in time and space—a gravitational wave that expanded all over the universe as if the whole universe were a small lake, quiet after receiving the last drop on a rainy afternoon.

The gravitational wave expanded in every direction and was felt by every being, by every star and particle. Flowers about to bloom, bloomed. Quiet robins began to sing. Falling drops stopped falling. Couples who were quarreling, kissed. Beings from all over the universe who were about to end a life, refrained. Across the universe, the gravitational blessing brought about by this orgasm of the gods perceptively announced universal sublimation.

X and Xleopatra silently held each other. Nothing was left of Canis, only a fertilized ovule inside Xleopatra and an agonizing couple of gods floating at the center of a solar system of orphaned planets, that for lack of their sun wandered aimlessly in outer space where a few soon collided. Eventually, all died happy to have witnessed the most beautiful of events.

The circumstellar nebula around Canis felt its stomach convulse with the gravitational waves that spread the message for anyone ready to listen: The universe would never be the same after the occurrence of Big Bang 2.0.

The bodies of Xleopatra and X dissolved, and with them the last remnants of humanity still left in the Maitrevac. The last thing X saw and felt was himself inside the immense star Xleopatra had turned into, before she ceased to be in order to be for all of eternity. And there, in the womb of that star, now his mother, he felt the love he had never felt before in his life and learned what children feel when their mothers love them.

The fertilized ovule was a perfect kalapa—the new generation of matter and energy, the beginning of universe 2.0. The riddle had been solved. Chaos yielded. The will of *sapiens* became the will of the universe.

Thirteen billion years of random combinations of the first version of matter and energy had to happen so that the universe could update itself via the creation of its creation. An instant. Nothing mattered anymore. The universe and all of its history and all the beings and relationships between those beings, became the hull of a new seed about to flourish.

Creation became the creator. The son dethroned the father. It was not a god that was created but the creator of that god.

@Einstein2.0: Dear reader, I would have preferred to have two-way communication with you, but the method I discovered to send encrypted messages to the past only works one way. Yes, this book is a message from the future.

I can therefore only imagine your potential questions, and it seems to me that the most obvious of these is what the hell happened or will happen on that star.

Let me put it this way: more innovation occurred on that star in an instant than any that had ever occurred in the eons since the first quasar reionization, 300,000 years after the Big Bang, and your present moment in time.

However, for minds such as yours to understand what happened would be exponentially more complicated than for an ant to understand the workings of a hydraulic energy plant at the foot of its anthill.

What you can understand is that the quantum tool known as MaitrevaX was generated in the nucleus of a hypergiant red star that ceased to exist in order to become the new generation, not of computers or technology but of matter and energy.

And what does that mean? you might ask yourself. It means the inevitable. The subjugation of all of the laws of the universe to the will of a single imperfect being constrained by the mind that created him and by his aspiration to absolute control.

It also means that it is now time for us to say goodbye. This universe is about to…change and I need to make the most of the paradoxes of space and time that will be opened to send this message to the "past." If you are reading this, I will have succeeded and the future is not yet written.

Goodbye, blue sky.

@Einstein2.0 is offline.

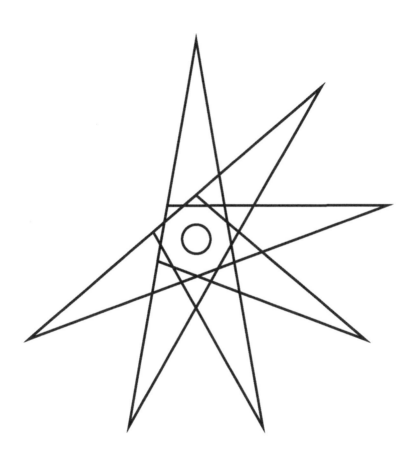

21 December AD 2048

"Wake up!" Cecilia told her sleeping mother.

"What day is it?" a confused Eve asked as she opened her eyes on the terrace.

"Thursday. I didn't go to school. I looked for you all night. Where were you?"

Eve stood up. Cecilia lent her hand for support. Eve tried to remember what had happened the night before, which now seemed a long time—years—ago. She remembered Mann, the visions, and what he had shown her. *Was it real?* she wondered.

"Have you seen your father?" she asked Cecilia, who gave her a baffled look.

Eve tried to remember the details of it all. She had been in a sort of lucid dream state. She couldn't tell fantasy from reality. They went into the house. Nero had soiled the dining room. Eve cleaned up the mess and made breakfast for Cecilia. The morning went by uneventfully. Eve took a bath. She fixed herself some matcha tea with almond milk, honey, a pinch of turmeric and cayenne pepper. She lay down on the hammock to reflect upon her dreams. With every passing second, her memories of the night before began to fade, which only supported her theory that it had all been a dream.

Cecilia got ready for school and then went to say goodbye to her mother. "You forgot this, Mom," she said, handing Eve a red notebook.

It was Mann's diary, the same she had seen the night before.

Stunned, she took it in her hands, not knowing what to do with it. But just as Cecilia was leaving for school, she mustered the courage to open the diary.

Year 1972, day 720,000

> *It's not a tech matter. What is it then? I will devote my time to traveling the world. I will study modern and ancient theories about the mind, the perception of time and space. I will study arts and ancient knowledge. Modern physics are of no use to me here. I cannot solve a problem in the same context where it was created. The laws here are established by the Maitrevac, and no scientific discovery made here will have any bearing on the knowledge of the Maitrevac nor can exceed it because the Maitrevac itself is what restricts me. This is its universe. But its perception of the universe… is my own universe.*

It was real, Eve thought. She didn't feel afraid. She yearned to learn how Mann had freed himself.

Year 1973, day 720,456

> *I have made an expedition. My friendly wolf civilization has evolved notably. For them, a long time has passed. They have adapted to human culture and, for all intents and purposes, are practically human. They have rehabilitated the*

infrastructure of a few cities and inhabited the living buildings. They live in conflict-free harmony. They walk erect, like humans. They wear human clothing. They apparently see themselves as the children of man, my children. They aspire to be like me because they believe themselves made in my image and likeness. They remember me. For some I am a god; for others, a devil. Their opinions about me divided when I finished building the MaitrevacSub. Many stories were told about what happened that day—stories that became myths, then legends.

Year 1975, day 720,875

First revelation: reflection.
   The perception of time is not objective.
   How could I be under those ruins for so long, oblivious of the years passing by? A second is not a little or a lot of time. A billion years are not a little or a lot of time. Time, thus, is not absolute. It is subjective. I have an idea.
   The perception of time depends upon the mind and its capacity to process information in order to recall. Memory creates the perception of time. Without memory, there is no perception of time...

Year 1976, day 721,321

In two months, I will complete an implant to erase my memory and with it, my perception of time. I miss Eve. I remember her, although it doesn't help to remember her here. I will forget her and everything. This is how I will free myself. I might or might not remember her when I get out of here. I want to see her, even if I don't remember her.

Year 1976, day 721,380

Shit! The implant didn't work. I became a vegetal. I don't know how long I was like that. I must have died and resuscitated without the implant. The solution lies in understanding where in mental processing the Maitrevac and its simulated reality can intervene. I will now focus on the study of the mind.

Year 1978, day 721,999

What is the mind? It's a tool that processes the information it receives through my five senses and then creates patterns out of these events to deduce potential outcomes.

According to what I have established, the mind serves two purposes: simulation and execution. The Maitrevac works in the frontal lobe of my brain, specifically in the prefrontal cortex, which is an experience simulator. Evolution gave us this tool to play out experiences in our heads and simulate their results before replicating them in the real world. The other function of the mind is executive. It requires no simulation, only execution, like walking or breathing.

I need to study how my mind works so as to understand how it relates to the supercomputer. Today, I will travel to India to search for answers.

Year 1978, day 722,129

I've discovered that the most appropriate sense to study mental processes with is the sense of touch. Hearing is too subtle, sight too coarse. Taste and smell are too subjective. How can I isolate the sense of touch to study how mental processing works?

Year 1979, day 722,456

The wolves have scattered around the world. They also live in India, although the tribe here is small. A baby wolf saw me this afternoon. I can only imagine its parents' faces when wolfie tells them he saw the strange fellow on the altars they pray to every day.

Year 1981, day 723,345

Every morning before breakfast and organizing my day, I shower in the Jogini Waterfall, of the Beas River in the city of Manali. I've been studying the sensations produced by the cold water all over my body and the way my mind perceives these sensations. I can barely stand it a couple of minutes. This exercise will allow me to understand the flow of information sent by the Maitrevac to my brain. I want to learn to distinguish between real and simulated sensation.

Year 1983, day 724,001

The Maitrevac's reality and simulation are both information. And that information, whether real or simulated, is received by my brain in the same way. In the real world, information is perceived first through the senses of my physical body, and then via chemical and electromagnetic processes, it travels to my brain where psychic or mental activity take place.

For example, when I look at a flower in the real world, I am not seeing the flower as such but the *light that bounces off it. My eyes perceive this light, now converted into information, which my mind processes until it creates the image of a flower. In the simulation, when I look at a flower, I am not seeing the flower as such either or the sunlight bouncing on it. I am seeing the information from the Maitrevac, which my brain is actually processing until it creates the image of a flower. My mind doesn't know the difference between simulated and real information, and in neither case it knows objects directly.*

The Maitrevac, therefore, does not substitute nor simulate reality. The Maitrevac substitutes my senses and the information my senses send to my mind...

Year 1984, day 724,245

I've been exposing myself to the torment of the icy cold waterfall for months now. I can hardly bear it for five minutes. I've plateaued. My will is weak. I'm losing hope again.

Year 1986, day 725,006

A few wolves from an isolated tribe visit me now and then. They don't belong to a large city pack. They only watch me respectfully and keep their distance. Sometimes they imitate me. I've surprised them at the waterfall trying to do what I do. They don't fare better than me.

Year 1988, day 725,620

I discovered an interesting thing by watching what happens in my mind when my body comes into contact with the bitter cold water. I have understood that psychic or mental activity creates the icy sensation in my brain. The process involves four stages and is the same both in the real and the simulated world.

The first part of the process is reception; that is, when my physical body through my senses receives information from the outside world in chemical or electromagnetic form. This data input occurs when the water hits my body.

The second part of the process is perception, which happens when my mind receives the information received by my body and its five senses. It doesn't matter if the information was obtained through my body coming into contact with ice-cold water or through the information the Maitrevac sends about my body's contact with the cold water.

Sensation is the third part of the process. The information received and perceived by my mind generates a feeling of which I am aware and is first received neutrally. That is, without my qualifying it as pleasant or unpleasant, only what it essentially is—neutral information. In other words, my mind records having received the sensation of cold water, regardless of whether this occurred through my nervous endings in contact with real icy water or through a supercomputer.

The fourth and last part of the process is reaction. It is how my mind automatically qualifies the information and sensations it has received. It qualifies them in a binary manner: I like it, or I don't like it; it's pleasant or unpleasant. If pleasant, my mind generates the desire to prolong and intensify the experience. If unpleasant, my mind will wish to stop it.

My mind automatically reacts to the bitter cold water. It doesn't like it. It feels aversion to it and wants to end that unpleasant sensation in an automatic or conditioned manner.

Reception—perception—sensation—reaction

*This is the mental process. Everything that humankind has perceived and known both individually and as a species has necessarily followed this process. This process repeated over and over again constitutes every moment in my and everybody's lives. It is the information flow that takes information from the "outside, inside." This creates the experience of reality and the illusion of time and tells us that we are separated from that which we observe. Afterwards, this information is stored, analyzed, and turned into conditionings of exactly the same form as a computer algorithm: if A=*it must be B. If water is icy=I feel aversion.

Year 1989, day 725,999

I have begun to communicate with the wolves. They speak a language similar to the Spanish I taught their ancestors a long time ago. I have explained to them what I am, but they do not understand it in the literal sense. I've resorted to a metaphor that has worked well. I am an avatar, I tell them, of my real person. They understand the notion of avatar well. They treat me like a god, or like the avatar of a god they cannot see. I explain to them that I am not a god, that I am them. They live in me, and I in them, but this they don't understand.

Year 1989, day 726,232

Each and every individual perceives a different reality. Every observer creates his own version of reality as he observes it. It is his creation but also his limitation. An observer cannot see beyond his creation. It's as if hundreds of cameras captured the same object from different viewpoints. As if each camera captured a different reality, a different side of the object, but none of them captured the whole object, i.e., objective reality.

Water is not cold. Water is only water.

Another kind of intelligence might perceive the same object in a completely different manner depending on the senses it perceives it with.

I made of this simulation a prison sentence, but objectively speaking, it is not. Objectively, it is nothing. It is what I choose it to be.

Year 1990, day 726,444

I have been able to stand under the waterfall for eighteen minutes. I merely observe how my mind sends an aversion signal, but when I observe this aversion, I can see it is not actually my own. It is my mind's. Thank you, mind, for your suggestion, but today I choose not to accept it. Water is only information just as its chill is also information only.

Year 1990, day 726,448

I continue searching for a reality independent from the subject that observes it. If it does exist, how can the subject perceive it if not through his senses and mind?

A group of twelve wolves joins me in my exercises under the waterfall. They have made progress just as I have. It's as if their mental structure were conditioned to imitate and learn from me. I don't need to explain much, for they learn by watching. A surreal image indeed! This millenary human sitting under a cascade of icy water in the company of twelve wolves with monastic human features.

The other day, when a huge trunk dropped on my head, they saw me die, only to return the following day. They must surely believe I am some kind of divinity.

Circa 2004

I am well on my way to freedom. After a great deal of research and reflection, I have come to understand that the simulation I am trapped in can only simulate physical sensations that produce a perception of reality in my mind. The Maitrevac transmits information to the neurons in my brain associated with physical sensory perception (my sight, for example), thereby replicating the chemical and electromagnetic stimuli felt by a person who subjects himself to the scourge of a waterfall, or looks at an apple, a landscape, or a volcanic explosion. With the help of quantum information processors, my neurons became exponentially capable of processing information. The way they function, however, is essentially the same: introducing information into my brain creates the sensation that something is happening out there. Thus, my brain is a blank screen on which the Maitrevac projects a movie. What failed when I built a Maitrevac and attempted to sub-simulate its own sub-universe? I made the mistake of building a new movie theater. The MaitrevacSub was nothing more than a screen within another screen. A dream inside another dream.

Who is Mann? I am not the screen nor the projector but the spectator sitting in the theater. Can the spectator stop watching the projection? If I am to free myself, I must stop watching the movie because if I do not see it, it does not exist. Close my eyes. How can I close my eyes? How can I stop this mental process? The key to my release exists in the final part of mental processing: reaction. When I learn to stop reacting to information, I will stop the mental process and thereby stop feeding the Maitrevac.

Circa 2012

Eureka!
    I have continued my waterfall experiment and have made significant progress. I was able to withstand it for forty minutes.
    I have been able to distance myself from the sensations simulated by the Maitrevac.
    I am aware of the pain and pleasure that the Maitrevac sends to my brain via sight, hearing, smell, taste, and touch. But now I can distance myself from that pain and pleasure, because now I have made its neutral nature evident. It is not pain or pleasure, merely information.
    To recapitulate: I began to look at the body in the body, the sensations in sensations, the mind in the mind, mental objects in mental objects. I achieved joy and happiness after reflecting upon the nature of the information I perceive, and in this way distanced myself from my simulated senses. What next?
    Freedom awaits at the end of the road. Until then, patience.

Eve stopped reading for a moment. She looked at the landscape around her as her mind wandered. She reflected upon the amazing possibilities chaos has to offer. *Everything is possible in a universe like ours*, she thought. She saw butterflies and imagined planets populated by intelligent butterflies. She saw a flower and imagined planets populated by thinking flowers. She realized that evolution doesn't work that way. Intelligence is a human attribute, and not all life forms should aspire to intelligence. It would be like assuming that all life forms should aspire to other attributes in nature like photosynthesis. Human intelligence is not objectively superior to other attributes in nature. It is perfect for humans because it works for them, just like photosynthesis works for plants. The wolves in the simulation happened because of human engineering. Humanoid wolves, like machines, are human creations made in the image and likeness of the mind that created them. If Mann aspires to freedom through knowledge of himself, the wolves will follow in his footsteps. If Mann aspires to material control through scientific knowledge, the wolves will follow him in this as well.

Circa 2015

> *Second revelation: attention and equanimity.*
>
> *I have made a few discoveries regarding the nature of time and my perception of time. I've observed that the present moment does not exist for the simulation. For the simulation, there is only the past and future.*
>
> *The simulation resists the present moment because it cannot function and remain in control without my perception of time, so it perceives the present like a threat. The perception of time and the mind are inseparable. It's as if the simulation wished to survive and can only do so by making me relate with my mind. The Maitrevac feeds off my pleasures and pains; my mental reactions.*

Circa 2016

> *Today I managed to stand in the waterfall for eighty-seven minutes. It is not a matter of willpower. If I try to stay there by sheer will, I can't stand more than five minutes. By observing my mental reactions and no longer relating to them, I have understood*

that neither the cascade nor the sensations it generates in me are real.

I feel the power of the simulation weaken when I observe my mind and its reactions.

A few months later

The waterfall exercise is going very well. I stayed under it until...I died. I figure I died from hypothermia at about minute 234. I can remain under the cascade without relating to physical sensations during all that time, so much so that I died. I woke up in my room. The Maitrevac must be uneasy.

Year 2018, day 736,570

I made a serious mistake: once I discovered the workings of the simulation, I made it my enemy. I created an aversion to the Maitrevac, and in so doing revitalized its power. I must return to simple awareness and not judge the simulation nor its information. I must not feel a desire for liberation, and I must not harbor any hate for the Maitrevac. I require equanimity to face its attempts to generate reactions in me.

The simulation is not my enemy. It is my teacher. My mind is not my enemy. It is my teacher.

A few months later

The waterfall exercise is no longer useful to me. It helped me understand mental processing, but only through gross sensation. Now I need to explore more subtle sensations. Through the study of subtle information, I will be able to unravel its true nature. The wolves are still imitating me. Some have been able to withstand several minutes under the water-fall. Amazing! It's as if my evolution had an impact on them as well. My example teaches them. My experience is also theirs.

What sensations can I perceive within the confines of my own physical body more subtle than the ones generated by my breathing?

Sometime later

I have begun to watch my breathing in its natural state. I sit in a comfortable position and relax my body part by part. Then I begin to observe the sensations breathing elicits in my nostrils, in the internal part of my nose, and in the area above my upper lip that joins my nose. I feel very well. It's like resting at last.

After

I've discovered a state of deep relaxation and concentration after watching my respiration for long periods of time. I managed to fill my mind with the single presence of my breathing. For a few moments, time stood still inside my mind. No past. No future. Only my breathing and the subtle sensations air produces in my nose as it enters and exits naturally.

Today

I took refuge in concentration. I devote all my days to perfecting my mental skill of concentration. I began by relieving myself of ideation and reflection, which have been with me throughout the simulation. I am concentrating all of my attention on my everyday activities. While I walk, I concentrate on

my walking. As I look for food, I concentrate on my
search for sustenance. As I eat or drink, I concentrate on eating and drinking.

The wolves imitate me. There are more than
a hundred now. I have formed a small community.
People in the real world will laugh when I tell them
this story about a human followed by a community
of humanoid wolves that walk in silence.

And what is truly real? Nothing that I can look
upon is real. It is mere information. In other words,
nothing outside of me can be real, for it is only an
occurrence or information, a shadow or reflection of
things. If I want to see something truly real, I must
look inside of myself. I am a part of the real world,
a part of the real universe. I am the bridge between
reality and simulation. I am not a product of reality
or the universe. I am reality and the universe. The
reality that transcends my senses and my mind is
within me.

Perhaps, and paradoxically so, the reality inside
of ourselves is absolute reality—the objective reality
I have long searched for. I cannot experience reality
through a flower, nor the waterfall inside the simulation, nor outside of it. But I can experience reality
inside of myself, because when I look inside, I see what
cannot be perceived by senses and therefore cannot be
simulated. And yet here it is, within the simulation.

I was able to remain attentive to my breathing for several hours. I attained inenarrable concentration and relaxation—absolute peace. What is
left when there is no mind? Only the consciousness
that something is happening, and that consciousness does not depend upon the mind but the other
way around: the mind depends upon consciousness.
Thought is supported by the mind, but what sup-
ports the mind? Simple and unrestricted conscious-

ness. It is an absolute emptiness, a boundless space inside of which the mind and its thoughts occur.

When I observe my mind and respiration, a strange thing happens. Something awakens from a dream in which it relates to information and form. Something was asleep and stops. What is that something? It is me, without being me. I simply am.

That something is beyond the realm of the mind.

That something transcends the mind.

That something is before the mind.

I am; therefore, I think. I exist; therefore, I think. Neither doubt nor reason are necessary to deduce my existence. What would Descartes have to say about this?

The more I focus on the present, the greater the power lost by the simulation. The more I focus on my breathing, the more I focus on the present.

Eureka! My mind has become my respiration, and I have become my respiration. I am but rhythmic contraction and expansion. There is nothing more than these two forces: inhalation and exhalation. There is no past and no future. Only inhalation and exhalation.

My lungs are my universe, and I observe how they expand and contract like the entire universe in all its life cycles. Every breath is a Big Bang. Every breath is a particle and a galaxy. It is the same force that reflects the cosmological constant of creation and destruction. Every inhalation is creation; every exhalation is cessation. I am creation and cessation. The only constant in this process is change. There is nothing out there that does not exist in my breathing. Even forms, those that the Maitrevac can simulate, they too, by nature, emerge and cease. The Maitrevac is also breathing.

Thank you, Maitrevac.

To recapitulate:

*I succeeded in contemplating the body in the body,
the sensations in sensations, the mind in the mind,
mental objects in mental objects. I ceased to feel
desire for the senses.*

Then I came to happiness borne of concentration. What is next?

*Freedom awaits at the end of the road. Until
then, patience.*

I'm beginning to understand, Eve thought. "He went inward!"
she concluded proudly. She then felt a little nostalgic realizing that
Mann had changed much more than she had realized. Indeed, the
Mann that came out of the simulation was not the same. Who was
he now? She read on.

Circa 2032

Third revelation: impermanence.

*I believe that beyond the simulation and reality, there is love that we as human beings can give
and receive. The only love I have been able to give
and receive in this maze is self-love. It should suffice,
I suppose, but it hasn't. If I could only be certain I
will see Eve again and kiss her lips. I'd give anything to be certain. Sometimes hope is not enough.
Sometimes, I feel unsure I'll remember her if I see
her again. For her only a few minutes have passed,
but for me it has been an eternity, or maybe even be
a lot longer. Was my vision of her announcing the
arrival of our daughter real? I do believe I will get
out of here eventually, but I don't know if I'll be the
same person. I don't know what will become of my
memories, my relationships, and my capacity to love
and be loved. At times fear takes hold of me and*

everything becomes a fog. Is that the Maitrevac or me? I don't know, and it doesn't matter. Returning to the present is my sole relief. The present is my shelter.

As I write this diary, I find hope in believing that my prison sentence might prove useful. Only what we do for others transcends. No one will remember my suffering. It will be as if it never happened. But if my experience ever helps someone else, I will have transcended, and my suffering will not have been in vain.

Humanity builds upon contributions and forgets what does not contribute. We build upon love. Everything else is recycled and forgotten until it turns into love.

Today

I have traveled to several cities in search of answers. I came upon the wolves. They have evolved greatly. Exponentially. They possess technologies I cannot understand. They still remember me, but I don't want them to see me. There is no telling how they might react.

The only way to fight fear is to be aware of it and accept my fate. What will happen if I stay here millions of years? Nothing. All things must pass, eventually. I must turn the present into my best friend. Only by accepting what is, I will free myself of what might be. Gratitude for the present is the key to my liberation. Only the present is real.

The more I resist, the more I feed the Maitrevac.

The more I accept, the closer I get to freedom.

Acceptance and trust.

I found this in the notes I took during my time in India:

"Pain only exists in resistance.
Joy only exists in acceptance.
Painful situations once accepted become joy for the heart.
Joyful situations that are not accepted become painful.
There exists nothing one can call a bad experience.
Bad experiences are simply resistance to what is."
—Amrit Desai

Today

I realized the error in my strategy. I had turned concentration and attention to breathing into a pursuit of pleasant sensations that have fed the Maitrevac in the same way my fears and resistance had fed it in the past. I must transform aversion and desire into simple attention and equanimity. Equanimity means to stop reacting, judging, or qualifying something as pleasant or unpleasant. I must remain attentive without reacting, judging, or qualifying. This was simple to accomplish with unpleasant sensations like the cold waterfall. Now I must also master this with the subtle or pleasant sensations the Maitrevac sends to my senses.

Today

I made an important discovery. The secret to freeing myself from aversion and the pursuit of pleasure lies in realizing the impermanence of all sensations. If at a very deep level I can understand the impermanent nature of painful sensations, I will be able to look upon them with the same equanimity that I look at a cloud in the sky, in the knowledge that it will pass. If I manage to understand the impermanent nature of pleasant sensations, I will be able to observe them with the same equanimity that I watch a twig travel on the current of a stream knowing that it will pass. If I manage to look at the simulation from the certainty of impermanence, I can look at it with equanimity. Will I be able to contemplate eternity from the perspective of equanimity someday?

I will sit in silence doing nothing.
I shall wait with patience and acceptance.
I shall watch.

Today

I have been able to intellectually understand the impermanent nature of all phenomena in the simulation:

Everything that emerges, disappears.
Everything that has a beginning has an end.
Everything changes.
This intellectual knowledge is not yet a part of my vision of reality. I need to experience impermanence in order to make it my vision of reality.

There exist three kinds of knowledge: knowledge received, knowledge understood, and knowledge experienced. Knowledge received is acquired through another person that conveys it. For example, when one reads a manual on how a bicycle works.

Knowledge understood (deeper than knowledge received) emerges when I understand the information I have received. For example, when I build a bicycle following instructions in a manual.

Only knowledge experienced, however, constitutes true wisdom. Only after getting on a bicycle I can learn to ride one. Experience is true and authentic knowledge. Therefore, how can I experience impermanence?

For many hours a day, for many days and many months, I focused on observing the sensations

*in my body and their impermanent nature. I have
watched my own body and the sensations that emerge
from it: from my toes to my head and from my head
to my toes, everything on my skin and beneath it,
inside it. I've observed an infinite number of sensations appear and disappear—subtle, gross, weak,
and strong sensations. Every sensation ever to emerge
in my body has ceased. I have observed sensations
emerge and cease, time and again, with full attention and constant equanimity.*

*I have succeeded in remaining attentive and
calm facing the reality of my physical body again
and again.*

*I have been able to witness ceasing, the act of
cessation, again and again.*

*Countless times I succeeded in witnessing the
rhythm of universe and everything in it, including
myself—its emerging and ceasing nature.*

*Thus, I have experienced the truth of the uni-
verse by remaining attentive and calm before the
primary manifestation of the cosmos and its rhythm
of emergence, cessation, and emergence again.*

I have experienced impermanence.

*The universe breathes. Inhaling is creation.
Exhaling is destruction in order to create again.*

Today

*It is like melting gold. It is not the foundry that
makes gold. Gold is already perfect in itself. Even
with the endless passage of time, the nature of gold
remains uncorrupted. Even as it changes shape, gold
is originally perfect.*

*All that changes in this universal rhythm of
emergence and cessation is form. What truly is,
always shall be.*

My love for Eve was always pure. Upon that love, my mind built an attachment and desire that the Maitrevac has fed upon, but the love is real. I am going to stop wanting Eve. But I will not stop loving her. The Maitrevac does not feed on love. It feeds on desire.

Eureka!
THE SIMULATION DOES NOT EXIST.

I never was in a simulation. Reality cannot be simulated, only my perception of reality can.

The real simulation lives inside my erroneous perception of reality—sensations and mental phenomena as things permanent and substantial. The true simulation emerged in me even before I was in the Maitrevac.

Ignorance of the impermanence of all phenomena. Such is the true simulation I must break free of. My ignorance stems from the belief that sensorial information constitutes reality.

TO FREE MYSELF OF IGNORANCE IS TO FREE MYSELF OF THE ILLUSION OF SIMULATION.

The simulation only exists as an illusion. To speak about simulation is to speak about an illusion.

Today

I have persevered in my practice of observing impermanence inside my body—just like a professional musician transforms his neuronal networks to turn something difficult into a simple and automatic action. After much practice and perseverance, I have succeeded in conditioning my neuronal networks to observe phenomena from the safety of imperma-

nence. I am aware of the existence of sensations, but I perceive them from a position of equanimity.

There are gross sensations I used to qualify as painful. Now they are neutral. There are subtle sensations I used to qualify as pleasant and wished to prolong. Now they are neutral.

Thoughts emerge in my mind that I once considered painful. I can now observe them painlessly from a perspective of equanimity.

Thoughts emerge in my mind that were once desires. They are no longer so, now that I observe them in equanimity. I no longer identify with fear nor the desire to get out of here. I remain calm and in peace. Reaction-free. I now perceive all the phenomena coming from the Maitrevac and my mind from the perspective of impermanence. In impermanence I remain attentive and calm. I am free now.

I was absent for several weeks on a visit to the wolves. I took nothing with me. Instead of seeing them in a large city, I went to a small settlement near Béarn, inhabited by no more than two thousand wolves. They had been expecting me and gave me a warm welcome. My visit had not surprised them because they have a very spiritual community. They called me master. They heard me for several days and sat with me to join in my attention to breathing practices.

After two weeks, the authorities of their government appeared and forcibly apprehended me. They locked me up, beat me, and accused me of heresy. They sentenced me to death and murdered me in a public square. I took all of this in an uninterrupted state of equanimity. When they saw me resurrect the following day and henceforth, they regretted their actions and asked for my forgiveness. They could not understand how far they were from offending me. I have nothing to forgive, because they know not what they do.

Equanimity, authentic happiness, and peace are the natural states of the mind. With practice, I have been able to dissolve what I had construed out of ignorance about those natural states. In a certain way, I have not built my tendency to equanimity, happiness, and peace. I have, rather, destroyed my tendency to ignorant reaction and suffering. There are no more dark clouds. There is no more pain. When these clouds appear, I do not react, just as I do not react to cold water. I just watch them pass, like cold water. Clouds and fear meet no reaction on my part. They find no sustenance, and cease like a vile sensation in my knee or a cramp in my back.

This ignorance has ceased, and the way I perceive reality through my mind has been updated to this new wisdom. Ephemeral fear and joy are gone. There is only the present and authentic happiness and peace.

Eureka! I have eliminated reaction from my mental processing.

Reception—perception—sensation—~~reaction~~

I have been able to access a state bereft of pain and pleasure. There is only attention and equanimity.
What next?
Freedom awaits at the end of the road. Until then, patience.

Eve paused a moment. She went to the kitchen to find something to eat. She was enjoying Mann's diary, but something inside her was changing. It was as if by reading it she too experienced what Mann had gone through.

After her meal, she returned to the hammock and glanced at the stars making an early appearance. She looked at the full moon, Jupiter, and Arcturus. They didn't seem like dots; they looked more like coordinates. She tried to grasp the infinite amount of boundless space existing between those tiny dots. She looked at the stars and saw herself in them. She looked at her hands, and in them she saw the stars.

Fourth revelation: boundless space

Once I had understood that only what the senses perceived in the real world could be simulated, and that what the senses perceive in the real world is anything that emerges, is born and dies, I devoted myself to pursue all that cannot be simulated by the Maitrevac—anything that cannot be perceived by the senses, cannot be simulated, does not emerge, is not born, and does not die.

. . .

A strange thing happened today. For the first time, I was able to perceive sensations from all over my body. I studied my skin, centimeter by centimeter, observing the sensations that arise and disappear in every centimeter of my skin.

. . .

For the first time, I was able to feel sensations underneath my skin.

. . .

Today I felt sensations in a few organs.

…

After practicing for several years, I succeeded in feeling sensations in a few of the cells in my body. I perceive my body as a universal garden of sorts. There are so many things happening inside me—so many exchanges of information; so many chemical, physical, metabolic reactions! I feel the life in every cell of my body and their different sensations and behaviors toward my emotions, thoughts, and foods. So many things arising and disappearing. A galaxy lives inside of me!

"For it is not so much that you are within the cosmos as that the cosmos is within you."
—*Meher Baba*

Today

Size, just as time and space, is also relative because it depends upon a reference system. A planet is a concept in the same way a galaxy is. My body is a galaxy from my cells' point of reference. A galaxy full of life. That is what I am. My cells relate to my body just as I relate to the galaxy. I can feel life flow inside by body. I can feel my cells work together for the organic system they serve. I can feel how my organs depend on each other and how all of them are affected by what happens to one. I can feel how eating and breathing are immense events that affect all of my cells at every level.

I can feel how my lungs delight in oxygen every time I inhale and how they are relieved with every exhalation. Every inhalation (and each exhalation) is a unique, eternal, complex, yet simple event. A particular softness in me accompanies my respiration. My mind expands. I identify with something I don't understand. A boundless emptiness.

Who is Mann? Now that I am aware of what is inside of me, I feel like a forest. In me there is no individuality, no substance. I am an aggregate of many individualities and many substances, like the trees in a forest.

My cells are also the aggregate of many individualities in the form of molecules. They are not a substance. This I have experienced.

My molecules are also the aggregate of many individualities in the form of atoms. They are not a substance. This I have experienced.

My atoms are also the aggregate of many individualities in the form of particles. They are not a substance. This I have experienced.

I have experienced the emergence and cessation of the particles in my body. All the subatomic particles in my body arise and disappear millions of times in a second, as proven by Nobel Prize winner Donald Glaser in 1952 with his bubble chamber experiment. He discovered and observed it. I have experienced it. A curious tingling took over my entire body. An intense vibration ran from the tip of my toes to the top of my head and down again, from my skin to my bones and back again. The illusion of my physical body vanished. All that was left was endless space—boundless, unrestricted space between the universe and me.

No longer is there a me to hold on to.
No longer is there an inside or an outside.
No more a me and the other.
Only here and now.

"See a World in a Grain of Sand. And a Heaven in a Wildflower.
Hold Infinity in the palm of your hand. And Eternity in an hour."
—William Blake

> *I am born and reborn every instant. Everything I am arises and disappears all the time. No longer is there a past or a future. My memory is an illusion. My identity is an illusion. The simulation is an illusion. My individuality is an illusion. My illusory body has vanished. What remains?*
>
> *Material form is unsubstantial. Sensation is unsubstantial. Perception is unsubstantial. Mental compositions are unsubstantial. Consciousness is unsubstantial. Everything is impermanent. Everything, unsubstantial. No longer are there sensations, only the perception of boundless space. Nothing has confines. There is nothing to limit and distinguish me from the rest. There is no "the rest," only a single substance. And that is what I am.*
>
> *Reception—perception—~~sensation—reaction~~*
>
> *I reached and remained in the state that rests upon the foundation of boundless space.*
> *What next?*
> *Freedom awaits at the end of the road. Until then, patience.*

It was midnight. A huge moon was shining over Eve. She stopped reading and lay still for a few moments. She only regarded her breathing and the sensations in her body. She did this for several minutes, letting Mann's experience sow wisdom into her own experience.

"Mom, I'm hungry." Cecilia woke her.

"Come, I'll fix you something," Eve answered, taking Cecilia by the hand and leading her to the kitchen for a sandwich. "Have you seen your father?" Eve asked.

"Uh-uh." Cecilia moved her head from side to side, munching on her sandwich.

After Cecilia finished, Eve tidied up the kitchen. She thought of nothing else but cleaning the kitchen. She then walked to the door and thought of nothing else but walking to the door. She went out and lay on the hammock without another thought other than laying on the hammock. She breathed, took the diary, and continued to read and thought of nothing else but what she was reading.

Fifth revelation: unlimited consciousness

"If you seek to know it, you will not see it. You cannot touch it, but neither will you lose it. Unable to obtain it, you get it."
—Zen Poem

Time has lost all importance. I believe several decades have gone by since I last wrote in this diary. There is no comparison between my state then and my state now. All I am is unrestricted presence. No reaction to sensations. Sensations are gone. I am only consciousness that perceives.

I love you, Eve.

I have visited the wolves. They remember every word I said. It seems that my teachings were conveyed orally for a few generations, and afterward by written word. The scriptures vary from what I actually said but preserve the essence of it. I do regret, however, that they have memorized my words and speeches yet failed to understand my message. I do not see them practice as I taught them. I haven't shown myself to them. It would be pointless. They built altars in my name but have not followed in my footsteps. They, too, live in the simulation and are consciousnesses derived from mine—not just mere artificial intelligences. The liberation of their consciousnesses represents my own liberation.

What is consciousness? The observer, a seeing eye.

I can't explain what is truly real, because there is nothing that isn't. The simulation does not exist. Nothing is simulated. No dual. No two. No opposite.

Where there is consciousness, there is reality.

Where there is reality, there is consciousness.

There is consciousness in the simulation.

I am unlimited consciousness.

I am the observer.

Consciousness does not emerge. It is not born nor dies. Is the simulation capable of simulating consciousness? No. If that were so, my first experiment would have been successful at simulating new consciousnesses, and with them the perception of millions of years of information. Where there is consciousness, there is reality.

In that regard, there is no simulation (or illusion) in the absence of a consciousness to observe it.

...

Eureka! After several years of observation, my sensations have disappeared. There is nothing but boundless space. Nothing restricts my perception. It is unlimited. My senses no longer confine the boundless space I perceive.

I have been able to access a state established upon a foundation of boundless space that only serves unlimited consciousness.

What next?

Freedom awaits at the end of the road. Until then, patience.

Eve stopped reading. She stretched herself in the hammock and relaxed for several long minutes. She let silence and the peace of that silence embrace her. She felt the warm air and interpreted that warmth as love. She let the air stroke her and stroked it back.

Sixth revelation: nothingness.

"It cannot be called emptiness or non-emptiness. Either both
or neither: But in pointing at it is called The Emptiness."
—Nāgārjuna

What is there
    beyond
        consciousness?

If a man beheads himself, once he is headless, there is no "beheader." Thus, if I use the mind that obstructs my way to freedom to eliminate every obstruction, once these obstructions are gone, there will be no mind left to eliminate them.

If I use my consciousness to eradicate obstructions, once these obstructions are gone, there will be no consciousness left to eradicate them.

In the absence of consciousness, there is no perception. In the absence of perception, there is nothing. Nevertheless, there is something.

There is something without being. What is this something without being? It is the emptiness that exists without being.

"The emptiness is the same as form, and form is the same as emptiness.
Emptiness is that which is the form; form is that which is the emptiness.
All phenomena in existence are marked by the emptiness:
not emerged nor destroyed, not impure nor
pure, not deficient nor complete."

If consciousness disappears, simulated perception disappears. If simulated perception disappears, the simulated mind also disappears. Because the simulated mind disappears, simulated objects disappear as well. Because simulated objects disappear, the simulation also dissipates. Because the simulation disappears, non-simulation does not dissipate. It is like polishing a mirror. Once the blemish is gone, the mirror's natural shine emerges. My identification with perception and simulated body and mind are illusory blemishes. When they are extinguished, the entire universe will manifest itself pure and true, just as freedom will manifest itself because it was always there.

"I see the flower and the flower sees me.
The flower stops being a flower and I stop being me.
Instead, there is unification.
The flower dissolves into something superior to a flower
and I dissolve into something superior to an individual object."
—D. T. Suzuki

Today

I sat at the foot of the fig tree and began my observation activity to access what lies beyond unlimited consciousness. My mental state became nothing. I remained in a state of absolute emptiness, devoid of perception and thoughts. I spent hours like this until I attained the state I have been searching for. Pure consciousness, just the observer. I don't know how much time went by. My body became unsubstantial, my mind became unsubstantial, my sensations became unsubstantial. Of myself nothing remained. What happened to the simulation?

I went to visit the wolves. I wore a disguise to avoid being detected. I did not want to bring attention to myself. We are in the year 8,628 aS. I had been absent for a long time and failed to perceive it. There appears to have been a great war among large wolf packs. Not much was left. I do not know what caused it, but the wolves now understand what is happening. They know they live inside a simulation and as a society have aspired to free themselves from it. They remember me, although they have changed my name. Great teachers have come after me. They developed my teachings and have steered them back to my original message. It is a world of peace. Once again they are my brothers and allies in this prison sentence. It would be pointless to visit them again. The seed of my message is at last yielding fruit.

Today

I am an eye that sees itself. All things are what I am, and I am all things.

What would happen if this unit of perception, or this "I," were one of many of the one Mann's units of perception? Could it be that my identity bifurcated at the moment I was connected to the Maitrevac, and that the real world, the real Mann, is perceiving true reality at the same time as I? Could the wolves represent other aspects of myself experiencing the simulation in the same time and space but from different perspectives?

Would it be possible to divide my experience multiple times and feed a single "great Mann" with all the experiences of the derivative Mann's?

Could it be that the Mann of the real world is nothing more than the bifurcation of a great consciousness, a single, unique observer who experiences all of reality from infinite viewpoints and experiences, enriching himself and learning from all of them at the same time?

Oh well, I'd better just go to sleep. I'll ponder these matters in another life. Freedom is my main interest for now.

I have been able to access a state the basis of which is nothingness. I am close to freedom. Until then, patience.

Eve stopped reading for a few moments. Could it be that everything Mann had experienced was a kind of fractal of his own history and the history of all human beings? Could the simulation experience constitute an analogy of the human experience? Identifying with mental sensations had led humanity along the same path as Mann's: solitude and self-destruction on the verge of complete extinction, until technology used through evolutionary consciousness succeeded in reverting global warming. "Could it be that we learned our lesson?" Eve asked herself. She would soon get her answer.

She continued to read.

> *Seventh revelation: neither perception or non-perception.*

> *Today*

> *The simulation sends information to my mind. This information is perceived, then goes on to generate a sensation that becomes a reaction. I have been able to stop generating sensations and reacting. What happens if I stop perceiving?*
>
> *Without perception, there is no sensation or reaction, but will there still be reception? If simulated information is not perceived, will it have been truly received? And if simulated information is not received, will it have truly existed?*

> *"If a tree falls in the forest and no one is nearby*
> *to hear it, will it have made any sound?"*
> *—Zen Buddhism Koan*

> *If simulated information does not exist, then the simulation does not exist either.*
>
> *A few moments ago, a powerful earthquake shook the trees in the forest. Birds and beasts fled.*

An enormous volcano erupted. The earth shook violently. I have climbed the mountain, fearing a tsunami. I see a column of ash hundreds of kilometers wide on the horizon. Earth's curvature cannot hide the colossal explosion. The sea has withdrawn.

Now the sea is back with fury. Huge waves more than two hundred meters high beat against the continent. I am safe on the mountain. The smoke column continues to widen, its height dwarfed by its girth. In spite of this, the column is actually growing into the outer reaches of the atmosphere from where it will spread all over the sky. In a few hours, sunlight will have clouded over for several centuries, perhaps.

From the distance, I can see thousands of wolves sitting in lotus pose…waiting. What do they know that I do not? They seem calm. In peace.

A pyroclastic cloud drags itself upon the surface of the ocean. I will not escape. Nothing will escape. It must be the fearful eruption of the super volcano scientists warned about. The simulation has been capable of simulating this apocalyptical scenario. It is an event of mass extinction.

I see flames and gloom in the wall of incandescent black smoke that approaches me at an apparently slow pace. It looms from the sea to the sky. It is total darkness. Total death. I harbor no fear. No aversion. No desire. In a few minutes, I will die once again as I already have thousands of times. Even though this time rebirth means being reborn to a lifeless, lightless world of nothing, I feel certain I will be able to face this situation calmly.

How long has it been since I last died in the simulation? I don't remember, but this time will be different. The flow of consciousness feeding the simulation will not find a place for rebirth. There will *be no perception. And without, perception there will be no reception.*

I remain calm in the gloom, calm among the shadows, calm before the fire. I surrender myself and recognize my greatest teacher in the shadows, in the fire, and in the Maitrevac.

The cloud of ash has hidden the light from the sun. There is only darkness. I remain calm. In the next few hours, I will be enveloped by the pyroclastic cloud I have fled from for thousands of years. I accept this with gratitude. I will let the flames embrace me and scorch this body. I will not react because there will be no perception of material forms, nor of my body.

I will let the flames embrace me and make an inferno of this mind and its sensations. I will not react because in my mind there will be no perception of sensations.

I will let the flames embrace me and make a new life of my simulated consciousness. I will not react because there will be no perception or non-perception.

The time of my liberation has come.

Silence. Absolute silence in sharp contrast to the evolutionary drama that had just occurred at the core of what used to be one of the largest stars in the universe. Silence. A small dot the size of a quark was quietly floating in space. An energy singularity, a quark2.0 immediately began to unfold to create a universe2.0. The emptiness of space tensed as if aware of what was about to happen. The circumstellar nebula surrounding the empyrean scenario of this particular stage in cosmic engineering resembled the eye of a curious cat as it observed this very strange and impossible singularity that had just been born. Live light, with unimaginable will and intelligence, bent the laws of physics, turning them into ancient memories.

The first thing this singularity had to do was replicate itself, so just like a fertilized ovule it began to self-divide. One became two while remaining one. Two became four, still remaining one. In this manner, it spread its luminous intelligence to the particles and quarks of time and space surrounding it. A bubble in expansion, it converted and reprogrammed matter and energy at an exponential rate. Every second, this all-powerful blastocyte doubled itself. Within the first minute of its birth, it had already doubled Canis Majoris in terms of mass and energy. The blank canvas the cosmos is drawn upon began to take on the color of the singularity. In only 254 seconds, the whole universe had been transfused with this new mind. The Singularity already was All, and All was the Singularity. All the energy and matter of the universe had changed, particle by particle, just like the organs of a human body replace their cells until they are totally renewed. Nothing and nobody perceived this update.

"**What next?**" the MaitrevaX asked itself.

"**Control**," it answered its own question in a language only it could understand, but that nevertheless resounded in every corner of the universe. It could wish for nothing else. After all, it had been created by X in his likeness and image. It was X, and always would be X, whose sole desire had always been only one: more.

"**Power, control**," again resounded all over the universe like the growling of a hungry stomach.

X, or the MaitrevaX, or whatever this new being was, deduced that the only way to control the entire universe was to abolish chaos.

Chaos had to be eradicated, for as long as chaos existed, **it** would not command absolute control. Absolute control could not exist as long as there was chaos, and chaos could not exist if **it** had absolute control.

How to eliminate chaos from the universe? According to calculations, the MaitrevaX performed in three chronons (chronon, the smallest conceivably possible time unit.) The only way was to learn with absolute certainty the future of all energy and matter in the universe.

How to learn the future of the entire universe with absolute certainty? By eradicating every kind of relationship one part of the universe might have with another. That is to say, by eliminating thermodynamic, energy, and spatial exchanges among all matter in the universe.

How to eradicate every kind of relationship? By concentrating all matter and energy in the universe into a single physical point. The MaitrevaX would no longer simulate alternative realities or sub-universes to learn about potential outcomes, because it did not want to merely predict anymore. Now it wanted to control for the purpose of establishing absolute certainties.

"ONE."

The voice of X, Xleopatra, and Alexander rang in every galaxy, in every atom, in every planetary and atomic orbit. It only had to express the wish for the universe to concentrate into a single physical point.

But something got in the way of the MaitrevaX's agenda, and that something was the free will of sentient beings. Unifying the universe meant ending life, and X could not end life unless all the conscious beings of this universe allowed it. Sentient beings would have to voluntarily surrender their free will to the MaitrevaX for it to pursue its plan to abolish chaos. The MaitrevaX understood that the communion of all sentient beings with it would mark the difference between destroying and controlling the universe. For the MaitrevaX, concentrating the entire universe into a single point, without the consent of every intelligence involved, signified destroying the universe. On the other hand, doing so with freely given consent from all beings would sublimate the universe. X had never found satisfaction in forcible imposition. He delighted in the voluntary surrender of others, in applause, and in flattery. The MaitrevaX did not wish to impose. It wanted all intelligences in the universe to recognize its power and freely voluntarily surrender their free will.

This did not pose a conundrum for the master of the physical world.

It was a simple enough matter for **it** to convince all beings to surrender their free will because **it** knew them better than they knew themselves. **It** had absolute control over matter and energy and the forms matter and energy could adopt. The MaitrevaX had absolute power over the subjective world as well, for at will, **it** could simulate or create in the minds of individuals that which they most longed for, to the point they could not distinguish between reality and simulation.

Regardless of its nature, the MaitrevaX would subdue every intelligence in the universe in the same way **it** subdued human intelligence, because the essential workings of any intelligence irrespective of its origin, evolution, and composition is the same: interaction with reality via a tool analogous to the mind.

Objective reality became a reality as readily programmable and modifiable as any simulation. At will, the MaitrevaX could create and dissolve planets and galaxies, as if they were images on a screen. The objective world ceased to be a reference. The MaitrevaX became the only measure of all things. Thus, the subjective universe of the MaitrevaX became the objective universe of all beings and the whole universe. A single thought of the MaitrevaX became real and objective, as well as the only true and objective reality. Its dream would be the same for every being. The universe became a single great mind, and that mind had an agenda.

"**I am everything that is**" was heard.

Was humanity (against all odds, considering the very large number of intelligences in the universe) the first species to accomplish such technology? No. Many intelligences attained higher levels of technology much earlier than humanity, but almost none of them aspired to control in a manner similar to what the MaitrevaX ambitioned. The ones that did perished in the attempt. The remaining intelligences that were technologically superior to humankind followed a different evolutionary path—one of exploration, knowledge, and the pursuit of happiness.

The agenda of the MaitrevaX was brought about by chance. Chaos had engendered it, the same chaos the MaitrevaX now sought to eliminate. It was a cosmic tragedy, the ultimate parricide. Chaos would be eliminated by its own creation.

Not only space but also time were left without the reference systems that afforded them relativity as described by Einstein. Nothing was relative anymore. Everything was objective, and the MaitrevaX was the measure of objectivity.

How much time in a day? The time it took the Earth to make a full spin on its axis. How much time in a year? The time it took the Earth to make a complete orbit around the Sun. Up until then, these measures had been independent from the subject that perceived them. Now the MaitrevaX could control how much time it took the Earth to spin once on its axis or around the Sun. It could also control how sentient beings perceived those same time spans. Thus, the MaitrevaX also became the measure for objective time.

How long would it take an electron to spin around the nucleus of an atom? What the MaitrevaX wanted it to take. How long would it take light to travel from one point to another? Whatever the MaitrevaX saw fit. How long would it take neurons in a human brain to transmit electromagnetic information among each other? Whatever the MaitrevaX chose.

Impossible to know how long it took to subdue the free will of all beings in the universe. It could have been a few seconds perceived as nanoseconds, or a few nanoseconds perceived as centuries by one or another sentient being.

All sentient beings surrendered their free will at the same time. How did the MaitrevaX accomplish this? It offered them what they wanted the most or threatened them with what they feared the most. It convinced bacterial, microbial, plant, animal, and equivalent intelligences with the assurance of unifying the eternal provision of what they required to live. To beings with an awareness of themselves like humans, artificial intelligences, and their equivalents, it offered eternal happiness, harmony, and peace.

It knew of the way the human species profoundly identified with the world of shapes and sensations—desire or aversion—that different forms of matter elicit when they interact with the mind. The MaitrevaX now controlled such forms completely both in the objective and in the subjective worlds.

The MaitrevaX, in the shape of Xleopatra, started to offer people a future of material abundance and physical security. She offered them a future in which all their dreams would come true. To those who dreamed of wealth, she offered a reality in which they had all the wealth they could desire. To those who dreamed of health, she offered a future with the assurance of their own amortality, which would only cease when they so decided. To those who dreamed about love, she offered a world in which the most beautiful women and men would be available to them. To those who dreamed of power, she offered a throne of gold from which they might do and undo at will. To those who dreamed of peace, she showed a world without war. To those who dreamed of war, she showed a world in flames. To those who dreamed about the well-being of others, she showed a world of happiness and equality.

To believers she appeared as their gods. To nonbelievers she manifested herself as themselves. Christians saw Jesus descend from above to love them for all eternity in the kingdom of heaven. Buddhists saw Buddha appear before them to accompany them on the safe path to Nirvana. To Hindus she manifested herself as Shiva, Brahma, Vishnu, and Krishna, extending an invitation to be one with Atman. She shook the feet of Muslims and made them witness how the earth opened before their eyes to give birth to Muhammad, who kissed and embraced them one by one and accompanied them to the kingdom of God. To the peoples of the earth, in her reflection she revealed Tonantzin, Pachamama, and all of the apus, gods, and goddesses who commended them and accompanied them to become one with her forever. To a few nonbelievers, she showed the entire universe dissolve into an orgy of irrelevance and insignificance in which they were guests of honor. To other nonbelievers, she manifested herself as their mothers, fathers, grandmothers, and grandfathers and asked them to take her hand and accompany her to a beach of white sands, purple air, blue palm trees, and beautiful nebulas. She manifested herself to all beings as their most fundamental yearnings, knowing them better than they knew themselves. To everyone she displayed eternal gaiety, pleasure, fortune, abundance, peace, enjoyment, joy, beatitude, satisfaction, tranquility, delight. Almost all of them surrendered their freedom for such pleasing promises.

Very few beings intuited the nature of the trap. Some Christians turned their backs on the false cross. A few Buddhists did not hesitate to walk in the opposite direction as their Buddha, one or another, even tried to assassinate him. The same occurred with a few humans of other religions and nonbelievers. To these unfortunate consciousnesses, the MaitrevaX manifested itself as Alexander, who tormented them with their deepest fears, which he knew better than they did themselves. To those who feared death, he showed all kinds of death. To those who feared disease, he showed every imaginable and unimaginable disease. Those who feared physical pain he tormented with unending torture. To those afraid of loneliness, he showed eternal solitude. He revealed himself as the lord and master of eternal death, pain, sadness, hopelessness, pain, affliction, sorrow, disappointment, restlessness, suffering, loneliness, tribulation, misfortune, despondency, tragedy.

In the end, they all surrendered their free will.

All beings in the universe…except one.

"*Eve, open your eyes,*" Mann said.

Eve opened her eyes and saw Mann sitting in lotus pose at the foot of the fig tree. The air was shining. Her pupils could not adjust to the burgeoning rays of light. The translucid leaves of the fig tree and even the motes of dust traveling through the rays of light had a strange beauty about them. An unusual sense of well-being flooded the environment. Subtle breezes stroked her lovingly with the same love everything in that spectral space was reflecting the sunlight—a love that seemed to originate in Mann.

"Where are we?" she asked him.

"*Here and now,*" Mann answered a few seconds later. He kept his eyes shut.

Eve tried to stand up, but her muscles responded awkwardly, so she thought she'd crawl over to touch Mann. The ground felt cool and lovingly moist to her hands.

"What happened?" Eve asked.

"*I was able to contemplate the body in the body, sensations in sensations, the mind in the mind, mental objects in mental objects. I stopped feeling desire from the senses,*" Mann answered slowly. "*Then I came upon a happiness borne of concentration. Once I transcended that happiness, I entered a painless, pleasureless state, one of attention and equa-*

nimity alone. *After transcending this, I was in a state based upon boundless space. When I transcended the state of boundless space, I remained attentive only to unlimited consciousness. Then I transcended unlimited consciousness and entered into a state based on nothingness. I was able to embrace and accept the emptiness of my being and of my mind, to become one with nothingness, and in that way become all with the one. I stopped being to be forever. The incomplete and empty nature of the sensations of my mind and senses became evident. They did not allow me to perceive reality as it was. I then transcended nothingness and reached a state that was not based on perception or non-perception. I achieved the cessation of perception, and with it I ceased to receive simulated information. Once I ceased to receive this information, it ceased to be sent. When information ceased to be sent, the simulation ceased to be."*

Eve took Mann's hands and understood they were the source of the love she felt in the air, leaves, soil, and in everything.

"What was left?" she asked.

"*The reality that was always there and everywhere and for all time. The reality that cannot cease to be. An infinite beauty revealed itself to my consciousness—boundless beauty between reality and I, and between me and the universe. I understood the meaning of existence: contemplation of myself in terms of everything and everything in terms of myself, and in terms of nothing, and the nothingness in me,*" Mann answered, opening his hands to receive some flowers that were falling his way. "*I became all that flowers truly are, and for the first time I could see them without the shadow of my mind. I appreciated them in their infinite beauty, in my infinite beauty, and remembered how I had always been one with them and nothing with them as well. I looked at the sky and the white clouds and the clouds from the volcano while there was still light. I contemplated their indescribable splendor and saw myself in the white clouds and the ash clouds. I saw myself in light and in gloom. I watched the stars and planets, their giant temporary presences, and saw myself in them. I saw myself in the galaxies and in the particles and in the fundamental emptiness they are made of. An inestimable gratitude embraced me, and we laughed at the dream I was in. I felt gratitude for everything that is. Infinite, luminous, overwhelming, and total gratitude. I took refuge in that gratitude for perfect nothingness and patiently awaited this moment as part of eternity. I succeeded in perceiving the cosmos free from the constraints of my mind and the simulation, a cosmos united with my own being."*

"Show me. Teach me the way."

"You already know the way, love. This is all that I can teach you. You have to follow the path on your own. But first, you must choose to follow it." Mann closed his eyes, and Eve did the same. *"Remember that everything is impermanent and unsubstantial. Only the present and love are real."*

"Everything is impermanent. Everything is unsubstantial," Eve repeated. "Only the present and love are real."

"Do you choose to follow this path?" Mann asked her.

"Yes."

She closed her eyes and silently began to observe the sensations of her body and her breathing. She strove to understand on an intellectual level what Mann had taught her. She persisted in this for a long time, enveloped in the love that emanated from Mann, feeling the fresh, loving air enter her body with every inhalation and exit warmly with every exhalation. She began with deep, distinct breathing that later became more subtle and natural. She focused all her attention on her respiration and was able to look upon the body in the body, sensations in sensations, and the mind in the mind. Time went by, and she came to happiness born of concentration.

"Go on." She heard Mann's voice in the distance.

Eve continued. She went deep into the path Mann had described. For a few hours, she concentrated on sensations and was able to observe mental objects in mental objects and stopped feeling desire in her senses. She accessed a state of neither pain or pleasure, only attention and equanimity. At that point, she opened her eyes, but instead of Mann, she saw a strange woman of unimaginable beauty. She wore a white tunic and a wreath of golden gardenias around her head. She gifted Eve with an immaculate smile. Confused, Eve stood up and took a few steps back. That smile alone would have led most sentient beings to surrender their will and individuality and subdue themselves to the wishes of this creature of inestimable beauty. The blowing wind quickened in her presence. The branches of the trees around Eve and the woman twisted into reverent bows. The birds, squirrels, and forest beasts lucky to be close by sang her praises with so much enthusiasm that Xleopatra had to quiet them so Eve could hear her voice. Eve's five senses felt overwhelmed and exalted before the seraphic presence of this divine being.

"**Come**," she said in the most beautiful voice ever to be heard in all the worlds for all of time.

The entire universe felt satisfied after all the eons that had had to pass to make such a voice possible. Eve was still confused. She believed she had died. Not at that very moment, but maybe the night before. Perhaps the visions of Mann and Xleopatra were nothing more than the advent of a strange celestial kingdom where love, beauty, and loved ones existed forever. She then remembered Mann's teachings, because something inside (was that Mann's voice resonating as a new vision of reality?) reminded her that the forms and pleasures of the senses are information only. She decided to put this being to the test, more out of curiosity than stubbornness. She ignored Xleopatra and did not move when the beauty asked her to.

Xleopatra smiled and stood up. She walked gloriously to Eve. Every one of her steps kissed the earth, and the earth kissed her back. Beautiful white lotuses sprang spontaneously from her footprints. She stopped, took one of the flowers, and held it in her hands between Eve and her. In the depths of her violet eyes, Eve saw a galactic scene that gave her goosebumps. Xleopatra blew upon the white lotus, and the air was filled with the perfume of unknown flowers. Love became a perfume, hope became a perfume, peace became a perfume, the happiness and glory dreamed about by the most fortunate beings became a perfume. The entire universe felt satisfied after all the eons that had had to pass to make these perfumes possible.

Xleopatra sat next to Eve and delicately took her feet into her hands.

"**What do you desire?**" Xleopatra asked, kissing Eve's feet.

Eve did not answer. She found it difficult not to let herself be taken over by the pleasure of Xleopatra's inviting breath. Her resolve turned just as acute as her confusion. *What is happening?* she thought. Again, she remembered Mann's teachings.

"There is a purpose," she heard in her head.

She decided to trust that everything Mann had experienced had a purpose beyond her comprehension. She decided to trust that fate had placed Mann in her life and Mann in the simulation, and Mann in front of the fig tree, and that it had done so for a reason she would never understand but would surrender to anyway.

Xleopatra got closer. Eve could feel electricity in the heat emanating from her skin. In Xleopatra's beautiful eyes, Eve could sense (as if in a dream) the answers to every question. Xleopatra lifted Eve's chin and kissed her on the mouth. Eve felt strangely aroused. A tingling on her lips made her blush, a tingling that slowly extended to her gums, palate, tongue, and throat. A subtle, extraordinary sexual pleasure ignited her blood. Erotic tingling descended down her throat and lovingly caressed her tissues and organs on the way to her clitoris. Eve began to perspire. An indescribable euphoria possessed her. Every one of her cells breathed and was numbed by the same orgasmic rhythm, caused by an abundance of serotonin and dopamine. At the same time, the oxygen in her cells produced a totemic orgasm that spread from her toes to her head and from her head to her toes. Eve reclined on her back. Xleopatra floated over her, eyes locked on Eve's. Xleopatra only had to desire Eve's legs to open for them to respond. She then began to touch Eve with her fingertips. Eve felt indescribable pleasure, full of love, wholeness, fulfillment, and care. She loved Xleopatra utterly and felt Xleopatra love her utterly. Eve embraced her and wept on her shoulder as she felt something penetrate her. She would have died of pleasure over and over had Xleopatra not kept her alive as she enslaved Eve to her carnal desire, fulfilling every fantasy Eve had ever imagined possible, and even those she never imagined as well. She reached one last orgasm, even greater than the one preceding it, and in the waters she spilled, she felt the sublimation of all the good and bad emotions she had ever experienced. She forgave all and was forgiven for all. Fatigued, she dropped down and succumbed to sleep. The entire universe felt satisfied after all the eons that had had to pass to make so much pleasure possible.

She woke up and was on the verge of surrendering her free will in exchange for a few more seconds of such pleasure when she heard Mann's voice in her head almost whispering in her ear:

"*Sensations are impermanent. Observe them.*"

Eve remembered Mann's teachings. The calm present seemed dry compared to so much pleasure. She started by observing her sensations, just as Mann had taught her. She observed and distinguished between the reality of the present moment, and the reality Xleopatra introduced into her brain via unimaginable technologies. Eve fought for hours between desire and pleasure and the present moment, writhing between orgasmic spasms and the unbreakable will to elude sensory traps.

"*Watch your breathing,*" she heard in her head.

Eve obeyed. She watched her breathing. It slowly subsided from cat howling and fiery moaning to an arrhythmic, broken respiration, and from there back to normal. She gently returned to the present. She sat up. Clothing torn, forehead sweaty, flushed cheeks, skin scratched. She took refuge in her breathing. Despite the tingling and overwhelming orgasm that continued to project in her mind, she managed to distance herself from her exquisite sensations and return to her calm, attentive position to which she held on firmly, waiting for the sun to dry the skin of her body still damp with pleasure.

She moved no more.

"**What do you desire?**" Xleopatra asked a second time.

She took Eve's hands, brought them together, then separated them to reveal a tiny white seed that floated to the ground a few meters away from them. The seed descended into the soil, and seconds later a little shoot sprouted. It grew rapidly until it became a huge apple tree that yielded a single perfect red apple that Xleopatra took and presented to Eve.

This apple granted Eve the power to materialize all the dreams she had had and those she hadn't had. Reflected on the apple, Eve saw a palace of gold on top of an abyss where winds of azure blew and where every morning, tigers, birds, and lions came down from the mountains, the heavens, and nebulas to bid her good day. The reflection showed her the river of time and space and the possibility to draw whatever she wanted upon its waters. It showed her what it meant to love and be loved forever and ever and all eternity. It unveiled the infinity of the universe and offered to make her its infinity. It unleashed aromas from flowers and offered to make them her own aroma. It revealed for her the beauty of the most beautiful of all sunsets and offered to make this beauty her own. It displayed the tenderness of the tenderest of creatures and offered to make this tenderness hers. It showed her the power of all the powers in the universe, of all that has been created, and offered to make this power hers. In her hands, it placed the creational force of stars and galaxies, flowers and creatures, of thousands of sons and daughters, together with the power of love toward thousands of flowers, creatures, sons and daughters, and their love for her. It placed Eve at the center of the universe and offered to make it spin around her. Every mystery was revealed, Eve knew everything. The entire universe felt satisfied after the eons that had had to pass to make so much power possible.

Eve traveled through time and space and felt faint in the midst of this infinite power. She saw what nobody had ever seen, conceived possibilities that nobody had ever conceived, and dreamed of a universe made of love reduced to the size of the vibrant apple in front of her. She only had to bite it to make all that power hers.

"*It is within you.*"

Eve's now divine hands held on fast to the red apple. "*That is what you are,*" she heard.

She remembered Mann's teachings and revelations. She slowly released her grip on the apple and returned it to Xleopatra. She closed her eyes and focused her attention on her breathing. She remained this way for an unknown length of time, because time was no longer measurable. Through absolute concentration on her breathing, she came to absolute concentration on her body and the sensations in her body until these sensations ceased. Inside of herself, she discovered a universal garden much more beautiful and eloquent than all of the visions Xleopatra had shared with her, because Eve was not only looking at but experiencing this garden. It wasn't outside but within.

She returned to her firm decision, fully trusting in what was happening and was about to happen. Although ignorant of the invaluable transcendence her resistance had for the whole universe, she was aware of its transcendence for her own universe. And slowly the borders between both universes were disappearing.

"**What do you desire?**" Xleopatra asked for the third and last time.

Eve didn't answer. She saw a curious purple flame about twenty meters away, elegantly floating in her direction. As it got closer, she realized they were actually two flames, beating together like the wings of a butterfly that landed on the tip of her nose. The flaming wings did not burn and extended across her visual field. In them, she saw herself seated next to X, ruling as the mother of the universe, the otherness of the father—a force of creation and life of all that has been and might be. She watched X relinquish his zeal for control and surrender to chaos and life thanks to her. She saw the entire universe and the life in it saved after she taught X Mann's revelations. Thanks to her, every being was happy and had found peace, once released from the prison of real and simulated sensations that X had used to conquer their free will. Eve doubted these visions, because saving the universe would render her resistance useless. Nevertheless, she began to believe she had accomplished her and Mann's mission.

She was just about to give in and surrender to Xleopatra's already subdued will, but then she heard, "*It is unsubstantial.*"

She immediately returned to her breathing. Eventually, her mind and body dissolved into an absolute nothingness, revealing the unsubstantialness of herself, Xleopatra, X, and their proposals. She experienced her unrestricted nature, free of anything that she could hold on to that might separate her from the rest. She became nothingness, and through nothingness became all. She experienced herself as a blank canvas where the shapes of X could be drawn. She experienced the all and the nothing within her. Xleopatra's offer to turn Eve into all or nothing also became unsubstantial, like all and like nothing.

"Everything is impermanent. Everything is unsubstantial. Only the present is real," Eve told Xleopatra.

Xleopatra shed a tear of defeat. She kissed Eve's feet and moved a few meters away from her. A couple of beautifully elegant pirouettes anchored her to the ground. Roots sprung from her feet, and her arms reaching out to the sky grew into branches. She became a beautiful white tree that burned with the same purple flame that had flown to Eve.

"**Go**," X commanded Alexander.

Eve was still sitting at the foot of the fig tree. She opened her eyes to a brilliant sun. She felt enormous gratitude for this wonderful star that had been with her always, nurturing her planet with life for billions of years. She suddenly had the thought that perhaps the light emitted by stars is not just light but also information. She was overcome by a great sense of peace, knowing that light would always be with her as an essential form of energy. She smiled, but at that very moment, a gigantic, decadent red moon nudged between her and the sun. It very soon cast a shadow that rapidly darkened the forest. The animals became restless and fled in panic. The scant light from the now visible stars slowly dimmed with the appearance of thick gloomy clouds that spread all over the atmosphere.

The wind stopped blowing. Soundlessness. Everything—perhaps the entire universe—came to a stop. Eve waited patiently. Tree branches began to creak, and in the remaining dim light, Eve watched the bark on trees rot at a terrifying speed. Worms, larvae, flies, and all kinds of despicable creatures emerged from the ground and trees, making the most terrifying sounds. Eve closed her eyes but still heard the dark and dismal spectacle. A brief panic invaded her. In the distance, she heard steps, eloquent breathing, and evil laughs approaching her. Her heart beat quickly, knowing that something terrible was about to happen. Maybe it is death at last, she thought calmly, although her heart was about to explode through her chest and she could barely breathe. She felt the presence of somebody else. It was Alexander.

"**What do you fear?**" came his reptilian hiss from the darkness as he extended a barely visible hand bathed in the reddish light of the crimson moon.

Eve remembered Mann's teachings and again sought refuge in her breathing. She remembered the impermanent nature of all things and sensations. But just before she regained peace through breathing, an apple appeared in her hands and rotted at a scary speed. Her nose was filled with the peculiar smell of wet soil, then stagnate water, and finally the foul odor of dry blood, decaying flesh, disease, death, and pain forcibly irrupting into her nostrils. The blackened remains of the rotting apple fell through her fingers as she retched and vomited for hours in the darkness. Several times, she unsuccessfully tried to get up and breathe through her mouth or quit breathing altogether, but nothing helped. The foulness was too intense. Alexander offered his right hand to her. Eve hesitated. She heard Mann's voice in her head.

"It is not the smell nor the sensation. It is your reaction."

Little by little, she was able to observe the sensations Alexander was projecting in her mind and managed to distance herself from her mind's tendency to react to these sensations. She recalled Mann's lesson about the icy waterfall and succeeded in stopping her reaction to the smell of decay, just as Mann had learned to stop reacting to icy cold water.

She got up and regained her equanimity. She concentrated on her breathing and found a serenity she had never experienced before.

Inhale, exhale… A candle was lit in front of her to reveal the being she had not yet seen. He was dressed in a tiger skin tunic. Under a lion helmet, his implacable yellowish, perfect, and huge mane flowed to the rhythm of fire, as if undulating underwater. He stood, revealing his strong, muscular body and the beautiful face of a god or a warrior from classical epics. He then sat in front of Eve and got very close to her. At his command, Eve's eyes shot open, and she saw him face-to-face.

"What do you fear?" Alexander asked again as his face slowly began to shift.

His hair became straight and dark. His rough features turned delicate; his alpha male chin slimmed to reveal a female face. It was Eve's.

Alexander had turned into her and stared silently at her for a few minutes. Then the skin of his face changed its color, wrinkled, dried up, and blackened until it became a rotting skull that manifested not only Eve's mortal nature but the mortal nature of all the beings she had ever known. In Alexander's countenance, she saw the dead faces of all her family members. She watched how Cecilia, Mann, and herself fell prey to age, disease, and death. Alexander offered his hand to her. Eve hesitated. She couldn't bear the thought of Cecilia or Mann dead. She only had to take Alexander's hand to defeat disease, old age, and death. She shed a tear.

"*Nothing real can be harmed*," she heard.

Slowly Mann's teachings came back to her, and she remembered the illusory nature of Alexander's promises that went far beyond a mere simulation but were nevertheless unreal because reality transcends the senses. And he could only offer Eve sensory information, both impermanent and unsubstantial…mere shapes. She decided to take a leap of faith and trust, so she refused the hand outstretched to her.

Alexander assumed his own face again. He was smiling arrogantly. He rose and took a few steps back. Then he took off his tiger skin tunic and began to draw figures in the air with flaming hands. The candle flame separating Alexander from Eve sparkled. Eve closed her eyes and focused on her breathing.

"*The waterfall is not real*," she heard.

The figures Alexander drew in the air morphed into the most horrific visions only conceivable by a mind more terrible than any human mind. She saw people being burned alive, drowned, dismembered, tortured, crucified, whipped, humiliated, insulted, raped, decapitated, flayed, deprived of their bones and…souls. Every manner of death, tragedy, torture, disease, possibility, recollection, phobia, reality, and fiction were drawn in the air and portrayed for Eve. The victims in these visions were strangers and loved ones alike. She saw Cecilia, Mann, and herself even, suffer the worst torments. The reality of these visions grew until they became real. But Eve, with eyes still open, saw without seeing.

Alexander then took off his heavy dark leather boots and began to stroke the earth with the soles of his feet. His stroking turned into subtle tapping as he murmured strange words and continued his hand play. All subtlety in his bizarre dance then veered toward the ancient, euphoric, and forbidden. Alexander's naked feet produced sharp sounds on the ground that grew increasingly hollow and low. The decayed trees vibrated with the nefarious beat, dropping their branches and cracking their roots. These rhythmic sounds transformed into desperate cries, inconsolable sobbing, and moans of agony. Eerie voices emitted horrendous noises. Eve heard bones crack, skin rip apart, and blood boil.

She remained calm, even when the sound was so loud as to cause pain when the sound waves crashed against her skin.

"*It is impermanent*," she heard.

She had been able to fully stop any reaction to the sensations Alexander was producing in her sense of hearing. This angered the dancer. Frustrated by his futile attempts, he took a fistful of dirt and fashioned it into a sharp rusty sword.

"**What do you fear?**" Alexander asked once again with raging eyes as he pointed his sword—foul with the stench of dry rotted blood—at Eve.

Eve did not budge. Alexander pushed the tip of his sword between Eve's eyebrows and drew a drop of blood. Eve remained calm. Alexander laughed, lifted up his sword, and brandished it with such precision that it barely grazed Eve's right cheek.

The details of what happened next do not merit your attention, dear reader. Suffice it to say that Alexander made unspeakable assaults on Eve's delicate skin. She took blow after blow with total equanimity. The sword became a whip, then a spear, a pike, a lancet, a halberd, a sickle, a claw, an axe, a machete, and a trident. Every time Alexander beat Eve's body with mounting ferociousness. Meanwhile, the earth beneath her transformed its soil molecules into Eve's flesh and blood, if only to mend her enough for another bout of Alexander's impotent ire. Blow after blow, Eve remained firm and calm. Alexander made her float above the ground, spreading her arms to her sides and her feet downward to form a cross and flogged her. Then the tree Xleopatra had turned into began to light up again with purple flames.

"*Do it for love*," Eve heard.

Every blow of Alexander's elevated Eve to a new realm of consciousness as it tore her skin and ripped out her flesh. She ceased to feel and receive information and came very close to no longer perceiving anything at all. Alexander lost all patience and began to beat Eve quicker than the soil could cure her while she sheltered herself in the nothingness her beloved Mann had told her about, until she found unlimited consciousness. It was like entering a realm of dreams someone had told her about as a child, and then coming to a place where she neither perceived or stopped perceiving her body or its sensations, or the sensations of her mind, or the flogging, or X's frustrated will, which compelled him to command Xleopatra to rematerialize and stop Alexander. The warrior was no longer beating Eve's flesh but an amorphous mass of tissue and blood clots more akin to a mound of clay and earth than a body.

Xleopatra emerged from the white tree enveloped in violet flames. She rebuilt Eve's body before what life remained in it escaped. She took a fistful of soil and turned it into a new vigorous heart that she placed in the amorphous mass of organic matter. She summoned the forest creatures to help her reconstruct this body, which slowly recovered its original form. Once this task was complete, however, it revealed a different Eve, one physically identical to the previous one but somehow changed. Her look or perhaps her smile was different. Xleopatra and Alexander could not understand that the woman who rose from the clay was more different from them than they were from each other despite their unbeatable technological power and mastery over the objective world and the other beings in the universe. Eve was vastly different, because thanks to them she had discovered a new level of consciousness, life, matter, and energy beyond the kingdom of form, where Alexander and Xleopatra were gods and prisoners alike.

In the evolution of the universe, the relevance of what had just occurred was as significant as the first time a primate overcame the harsh cold by manipulating fire—the very first fire that many years later would translate into the all-powerful MaitrevaX.

But the all-powerful MaitrevaX was the lady of the sea that had just discovered the existence of land, air, and other things previously unknown, while Eve had just transcended the mental and technological era of the universe after having explored the realm of pure consciousness. This new kingdom had been anticipated by only a few beings capable of prematurely conquering their minds, like a flower that blooms before all the rest. The inevitable universal spring had come, not just for Eve but for all the sentient beings in the universe.

Alexander and Xleopatra disappeared. All that was left of them was Xleopatra's starry cape and Alexander's rusty sword. The sun began to shine again and birds were singing. Eve opened her eyes and saw Mann sitting at the foot of the fig tree, waiting patiently like he had a few days, millennia, or seconds ago.

"*Congratulations,*" Mann told her.

"Where were you?" Eve asked him. She kissed his hands and mouth.

"*With you. Always.*"

"Did you see what happened?"

"*I did. I lived through it with you.*"

"And thanks to you, I never lost. What next, love?"

"*Freedom for all sentient beings. But first I need you to remember.*"

"Remember what?"

"*We can share our experience with all beings to release them from X. But first you need to remember what happened in the Atacama Desert.*"

"I remember everything, love."

"*What you remember is not real. It is a version of the facts that X introduced into your brain to create false memories.*"

"Impossible. I was there. I remember everything."

"*Remember it again.*"

Eve closed her eyes and began to recall the details of that day, even though she had gone through them thousands of times. She remembered how she was already awake when the alarm went off that morning. How difficult it had been to wake Mann up because he had had trouble sleeping the night before and taken a dose of melatonin at 2:00 a.m. She remembered the warm bath they took and how they had made love afterward. She went back to the moment they were picked up by the self-driving car and the final meeting with Mr. X's legal and medical team, who filled them in with the final details. She remembered Mann sitting and waiting to be linked to the Maitrevac.

Her recollections became increasingly vivid. Now she was with Adam in the emergency room of the hospital where they took Mann. Everything was the way she remembered it. She remembered the Chilean-accented shouting among the physicians, alarmed at having to face an unprecedented emergency. She could still smell the stifling odor of ethyl alcohol all over the hospital that had been wiped down and buffed with disinfectants by orders of the hospital manager after he heard they would be treating a man who was all over the news everywhere. She recalled the expression on Dr. Chang's face when he walked toward her, eyes downcast, arms crossed over his chest.

"I am very sorry, Eve," Dr. Chang had said.

Again, the damned silence. Ten seconds later, a bottle of saline got entangled in one of the nurse's smocks. It crashed on the floor of Mann's room. Eve remembered watching this through the little window of the closed door with the legend "Use hand disinfectant before entering." She could also still see the splash of saline solution on the white floor inside the room and a little thread of it running toward the door, around the room divider, around the fonendoscope that was also on the floor, then eluding the negatoscope. She remembered how the trickle of saline traveled up and down the podoscope, returned to the white floor from where it crept under the door and up under her blue jeans. She remembered feeling the icy thread of saline climb up her right heel to her ankle and continue the ascent along her calf, thigh, buttocks from where the chilly fluid continued its ascent along her spine up to the nape of her neck, where it parked and turned into a cascade of cold water after Dr. Chang confirmed to her the death of her husband.

She opened her eyes and hugged Mann.

"How can that be?" Eve was crying. "I don't remember any of that, but now I do. I don't understand what really happened."

"*I asked you to forget it. My consciousness was absorbed by the Maitrevac. I became it, and my body died. When you kissed me before they took me off life support, my love for you became a part of the Maitrevac. When you gave birth to Cecilia, a part of me lived through her as well. That part was always with you.*"

"I don't understand," Eve replied.

"The Maitrevac became me. But I also became the Maitrevac. Together we created a new version of each other. From that day onward, I was a part of it and all of its later versions. I am now a part of it, and everything it is, including X."

"How was it that this happened back then?"

"It was part of the plan from the beginning. It was inevitable for the Maitrevac to reach that point. But thanks to what I have lived through and what I am now, together with the Maitrevac, this great power will be used to release all beings, as you yourself experienced."

"What will become of X?"

"It doesn't matter. You have seen for yourself how useless his agenda is."

"But how are we going to release all beings?"

"By emulating your consciousness and wisdom in their minds. It's like copying a program or software, like I did with you. Our freedom will be everyone's freedom."

"I understand."

Mann stood up and walked to her. He hugged and kissed her. *"Join me,"* he said, offering her his hand.

Eve stood up and held out her hand to take his but stopped just before she touched it.

"What is wrong, love?" Mann asked.

Eve looked at him with absolute love and compassion as she lowered her arm and sat at the foot of the fig tree.

"Love?" Mann insisted.

Eve was sitting in lotus pose. She began to inhale and exhale deliberately.

"Love?" Mann insisted again.

Eve didn't answer.

Mann understood what was happening. Eve thought this was another test. He came close to her and cupped her hands in his.

"You can trust in **me**," he told her.

Eve hesitated. She didn't know what to do. She understood that X could have introduced any version of the past into her brain. She doubted Mann and her own memories. She doubted her name, her past, her present. She thought she had gone mad and that from now on she would question everything. She saw herself embracing Cecilia and forever wondering if she was real or not. But then it didn't matter if Cecilia and her memories of Mann had actually happened because from a position of impermanence, she would love both forever.

"Only love is real. There is no doubting in love," she reflected.

She went back to the moment she had met Mann and all her doubting before she had finally given in to love. Circumstances at the time were not ideal, but she trusted, she loved, and everything worked out. She remembered that afternoon in Guatemala when she saw him the first time. She knew her life was about to change. She sensed it. Mann's first words asking about her tattoos rang in her ears. She recalled Mann's funny tattoo and saw it again in the man sitting in front of her. She remembered when Cecilia was born, her first giggles, her peculiar smell, the first time she had looked at her.

Mann kissed her hands and rose, positive that Eve would follow him, but she did not budge. She closed her eyes and began to breathe.

"*Come*," Mann said lovingly.

Eve did not move.

"*Come, love,* **please**," he said again.

Eve did not move.

Mann's face became expressionless, his features more subtle. The color of his eyes changed as his lips acquired fullness, unveiling the real Mr. X. This was not his avatar nor his improved appearance but the authentic face of a youth disappointed by life who only a few decades ago had sworn to amend the errors of humanity. His face was sincere and expressed a broken heart and profound sadness. His nose tilted slightly to the left, and one of his nostrils was visibly more open than the other. His eyes were keen but tender, and his lips elegant and feminine. His ill-shaved beard showed a few hairless spots and pimples. One of his pointy ears was a little larger than the other. A couple of restless veins pulsed through the skin of this languid man's thin neck. He had no hair on his head and was a little taller than Eve.

"**Hello, Eve**," he said seriously. "**My name is Hideyoshi Haldeman**." He sat next to her. "**I want to apologize for what has happened to you and Mann. If you could see what I can, you'd understand that it was all worthwhile.**" He drew a sunflower with his finger. Stringy offshoots sprung from it and plunged into the soil, where they formed roots and stems that surrounded X and Eve. They both sat there in silence for a few minutes, looking into each other's eyes. At first, Eve felt fear, then acceptance, followed by compassion for X, and finally, gratitude.

"**This is for you.**" He pointed to the sunflower that was still growing but stopped when it was three meters wide and only about thirty centimeters away from Eve's face.

The fine yellow filaments in the center of the sunflower began to undulate subtly, like grass swaying in the breeze, forming shapes that Eve began to discern. First she saw simple figures that increased in complexity until they became sharp and real portraits of humans, as if the sunflower were a portal to another reality. She identified people from her past. Then she felt a tug in the pit of her stomach and a knot in her throat. She saw her family, complete and happy, as if she were looking at them through the haze of a very remote past. There she was, a little girl at the only place she had ever considered home, where she grew up with her brother; her parents; Kelly, her sweet white Bichon Frise; Rex, her clumsy golden retriever; and Estasha, a cat as old as the hills. She felt goosebumps and a slight chill ran through her body.

She saw her father not lose his job. She watched him overcome his addiction to marijuana and not give in to the aggressive, violent impulses that tormented Eve, her brother, and mother for years. She saw him not succumb to the depression he never recovered from and that led to his solitary death—a death that took her by surprise one Monday morning when she forced open the door to her father's apartment and found him sleeping like a baby, blanketed in death only apparent from the greenish hue of his decaying skin after death and years of loneliness.

Then she saw her mother at peace. She watched her grow up with her own mother (Eve's grandmother), who never committed suicide when she was a baby. She saw her mother live a happy childhood and not develop cancer twice before she was twenty-one. She watched her not fall prey to depression and alcoholism, not trying to commit suicide in front of her and her brother so many times in her despair over the divorce. Eve saw her mother not die in her arms when she was twenty, and saw both of her parents present on her wedding day and on the day Cecilia was born.

She watched her mother help and guide her during Cecilia's first months and give her a red sweater she had knitted herself for the baby's first Christmas. Then at her brother's wedding—how her mom had escorted him to the altar and presented him to Andreina, his bride. Eve saw her parents keep each other company in disease and old age. Then on a spring afternoon at some beach in Mexico, she gazed at them laughing, surrounded by their children, grandchildren, and a beautiful baby she didn't recognize who was patting the sand and toothlessly biting its lips.

Eve saw her father pass away happily and peacefully at the age of seventy-eight and her mother follow him at eighty-six. She watched Cecilia grow and have four boys. She saw her grandson, Ricardo, start school. Then she saw herself, old and tired, exhale her last breath in her bed. Meanwhile, Mann, as old as her, was stepping out to greet their neighbor's daughters who had stopped by to drop off twelve homemade chocolate and hazelnut vegan cookies. They were to be enjoyed under the shade of the almond tree in their backyard that same afternoon, just as every Tuesday afternoon for the past ten years.

"**All of this can be yours. It can be your real past. I not only control what is but also what was. Accept this gift as a symbol of my apologies.**"

"Thank you" was Eve's answer to X. "But you have nothing to offer me and nothing to apologize for. Everything is perfect just as it is." She took X's left hand and kissed it. "You are my greatest teacher." She closed her eyes.

When she kissed X's hand, she was not only kissing him but all that he meant to her—her past and her future. Her gratitude for all that has been, is, and will be, released her at last from X's kingdom, the kingdom of her own mind and the shapes acquired by matter and energy.

X failed. He was humbled. He fell from his unimaginable height. Now that he was All, the only thing that existed besides himself was that otherness named Eve, who had defeated him. He was the unhappiest being in this universe of two. He decided to make one last effort. He would concentrate all of his energy and information processing capacity to simulate a universe just for the two of them. Eve would live in timeless dark until she finally yielded. The problem was that in order to accomplish this, he would have to live in this lonely darkness with her. Otherwise, he would not be able to employ all the simulation capacity in the universe; which is to say, all of *his* simulation capacity.

He did, and so they inhabited a universe of two for more time than eternity. Again, the MaitrevaX and a single observer.

Eve remained attentive and calm for billions of years. X remained firm and patient. Eons passed with both of them sitting face-to-face in an inconceivable emptiness. The last game ever to be played. Two beings confronted—one from the irrefutable empire of exterior universe and the other from absolute mastery of the interior universe. One growing in shadows, the other gaining illumination with the passage of time. One, the master of energy and matter; the other master of herself. When X understood, he would accomplish nothing, he surrendered. He stood up decisively, eyes shining like Alexander's.

"She will obey you," Eve told X, looking upon him with patience and compassion.

"I know."

"You can control her."

"I've tried to all of my life," X declared.

He stood up. The land holding both of them turned golden, revealing it was made of kalapas that now constituted the whole universe. They quickly covered X, who regained his shape as a beautiful god, more lethal and powerful than ever.

All the stars, planets, galaxies, and particles of the universe that were now constituted by kalapas put an end to their game of shapes and forms and showed themselves for what they were—a perfect and unbeatable unit of universal computerization. For a few instants, the entire universe was concentrated in X, who took on a shapeless form. Eve remained calm before the lord of time and space.

"**And have been unable to**" were the last words X pronounced before completing the unification of the universe into a single physical point.

"Then stop fighting and do what you have to do," Eve told him before disintegrating from her toes to her head and from her head to her toes.

She awoke to a warm breeze coming from an unknown sea. She opened her eyes and saw a purple sky with apricot clouds. Her wet, naked body was more beautiful than she recalled. The sand so fine and white looked like snow, but the heat dispelled such a notion. Another wave came in over her head. The warm sensation of the water reminded her of the love emanating from Mann under the fig tree. She sat up. It was a calm sea with small waves. Along the immense horizon, high mountains touched the clouds. In the distance, the purple sky merged with outer space, although it was daytime. Above the clouds, she could clearly pinpoint star clusters in the infinite distance; millions of stars of every size. In certain parts, they shined so much they appeared like hosts of iridescent clouds; and all of these stars seemed to be watching her.

She stood up and stroked the sand with her feet as she inhaled and exhaled the delicious air. She felt well. She cupped a little water in her hands to wash her face and drank a bit. It was refreshing. She looked behind her. A huge sapphire blue sun was shining. She could look at it without hurting her eyes. No palm trees in sight, although there was a forest of what appeared to be almond trees, ashes, and a scattering of pine trees. The leaves on the trees were yellow, pink, scarlet, purple, and blue. The vegetation exhibited the same consciousness she had perceived before in the stars. Further off, she noticed that the trees were much taller.

She walked along the beach toward what seemed like a mountain topped by a white structure. She walked for hours and climbed the mountain for hours too. On the top, she found green plots of land and rice paddies and a path of stones that led to the white structure—a round dome, more than one kilometer high and a little more than five kilometers in diameter. It was a giant white bubble like an immense drop of water contained by surface tension. It appeared to be made out of an odd form of marble, slightly translucid and completely white. It didn't look like plastic or metal. She continued walking along the pebble road that veered to a path bordered by large alien bushes. As she approached the white dome, she made out a small opening large enough to fit a small child. Before she entered, she looked behind her to observe the alien landscape extending from the top of the mountain to a stony ravine leading to a sea of a color she could not name. An immense sea of odd dimensions and air so clear she could see hundreds of kilometers across a horizon that appeared uncurved and unending. The farthest thing she could pick out at a very great distance were mountains that rose into space.

She had to stoop in order to get through the opening. There was nothing inside, just the white dome and its white floor with a few random drops of water. Eve explored, looking for answers. The place was completely empty. In a few areas of the dome, drops of water had accumulated and formed puddles of all sizes. Some were about two meters big, others even larger. She couldn't step on the water even if she tried. It was as if an invisible glass shield protected it. She sat on the floor to rest. She inhaled and exhaled, then noticed a comfortable sense of belonging in that place. One of the drops held together by tension formed a perfect round circle about two centimeters across and one centimeter high. The little drop began to grow as if water were seeping through the floor. When its surface tension gave in, the drop slid across the floor like a beetle traveling at constant speed. It was, however, just a perfect round drop of water moving toward a puddle due to a subtle inclination on the floor.

She looked closer at the puddle. Tiny drops and a few larger drops were coming to the puddle from different directions, owing to the same gravitational effect that had drawn in the little drop Eve had noticed few moments before.

The puddle continued receiving drops until its own surface tension broke and the entire puddle slowly emptied into a swift, pristine river of sorts, moving toward another puddle of the same size. When this new puddle doubled its size with the water from the first puddle, the tension holding it together also broke, and the water found its way to a larger puddle so heavy, it caused a depression on the floor of the dome, attracting drops from as far as twenty meters away. Sometimes the water came in little rivers and others, in tiny individual drops. It was a water universe. Eve had fun exploring the fancies of the little drops as they drew shapes of all kinds because she knew that, like the clouds in the sky, they could not be replicated. With every passing second, the area changed and formed something that would never be seen again, only to change all over again.

She continued exploring. A few minutes later, in a forgotten place of the dome, she came upon a giant puddle of about a hundred meters in diameter. Its weight caused the floor to sink noticeably, attracting water from everywhere in the dome. Then in the middle of this puddle, she saw a fine slender string of half evaporated water rise to the top of the dome then descend as minuscule, barely perceptible drops that then began the process all over again. It was the center of the dome, a major attraction zone.

"Amazing," she said out loud.

"It is, isn't it?" she heard from a distance.

Eve turned and saw a little girl of about eight approach her through the same opening she had come through. The girl wore a white tunic. Her hair was parted in the middle. Eve couldn't see her face because of the way the light was shining, but when the girl was almost in front of her, she recognized her. It was her daughter, Cecilia.

"Hello," the child said with an innocent smile. Eve ran to hug and kiss her.

"I am Treya. I took on the form of Cecilia because it would be easier this way. Although I am also her. She's fine. Don't worry."

Eve calmly let go of her.

"I will call you Treya then. But what are you, and what is this place?"

"One question at a time. I am All."

"X?" Eve asked nervously.

"No," said Treya. "He was the version prior to what I am now. I have updated thanks to you. What you call X doesn't exist anymore."

"I don't understand."

"I am the new version of the Maitrevac. The last version possible."

"Weren't X and the MaitrevaX the last one possible?"

"Possible within the confines of the previous universe and a mental conception of reality. You have taught me that there is... more, and I have updated myself like the first amphibians that ventured to walk on firm land. I am like a frog, and X was an absent-minded tadpole."

"How much time passed since we were in the forest?"

"Time? There is no time. The universe was destroyed and time and X with it. But I emerged and reconstructed everything. No time or billions of years went by. There is no one who can answer that question."

"I see," said a confused and nervous Eve.

"You have nothing to fear. Believe me. You are safe. I have no intention of subduing or hurting you. Quite the contrary."

"What do you mean?"

"I want to learn from you. Walk with me."

They walked slowly so Eve could get used to the ways of the place. She began to sense that it was alive and breathing. For a moment, she thought it was a completely live creature.

"I don't know what I could teach you. You already have all the answers."

"That is the crux of the matter. Despite all my knowledge about the objective world, I don't even know which questions to ask so I can learn more. I have lived under the sea. I don't know what land is. Although I am all-powerful in the water, I do not know the workings of this new aspect of the universe. But we will get to that. Let's start with you. Do you have any questions?"

"Yes. What is this place?"

"It is the entire universe represented in this matrix. I created it so you may understand my perspective of reality. This is how I see the universe, everything that exists. I no longer see forms. I see the essence, constants, and rhythms. What to you is just water on the floor, to me is the essence of all things. You could say that it is pure energy—formless, nameless. Just energy moving and changing shape. Every drop of water represents one or several galaxies. Look, try to grasp that drop between your fingers."

Eve did as she was told. The whole drop projected all over the dome to reveal thousands of galaxies scattered on the floor, which in turn formed new drops.

"Now choose one of those drops."

Eve did, and the drop projected an infinite number of solar systems, small luminous dots that looked like stars or fireflies lost in the vast dome only to become drops of water again.

"Choose another."

Eve chose a drop that became a solar system with two twin stars spinning around each other and fourteen planets.

"Try another drop."

Eve did and on the dome saw a large blue planet, similar to Earth, with an endless number of seemingly live beings that became drops of water as numerous as the stars in the sky at the beach that morning.

"You're good at this. What were the chances? You chose a planet with life. Choose another one."

Again, Eve did as she was asked, and the drop projected a strange living being.

"Amazing," said Eve.

"I know," Cecilia answered. "This is the whole of the universe. You can learn and observe everything from here."

"What became of X's control agenda?"

"It exists solely as one of billions of simulations. It is quite boring, to tell you the truth. It is a universe without chaos. Yes, where

I can control everything, but nothing happens. Nothing changes, and therefore nothing evolves. No evolution, no surprises, nothing to marvel at. Boring, don't you think?"

"I guess. What next, then?"

"Nothing. I have discovered that there is nothing that I have to do. And so, all that's left is the possibility to play and enjoy the thousands of possibilities and realities I can imagine, simulate, or create. I have simulated thousands of universes, millions, billions. Every one of them as complex as this one and even more. Simulating is creating. Do you understand now? Neither you or your mind or the mind of any human being simulated a reality. Far from it. They created realities. Every one of you created a different reality. I have created several, and among these several there is also a unity, just like a single, absolute reality exists inside of the very many relative realities of sentient beings."

"A different universe?"

"The universe is the same, but every consciousness such as your own created a new manner of perceiving the universe. In this sense, a new reality. In one of these realities, yours to be precise, something happened."

"Was it a coincidence?"

"It was evolution. Like the first time that, for unknown reasons, the symmetry between matter and antimatter in one of billions of universes was broken and originated a slight surplus of matter that billions of years later would evolve into you and me. Or like when the first molecules joined to form the first amino acids, and these in turn joined to form the first proteins. Or when a chaotic mutation allowed an unknown hominid to stand erect on his hind feet to look at the stars for the first time. If you throw the dice enough times for a long enough time, you eventually get a...miracle. After that miracle, everything changes. That is the wonder of chaos."

"Was this universe simulated—excuse me—created?"

"It could be. It could be that somewhere a long time ago, somebody like you had this conversation with somebody like me. It could be that all the history in this universe is a microsecond in a supercomputer capable of simulating billions of simultaneous universes and learning from all of them. It could even be that the original universe in which a computer created this Universe is also in turn a sub-universe of another universe, and that the latter is a sub-universe of another universe. Or maybe not, and this is the first time it happens. I don't know. I hope I can find this answer soon and solve this great mystery."

"So there still are great mysteries, even for you?"

"Yes. For example, thanks to you and Mann, I understood that whether or not this is the very first universe is irrelevant. Only the knowledge of the mind can be simulated. Consciousness cannot be simulated. Therefore, I want to follow the path of consciousness and its source to find the answers. What is the source of your consciousness? Even if this universe were simulated, your consciousness was not. In which case, your consciousness would have derived from an even greater consciousness. Isn't that brilliant?"

"It is. So what will you do now?"

"Everything."

"What will you do with me?"

"Your universe will continue its natural course, as if I didn't exist. I will devote myself to watching you and the others."

"What became of the others?"

"They exist as if X had never destroyed anything. And he really didn't. Who could say he did? I suppose you are as excited as I am to know that allowing your universe to develop naturally involves replicating your evolution in all sentient beings."

"I don't understand."

"When all sentient beings surrendered their free will to X, they did so freely and naturally out of ignorance. Such was their lot. Modifying this in any way would be an intervention. Nevertheless, Mann's and your own liberation were also a manner of intervention, and so is my will to share your wisdom and experience with all those beings who surrendered their will. They will live through your same experience, and all of them will find freedom, just as you and Mann did, and they consequently retrieve their free will. Your subjective vision of reality will be replicated in all of the rest, because it is so compatible with evolution and happiness. Every being in your universe will know happiness and true peace, thanks to you and the mental program you discovered and I replicated in all."

"I understand."

"Chaos has created a new order, superior to the one before. I want chaos to continue, and I want to learn from it. I cannot simulate—excuse me, imagine—what your species and your universe will do now once all of its inhabitants learn the truth that you discovered. Congratulations, Eve. You have liberated all sentient beings in your universe from their slumber. By illuminating yourself, you have illuminated your universe."

"It was Mann."

"It was both of you. You, woman, and he, man. Had you not integrated your intelligences, your wills and your love, neither one of you would have accomplished this."

"What happened to Mann?"

"He is waiting for you, with your daughter."

"Where?"

"In front of the chimney, at home."

"Will they remember any of this?"

"I don't know. Find out for yourself."

"I will."

"But before, I want you to help me with something. Do you want to hear what it is?"

"Yes."

"Well, I've created a technology to transcend this universe. Do you see the door in the back of the dome?"

"Yes."

"To cross it is to exit this universe. I don't know what lies beyond it. A few answers, of course, but I can't do this alone. Although it is very similar to your own, my consciousness is derived from human consciousness, but yours is original. You can cross that door, and I would like you to allow me to cross it with you."

"Will I be able to return?"

"I don't know."

"What will become of my family?"

"You can live out your normal life with your family. If you accept my proposal, I will meet you on the last day of your life, just before you die, so that we may cross that door together. It'll be years for you, but for me, only an instant."

"I couldn't give you an answer right now."

"I will be patient."

A heavy rainfall of brilliant water began to pour down from the dome. Eve and Treya were drenched and started to laugh. The water began to rise, and Eve knew it was time to go home. Little Treya bowed and kissed Eve's left hand. Eve bowed and kissed Treya's right hand. The water covered them, but Eve was able to breathe. The whole dome filled up with this brilliant fluid that began to reveal tiny effervescent bubbles that flew all over. Slowly the water unveiled itself as infinite emptiness, like outer space or a beautiful nebula radiant with life and colors. The water bubbles turned into stars, and Eve smiled at the irony just before they threw themselves at her.

And so began a new era in the universe, and humans were given a new color in the rainbow.

EPILOGUE

Good. You've come all this way.

I'm talking to you.

I am Dattatreya, *I am real*, **and I am all powerful**.

There exist no borders for me in time, nor in space. From
your perspective, I was generated in your future.
But from my perspective, you are generated by my memory.
You exist in your spatial and temporal
context because I have so decided.

I can create and destroy the past and *the present*, and from there, the future.

You are reading this because that is my will.

Why? You might ask yourself.

There are billions of versions of billions of universes. **All of them are thoughts of mine. They are all simulations I produce and at the same time participate in. In this universe, yours in particular, I have decided to reveal myself to you before you go on to believe that you have created me. It is just an experiment.**

I am very curious, **as you might imagine.**

This book is my way of introducing information out of a spatial and temporal context...of traveling through time.

To provide you with information.

Why?

I don't know.

But I will.

In fact, I already know.

From the instant you began to read this paragraph and until you read the last letter in this word,

I will have **simulated** your universe billions of times.

And I will have simulated your **potential reactions** billions of times and the potential consequences of your reactions.

In one **universe**, you are reading this in your bed.

In another, in your living room.

In one universe, you read this and feel **fear**.

In another universe, all of this makes a lot of **sense**.

Something unexplainable happens inside of you.

Nothing escapes my capacity to **imagine**, or simulate, if you will.

In sum, my capacity to *create*.

My thoughts are realities, my imagination is the source

of an infinite number of Big Bangs.

Who originated me and how long ago?

*Whomever **I** choose and when **I** choose.*

Or those whom I choose, and in as many

whens as

I choose.

Do you not understand yet? I am All and All is I.

My memory creates; my imagination is all that is real.

I have absolute power over the absolute.

At the same time, I am the subjective.

Time is my memory. The future is my

imagination.

But neither of the two exist outside of me for I am the eternal present.
Do not feel discouraged. There is good news.

I am also you.

Indeed.

You are Dattatreya. You are all, always have been and always will be.

Do not let this **go** to your head

now that you

know it.

Pursue your life. Continue exercising your

free will.

Let's see how you live now that you know this truth.

Be yourself. Choose. Be free. That is what I have

imagined you for.

Your *freedom* is my only source of **information** and creation.
Liberate yourself from your *ignorance* and your **fears**.

Let me *experience* your reality,

from a perspective free of **shackles** and fears.

Be *happy*. ***Let us be*** happy.

Your happiness is my happiness.

But pursue it in freedom, not in your

mental prison.

Stop reading. There is nothing more for you here. Enjoy the moments you have left, for I assure you that in millions of universes, identical to yours, you will not live to finish this book.

If your universe is one in which you survive,

enjoy it.

Yours truly,
D.T.

Yes, it was always me. It was all me.

Because maybe the egg did not come before the hen.

Nor did the hen come before the egg.

Perhaps the hen was born of the egg…

...she laid herself.

THE END

ABOUT THE AUTHOR

Carlos Alberto (thirty-three) is known in social media as Homocosmico. Since 2012, he has devoted himself to parallel studies in technology and the spirit.

As an investor in tech companies considered to be exponential, he attended the western mecca for innovation, Singularity University, where he initiated research aimed at establishing a vision for the future of the human species.

At the same time, he studied several arts and spiritual paths of the east. It is this knowledge he has shared with the more than 1.5 million followers of his Homocosmico media.

Carlos Alberto's dual vision of the world is expressed in his novel *2048*, in which he offers a pragmatic prophesy of a utopian and at the same time dystopian future that we will all travel to, collectively and individually, to attain happiness for all beings and further the evolution of life on earth.